BEACH, PLEASE

MELANIE SUMMERS

Copyright © 2023 Gretz Corp.

All rights reserved.

Published by Gretz Corp.

First edition

EBOOK ISBN: 978-1-988891-58-3

Paperback Edition ISBN: 978-1-988891-59-0

No part of this book may be used or reproduced in any manner whatsoever without the prior written permission of the publisher, except in the case of brief quotations embodied in reviews.

This is a work of fiction. Names, characters, businesses, places, events and incidents are either the products of the author's imagination or used in a fictitious manner. Any resemblance to actual persons, living or dead, or events is purely coincidental.

Praise For Melanie Summers

"A fun, often humorous, escapist tale that will have readers blushing, laughing and rooting for its characters." ~ ***Kirkus Reviews***

A gorgeously funny, romantic and seductive modern fairy tale...
I have never laughed out loud so much in my life. I don't think that I've ever said that about a book before, and yet that doesn't even seem accurate as to just how incredibly funny, witty, romantic, swoony…and other wonderfully charming and deliriously dreamy *The Royal Treatment* was. I was so gutted when this book finished, I still haven't even processed my sadness at having to temporarily say goodbye to my latest favourite Royal couple.
~ ***MammieBabbie Book Club***

The Royal Treatment is a quick and easy read with an in depth, well thought out plot. It's perfect for someone that needs a break from this world and wants to delve into a modern-day fairy tale that will keep them laughing and rooting for the main characters throughout the story. ~ ***ChickLit Café***

I have to HIGHLY HIGHLY HIGHLY RECOMMEND *The Royal Treatment* to EVERYONE!
    ~ *Jennifer,* The Power of Three Readers

I was totally gripped to this story. For the first time ever the Kindle came into the bath with me. This book is unputdownable. I absolutely loved it.
    ~ *Philomena (Two Friends, Read Along with Us)*

Very rarely does a book make me literally hold my breath or has me feeling that actual ache in my heart for a character, but I did both." **~ *Three Chicks Review for Netgalley***

Books by Melanie Summers

ROMANTIC COMEDIES

The Crown Jewels Series
The Royal Treatment
The Royal Wedding
The Royal Delivery

Paradise Bay Series
The Honeymooner
Whisked Away
The Suite Life
Resting Beach Face
Pride and Piña Coladas
Beach, Please

Crazy Royal Love Series
Royally Crushed
Royally Wild
Royally Tied

Stand-Alone Books
Even Better Than the Real Thing

WOMEN'S FICTION
The After Wife
I Used to Be Fun

For Lucy and Nelson,
My furry writing partners, who hang out in my office with me and nudge me to get up and go for a walk every few hours.
Thanks for being here.
Love,
Melanie

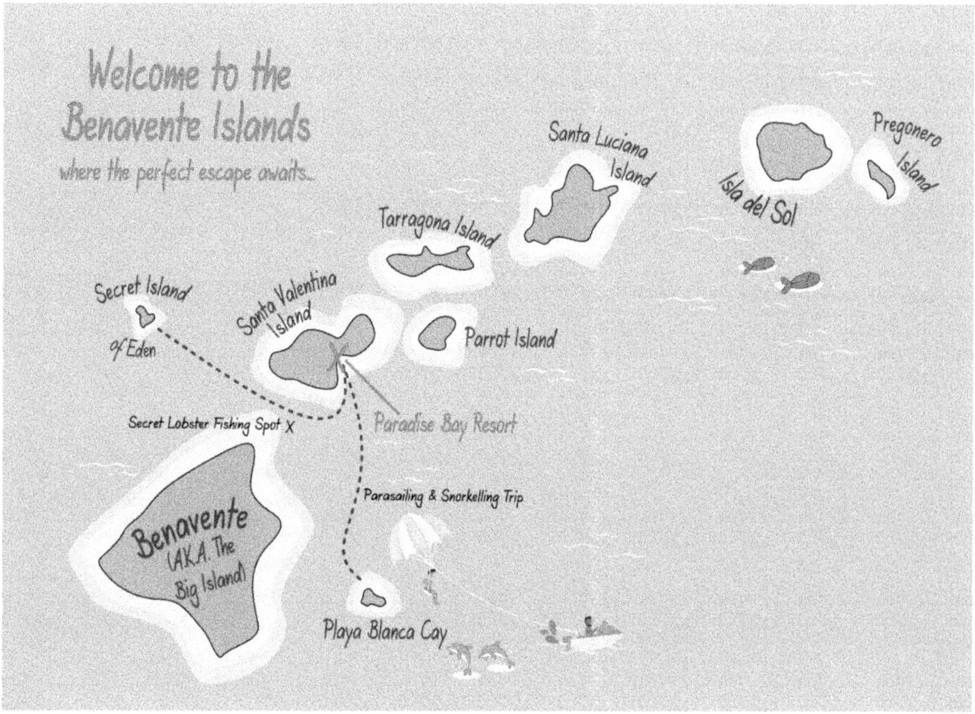
Welcome to the
Benavente Islands
where the perfect escape awaits...
Santa Luciana Island
Pregonero Island
Isla del Sol
Tarragona Island
Secret Island of Eden
Santa Valentina Island
Parrot Island
Secret Lobster Fishing Spot X
Paradise Bay Resort
Parasailing & Snorkelling Trip
Benavente (A.K.A. The Big Island)
Playa Blanca Cay

Santa Valentina Island

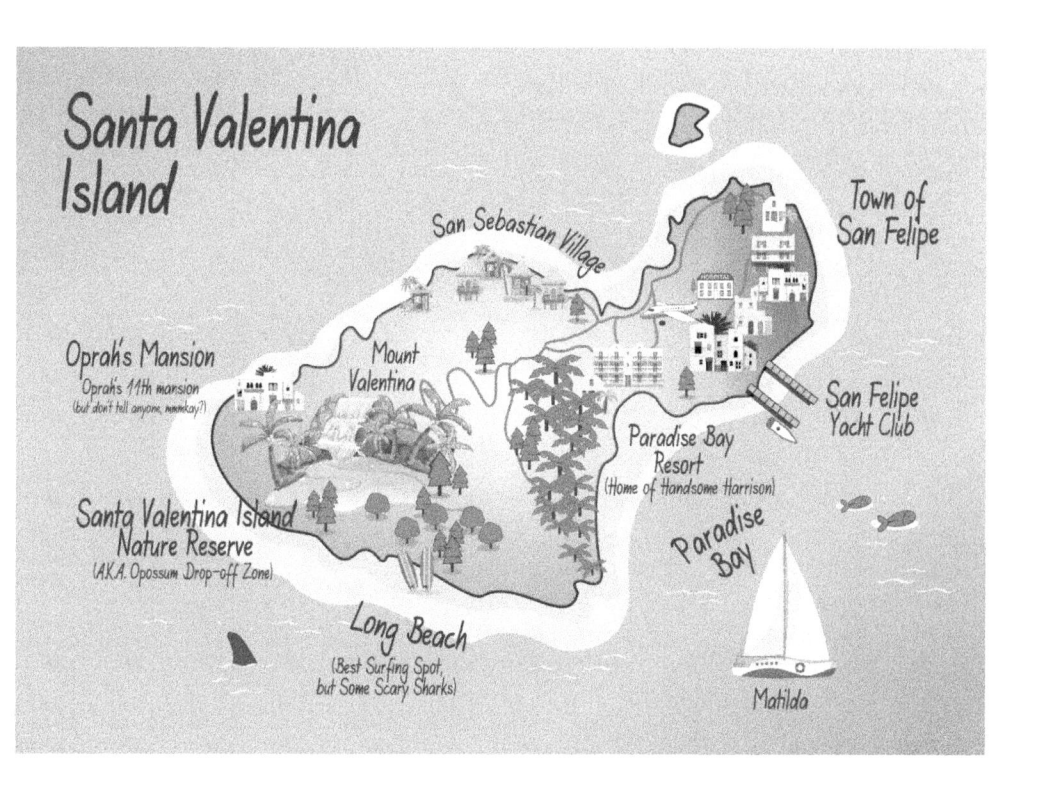

Town of San Felipe

San Sebastian Village

Oprah's Mansion
Oprah's 11th mansion
(but don't tell anyone, mmmkay?!)

Mount Valentina

San Felipe Yacht Club

Paradise Bay Resort
(Home of Handsome Harrison)

Santa Valentina Island Nature Reserve
(A.K.A. Opossum Drop-off Zone)

Paradise Bay

Long Beach
(Best Surfing Spot, but Some Scary Sharks)

Matilda

ISSUE NO. 326

MUSINGS OF A FANTASY MAN

THE WORLD'S BIGGEST AUTHORITY ON ALL THINGS FANTASY FICTION

THE COVER IS FINALLY OUT

HUGE news from Stone & Sullivan Publishing today. They've finally released the cover for the highly-anticipated prequel to *CLASH OF CROWNS*, *BLOOD OF DRAGONS*.

As you know, the prequel is set in Qadeathas four hundred years before *CLASH OF CROWNS* and features the ancestors of the Dalgaeron Family.

I, for one, am solidly in love with this cover. It's got all the classic Pierce Davenport features—the colors, the fonts, the excitement.

If the book is even half as good as this cover, I'll be completely satisfied. After such a long wait, I shall be chomping at the bit to get my hands on a hard cover copy. For now, I'm going to just sit and stare at this for another hour or so before I go reheat some leftovers.

ISSUE NO. 348

MUSINGS OF A FANTASY MAN

THE WORLD'S BIGGEST AUTHORITY ON ALL THINGS FANTASY FICTION

THIS IS NOT A DRILL!

It's official. NBO, along with Stone & Sullivan Publishing, are releasing the long-awaited prequel to *CLASH OF CROWNS* simultaneously! *BLOOD OF DRAGONS*, the prequel featuring the ancestors of the Dalgaeron Family, is almost here.

This is by far the most thrilling thing to ever happen to me. I have booked off work and will be sequestering myself for eight weeks while I read the novel, then watch the NBO series. If I get even a hint of a spoiler, I feel like my life will be forever ruined.

My sources at NBO have let me in on one secret that I'm happy to share with you. Tomorrow night, they will be making a huge announcement about the big launch. I can't say too much, but I will tell you it's got the words treasure and hunt in it...

Stay tuned for more right here on *Musings from a Fantasy Man* as I bring you the first, best, and most comprehensive *Blood of Dragons* news...

1

Party Boats, Life Goals, and Bachelorettes

Aidan Clarke

I won't do it today. I won't. It's been six months. Time to move on and shed the rituals that may have served me well in the past (or maybe only served to prolong the pain). Whichever it is, today, I have to stop. It will be a birthday gift to myself. And possibly a gift to the people on any nearby boats docked at the pier. I'm not sure if they can hear it, what with me doing it in the cabin, but I do get an awful lot of strange looks from people around here.

Not that I care what they think. That was the whole point of moving to Santa Valentina Island in the first place—to get away from people whose opinions matter to me. If I wanted to be judged—or worse, pitied—I'd still be living in Canada. I'd be back in Calgary with plans to drive out to my parents' ranch for a big birthday dinner with my four stupid professional hockey-playing millionaire brothers. But I'm not.

Instead, I'm here in paradise, starting over. Healing. Moving on. Which is why I *won't* do it today. I'm going to stand here in silence while I wait for the coffee to brew and prepare the snacks for today's snorkeling tour guests.

The thing is, I don't *need* to do it anymore. At first it started out as a way to soothe the pain. But now that I'm over her, I keep it up as a way to remind myself that falling in love is, without a doubt, the worst choice a human can make. Idiotic. Nonsensical. Not ever happening again. And because I know this deep in my bones, I don't need to keep doing it.

I've carved out an amazing life for myself here. When it all went down and I left Canada, I bought a catamaran and swapped out my previous life of working in cybersecurity for a major bank (hunched over a keyboard all day fending off hackers only to risk my life on the icy drive from my office to my condo) for something infinitely better. The perfectly free and easy, no-commitment life. I take two, three-hour tours out a day—one at nine a.m. and one at one p.m., which means I'm not even committed to serving them a meal. Just snacks. My morning guests get a variety of pastries, scones, and fresh fruit, while the afternoon crowd gets tortilla chips, salsa, fresh guacamole that I make myself, and cookies. Then I spend the rest of the day blissfully alone doing whatever the hell I want.

The inspiration for buying the catamaran was simple—it's a great way to meet women. Specifically, women who are here for a limited time and are looking for a little vacation fun with a free-spirited boat captain. But I'm not an animal. I have rules—no one vulnerable, no one intoxicated, and no one married or otherwise in a committed relationship. So far, it hasn't worked out exactly as I expected because at least half of my guests are families (so not my preferred demographic), and of those who are single women, a surprising amount of them are going through a bad break-up or some other tragic life moment which immediately makes them a hard no. On the odd occasion that I have met a woman who seems to tick off all the boxes, I inevitably wind up asking her a few questions about herself over a bottle of wine, only to realize that she's off limits. This means instead of a night of fun, I spend the entire evening listening to her talk about her ex/parents/whoever has hurt her, only to hug it out at the end and have her leave grateful while I head home to my little seaside cottage having not had the random hook-up for which I was hoping.

But there's always a chance, and today's group is looking pretty good—eight women who are here for a bachelorette party. Yes, ma'am, happy birthday to me. I'll start out the day feeding them and helping them fit their snorkels and fins, then at some point, mention my sad-but-true sob story—that my fiancée left me for my own brother. That'll garner some 'awww, you poor thing,' energy, which, with any luck, will turn into some hot, meaningless birthday sex.

The kettle reaches 200 degrees—the perfect temperature for French press coffee. I pour the water over the freshly-ground beans, then rest the plunger carefully on top while the coffee brews, its comforting scent tickling my nose. In precisely four minutes fifty-four seconds, it will be brewed to perfection, which is exactly the length of time to do it once.

Just once couldn't hurt, right?

Screw it. I know I said I wouldn't, but it's my birthday. I'll let myself do it this one last time. But I won't let myself sing along. That'll help me put a stop to this nonsense. After this, I really will move on forever.

Turning my head toward the speaker, I say, "Alexa, play 'The Winner Takes It All' by ABBA."

Alexa must be so sick of this by now. *I'm sorry, Alexa.* The keyboard starts up and I close my eyes, letting Agnetha's pain remind me of how awful it was when I first found out. Agnetha gets it. Even though, as far as I know, Bjorn didn't leave her for her own sister. I also doubt she grew up feeling like a complete reject on account of every single person in her family playing professional—or, in my mother's case, Olympic-level—hockey, but Agnetha was too uncoordinated to skate a straight line.

Don't sing. Do. Not. Sing.

"I was in your arms…"

Dammit, I'm singing.

I belt out every word until my throat is raw. When the song ends, I open my eyes, only to see one of the guys who runs fishing tours staring at me slack-jawed through the cabin window. He gives me a quick nod, then shakes his head as he walks down the pier to his boat.

Yeah, buddy, enjoy fishing with a bunch of old retired guys today. You weirdo who peeks into other people's cabins. I'll be hosting a group of beautiful ladies, hopefully at least one of whom will be looking for a little captain action.

That wasn't nice of me. Not very Canadian at all. Besides, technically I suppose *I'm* the weirdo. I should probably do that at home. Not that I'm doing it again because ... last time.

Plunging the coffee down with the exact pressure required to blend the oils to perfection, I tell Alexa, who just started playing Sinead O'Connor's "Nothing Compares," to shut off the music. Time to get prepared for the tour. These snack trays won't make themselves.

It'll be a bit of a tricky day because I'll be dodging birthday calls from my family, especially from Lawson the Betrayer. That's his new name. Fitting. He doesn't know I call him that though because I haven't spoken to him since it happened. He still tries calling me every two or three days, but I don't pick up. I should just block him already and get it over with. I will. Just not today.

Lawson always was an asshat. Two years older than me and forever determined to show me he could beat me at anything. Obviously he could beat me at anything. He was *two years older* than me.

All right, so he wasn't *always* an asshat. Not until six months ago when he started sleeping with the woman I was going to marry. In fact, of my four brothers, he and I were the closest. He was the only one in the family who seemed to have any appreciation of my skills—my ability to fix computer problems, the ease with which I could solve riddles and complete puzzles, and my mad Lego skills. Yes, my parents tried to encourage me, and my other three brothers certainly used me when they needed some tech nerd help. But Lawson actually seemed to like listening to me talk about my interests. He asked questions instead of giving me the cursory 'uh-huh, yeps' that my mom and dad would when I was excited about the latest version of *The Legend of Zelda*. So when he was the one who put my heart through the wood chipper, it was ... unexpected. And by that I mean the most painful experience in all my thirty-one years (and I'm including the time I broke my nose so badly it was sideways on my face).

It's a pathetically typical story. I got home a day early from an IT conference only to catch the two of them in bed. My bed. Where I used to snuggle up and inhale the scent of her right before I'd drift off into a peaceful sleep believing I was the luckiest man on earth to have a woman like her to love me. Cue the two of them scrambling to cover up, get dressed, and explain all at the same time. Caitlyn clutching my pillow to her chest and crying while he's on all fours searching for his briefs. Cue my world being shaken to the core, my lungs feeling like they were going to collapse, and my legs turning to mercury, which is both a liquid and one of the heaviest metals on earth.

Side note: Most people say lead in this scenario (as in, my legs felt like lead), but lead is light enough to sit on top of mercury. That's how heavy mercury is. But I digress.

Anyway, within a week, the story broke all over Canada. I'm not sure how the press found out that one of hockey's royal family had cuckholded his little brother, but they did and it was big news. That's when I decided to become an expat from Hockeylandia forever. I told Vivian, my overly sympathetic boss who will 'never cheer for the Cougars again,' that I was moving to Santa Valentina Island to become a boat captain. She felt so bad for me that she cried. Talk about an awkward Zoom call. It couldn't have been worse if she'd forgotten to wear her pants.

Fast forward to me literally living as far away from an ice rink as a guy can get while still remaining on planet Earth. Honestly, that's how much I hate hockey. I don't even get ice in my drinks. I'll suck back a lukewarm Coke rather than have that awful white stuff touch my lips.

After I get the snack trays set out on the counter and tidy up, I grab the freshly-laundered towels, roll them and set them up into pyramid shapes on various locations throughout the boat. Yes, if women love anything, it's neatly rolled towels within their grasp.

I'm just finishing the last towel when I smell the stench of a cigar. I turn to see Stew Milner standing on the pier next to my boat. Stogie Stew, as he's called by the locals, owns the biggest tour company on the island, Sandy Shores Snorkeling Adventures, which is honestly the dumbest name for a snorkeling tour company ever. It doesn't even make sense. *No one snorkels on the shore, Stew.*

He grins at me while he chews on the cigar he's holding between his finger and thumb (both of which are yellow—blech). "*Zelda*'s looking pretty fine. You almost ready to sell her to me?"

Zelda's my boat. She's a 47' Passenger Day Charter Catamaran that I bought off a fellow from St. Lucia. She's got seating for up to twenty-eight passengers, not including the trampoline. She has a small living quarters below deck including a galley, a bedroom with one double bed (and a cupboard full of condoms), a bathroom with a shower, and a tiny living room with a couch and TV. There are also another two toilets on the main deck for guest use. The best feature is a slide that drops people from the top deck into the warm Caribbean waters—a big hit, especially with kids. And I'm never selling her to Stogie Stew.

I involuntarily cringe, feeling somehow violated on *Zelda*'s behalf. "And give up the good life? Never."

"Oh, you'll sell her to me. It's just a matter of time before you get sick of ferrying drunks around." He turns to leave, calling over his shoulder, "I'll pay you a fair price for her! Just let me know when you're ready to give up!"

"Not going to happen," I call back. I'd rather burn *Zelda* to ash than sell her to that guy. *Sorry,* Zelda. *I didn't mean that.*

At ten minutes to nine, a taxi van pulls up next to the pier. And here they come, eight gorgeous women. I squint a little as they get closer. Are they ... old ladies? Based on the grey hair and the fact that one of them is using a walker, I'm going to say yes. Which means my hopes for a birthday romp are pretty much over. Unless…?

No. They're over, Aidan. Accept that.

I plaster a smile on my face and hold out my hand to help them climb the steps. "I'm Aidan, your captain for today. Which one of you lovely ladies is our blushing bride?"

They all titter and one of them shoots up her hand. "I am, but I'm not exactly blushing."

"No, Loretta's been with lots of men," the one with the walker says.

"Joyce, you're making me sound like a trollop."

"I'm just being honest," Joyce says.

"If I had known you were going to be honest, I wouldn't have invited you," Loretta says.

Joyce hands me her walker, then grabs hold of the railing and hoists herself up the steps while I stand, ready to help if needed. Once she's aboard, she smiles up at me. "Well, aren't you a tall drink of water?"

"Uh-oh, I can tell you're going to be trouble, aren't you?" I ask with a wink. God, I hate myself sometimes.

They all laugh and a few of them agree, although they don't sound too happy about it.

"Oooh! Look at the towels," Loretta says.

"So lovely."

"Where's the food? Your brochure said there would be pastries."

"Hold your horses, he can only do one thing at a time."

Oh dear, I have a feeling this is going to be an excruciatingly long three hours.

Yes, yes it was. So much bickering. And calling me Captain Hot Stuff. And asking me to 'do their backs,' meaning lather sunscreen on them. In more than one case, it meant lifting skin folds to make sure I could get in the cracks. To be honest, I'm not sure if I've just spent my birthday morning being sexually harassed or not. I think I was. Thank God I don't have a tour booked for the afternoon because I just want to go home and have a shower.

While I was out at sea (and out of range) I received the customary texts from my non-betraying brothers, Bennett, Hayden, and Wilder. But nothing from Lawson. Maybe his gift to me is a break from his pathetic attempts at reconciling. That would be surprisingly thoughtful, so clearly I'm going to have to keep my guard up.

By the time I clean up and head home, it's nearly three o'clock. I go for a long run on the beach before showering. Now I'm going to spend a delightful evening totally alone. I'll cook my birthday dinner of grilled snapper, brown rice, and veggies, then spend the evening binging the latest season of *Formula 1: Drive to Survive* while I play chess on my phone.

My phone rings and Scotia Dominion Bank appears on the screen. That'll be my ex-boss Vivian calling to wish me a happy birthday. She's so thoughtful. "Hey Vivian, how's life in Toronto today?"

There's a pause, then I hear, "It's me, Lawson. Please don't hang up. I had to beg the lady at the front desk to let me use one of their meeting rooms to call you."

My stomach lurches. My heart squeezes. So many emotions all at once. Humiliation at him going to my old place of work, where they will undoubtedly recognize him since he's an über-famous hockey god, then immediately remember that his brother used to work there. Red hot rage, searing pain, and inexplicably, guilt for having ignored him for so long, which is insane because I have every right to avoid him for the rest of my life. I open my mouth to tell him not to call me again, but nothing comes out. *Just say it. Then hang up. At least you'll have that one final thread of dignity you managed to salvage.*

"Aidan, please. I really need to talk to you. I've never felt so sorry about anything in my entire life. In fact, I'll never forgive myself."

"That makes two of us."

"I deserve that. I do. I just … really miss you, man. You're my little bro."

"A fact you conveniently forgot when you started banging my fiancée."

"Aid, I swear I never forgot. The entire time it was just killing me knowing—"

"If you called to tell me how hard this all been on you, I'm going to hang up now."

"That's not why I called," he says, letting out a heavy sigh. "I wanted to wish you a happy birthday, and I know it's a long shot, but I was hoping we could find a way to get through this mess. I miss you, man. The guilt is…" He lets out a groan. "I can't stop thinking about what we did to you. I'm worried about you. Mom's worried. Everybody's furious with me and with Cait. I'm playing like shit, to be honest. I don't even have one goal yet this season."

Cait. The sound of her name coming out of his mouth is like a sea urchin to the bottom of my foot. Clearly they're still together, which is just a real punch to the beans. "Well, you should have thought of that before you betrayed your own brother. Actions have consequences."

"I know. I know. I just…"

"What? Didn't care? Couldn't control yourself?"

"The second one. The thing is, I've been in love with her since the first time you brought her home to meet the family. For three years, man. I tried stuffing those feelings deep, deep down but…"

"But you failed miserably."

"Yeah, I did," he says. "I know I shouldn't say this because it'll probably come out wrong and piss you off even more, but I might be the only person who can actually understand how you feel."

"That's quite possibly the stupidest thing you've ever come up with, which is saying something." Now I'm just being nasty, and I won't lie—it feels fucking incredible.

"The thing is, if you're missing her even half as much as I wanted her for three long years, I get it. It was torture. Pure torture, which is why it's killing me to know how much pain you're in."

I pause while I try to make sense of his half-baked logic. My brain quickly decides it doesn't want me to admit how much this hurts. I'd rather have her think she didn't mean that much to me. "I'm not in any pain at all, actually."

"Come on, Aidan. It's me. I know you."

"No, for real. I'm totally over her. In fact, I've been having the time of my life. Meeting tons of women. Getting laid like crazy."

"Really?" He sounds hopeful.

"Yeah, and the best part so far is that none of them floss their teeth in bed or eat lettuce with their hands, like some other women I know."

He ignores my obvious digs at Caitlyn and says, "That's great, Aid. I'm really happy for you."

"I wish I could say the same," I tell him. "If that's all, I really have to go. I'm super busy with my catamaran business. Don't call me from the bank again. It's humiliating for both of us."

"Please wait. That's not all," he says.

I blow out a frustrated sigh, then snap, "What?"

"Caitlyn and I are … well, I'm not, she is. We're… having a baby and we're getting married." His voice sounds like it's coming out of a long tunnel. I hear the words but it's like I'm not really taking them all in. "We want you to be there. It would mean the world to us both."

I must have slid out of my seat because I'm now seated on the tile floor. Am I rocking back and forth like some sort of young child? Yes, yes, I am.

For God's sake, pull it together.

"Aidan? Are you still there?" he asks, his voice so quiet I can barely hear him.

I make some sort of sound. It comes from deep in my gut and resembles the lonely howl of a needy malamute who's been left out in the yard too long.

"Was that a … dog?"

"Yes, I'm outside."

"Oh, okay, it just sounded so close to the phone that I thought it was you. Look, I know it's a big ask—for you to come to the wedding—but I don't want to get married without my best friend by my side. And I can't stand the thought of you not being part of our daughter's life."

"Daughter?" I ask, finally rising to my feet. I walk over to the window on wobbly legs.

"Yeah," Lawson says, and I can hear the smile in his voice. How the fuck does he get to be so fucking happy? "We found out yesterday that we're having a little girl. But we're planning the wedding for after she's born. Cait wants some time to get back in shape again and I'm hoping it'll be enough time for you to decide you can be there. All I'm asking is that you think about it, okay?"

"Yeah, no. I'm not going to."

"Not going to think about it or not going to come?"

"Both." My gut flips. I'm taking a stand here and I don't know exactly what's going to happen, but I do know this is something he and I are not going to come back from. But then again, that ship has already sailed, hasn't it?

He blows out a long sigh. "Okay, I should have guessed that going in. I hope you'll change your mind. There's lots of time between now and then."

"I won't."

There's a long pause before he says anything. "For what it's worth, not having you in my life is like having my right arm cut off."

"Am I supposed to feel sorry for you?"

"No. I just want you to know how much you mean to me, and that I wish I had fallen in love with anyone else."

"Well, you didn't."

"No, I didn't. I guess I gotta play the cards I was dealt."

I let out a scoff. "How awful for you, especially since you dealt them yourself."

I can picture him rubbing the back of his neck, his face screwed up with regret. "I suppose I did. I'll let you go. Love you, man."

"Bye." I hang up before he can say anything else. I've heard about all I can handle from him for a lifetime. "Happy fucking birthday to me," I mutter.

This feeling, right now—this gut-churning, nauseous, too hot and too cold at the same time feeling that seems like it may last forever—is the reason I will never fall in love again. Because love is Not. Worth. It. Love doesn't care about you. Love will turn your life upside-down and leave you a complete mess. If life has taught me anything, it's that being alone is far better than being rejected. So alone, I shall stay.

New plan for this evening. I'm going to get piss-stinking drunk.

2

Nasty Bank Ladies, Trivia Champions, and Best Friends Forever...

Lola Gordon

From: Mary M. McNally
Benavente Credit Union
62 Main Street
San Felipe, Santa Valentina Island
B3A P2N
Phone: 248-355-2535

To: Lola Gordon
Owner/Proprietor of Soul Surfers Surf Shop and School
34 Sea Breeze Blvd.
San Felipe, Santa Valentina Island
B3B 4Y7

Re: Notice of Foreclosure Sale

Dear Ms. Gordon,

We regret to inform you that the property located at 34 Sea Breeze

Beach, Please

Boulevard, which is secured by a mortgage held by Benavente Credit Union, is scheduled for foreclosure sale on Friday, April 7th.

Despite repeated attempts to resolve the default on the mortgage, the property remains in default due to failure to make timely payments as per the mortgage agreement. The foreclosure sale will be conducted in accordance with the laws and regulations of San Felipe, Santa Valentina Island, and may result in the sale of the property and all contents located within the property including, but not limited to:

- all merchandise such as surf boards, clothing, towels, wax, sunscreens, stand-up paddleboards, wetsuits, swimwear, scuba equipment, and
- all retail-related equipment such as cash registers, display racks, shelving, sound system, seating, microwave, refrigerator, etc.

If the property is sold at the foreclosure sale, you may lose all rights to the property and all of the items within, and the bank may obtain a judgment for any remaining deficiency owed under the mortgage.

You have the right to redeem the property by paying off the outstanding loan amount, interest, and fees before the foreclosure sale takes place. We strongly recommend seeking legal advice and taking appropriate action to protect your interests in this matter.

If you have any questions or wish to discuss potential options to resolve the default, please contact our foreclosure department as soon as possible.

Thank you for your attention to this matter.

Sincerely,

Mary M. McNally
Foreclosure Specialist

Benavente Credit Union

———

Lola Gordon
Owner/Proprietor of Soul Surfers Surf Shop and School
34 Sea Breeze Blvd.
San Felipe, Santa Valentina Island
B3B 4Y7

To: Mary M. McNally
Benavente Credit Union
62 Main Street
San Felipe, Santa Valentina Island
B3A P2N

Re: Notice of Foreclosure Sale

Dear Ms. McNally,

I am reaching out to strenuously object to your proposed foreclosure sale of my surf shop and all the contents within. As you know from our previous conversations, my business partner (and world's worst ex-boyfriend) Reid Devonrow stole all the money from our business account and disappeared, thus creating the inability for me to pay the mortgage/business loan.

The police have a nation-wide warrant out for his arrest, and I have hired a private investigator to track him down, and when she finds him, I hope to get the money back. I have also obtained alternate employment at the Paradise Bay Resort and have been working as many extra shifts as a room service call center representative as they'll give me. In addition, I've been taking loads of side jobs to try to scrape together enough cash to pay you back and open the doors of Soul Surfers Surf Shop again as soon as possible. I'm literally working fourteen hours per day. I will pay you back.

Beach, Please

To that end, I have saved $1256.94 that I am happy to apply to the loan today. I promise I will pay it all back. I just need a little more time.

Let's stand together in sisterly solidarity.

Thank you for your patience and understanding,

Lola Gordon
Owner/Proprietor of Soul Surfers Surf Shop and Surf School

P.S. I also want to assure you that once I have my shop back, I hereby swear to never again have a business partner, and can promise you that I will never, ever have a business partner with whom I am romantically involved. As my business skills are much more honed than my skills for spotting bad men, please know that the bank's money will be in good hands from now on.

From: Mary M. McNally
Benavente Credit Union
62 Main Street
San Felipe, Santa Valentina Island
B3A P2N
Phone: 248-355-2535

To: Lola Gordon
Owner/Proprietor of Soul Surfers Surf Shop and School
34 Sea Breeze Blvd.
San Felipe, Santa Valentina Island
B3B 4Y7

Re: Notice of Foreclosure Sale

Dear Ms. Gordon,

As we've gone over several times, financial institutions cannot provide preferential treatment of clients due to 'sisterly solidarity.' We are beholden to our shareholders, and therefore must follow the law, as well as bank protocols.

Your offer of sending $1256.94 (that will only cover a fraction of the $386,973.21 outstanding) comes too late. Had you been able to make payments at stage one of the foreclosure process (notice of default), we may have been able to halt the process at that point (although you would have had to make payments of that size on an almost daily basis).

As much as I regret the unfortunate circumstances in which you find yourself, I cannot change them. The foreclosure sale will go ahead as scheduled unless you can come up with the *entire* amount outstanding.

Sincerely,

Mary M. McNally
Foreclosure Specialist
Benavente Credit Union

I SIT in the driver's seat of Bessy, my short school bus, sweat trailing down my spine as I wait for the light to change. The thing no one tells you when you get all excited about buying a vintage bus to paint up for your surf business is that they didn't make 'em with air conditioning back in the day. And if there's one thing that would feel soooo good right now, it would be 1000 BTUs of cold air blasting out of the vents. Or whatever unit they use to measure air conditioning. I don't know and I'm too hot to care.

Bessy wasn't supposed to become my sole means of transportation. Back when life was just taking off, I only used her to load up boards and surf students (boards on top, surfers in the seats) for the trek from my shop on Sea Breeze Boulevard to Long Beach, where you can catch the best waves on the island. Bessy took two round trips a day—one at ten a.m. (for the beginners needing smaller waves) and a two o'clock group who could handle the big swells brought in by the trade winds every afternoon.

Otherwise, my boyfriend, who shall forever be known as The Dirtbag, would drive me around in his Jeep. Top down, tunes playing, the two of us living the good life. Or so I thought.

But since he's gone (and so is my money), I now drive a bus that bears the name of my now-defunct surf shop. It's like a little kick in the hoo-hah every time I walk out of my basement suite and see it parked on the street. My bright pink, purple, and teal bus with the Soul Surfers logo painted in loopy graffiti-style letters across the side. She's the sign of a dream that I may never get back. But hey, she's paid for and she gets me from here to there.

The light turns green and I pop the clutch and hit the gas. Bessy lurches and complains but ultimately gets going in the direction of The Turtle's Head Pub, where I shall spend the evening with my trivia team, kicking ass, so I can walk out fifty dollars richer (all of which will go to feed Bessy).

One might think I'd be super depressed about my current state of affairs, but one would be wrong. I'm fine. Well, not fine exactly, but I'm certainly not giving up. The situation may be dire, sure, but it ain't over 'til it's over. It's darkest just before dawn. And a bunch of other platitudes that have kept me going over the last eight months since The Dirtbag did me dirty.

I circle the block three times before I find a spot I can squeeze Bessy into, then hurry to the pub where my best friend, Penelope Nilsson, will be waiting. She and I met back in grade eight when her father, a Norwegian popstar, became my mother's fourth husband. Of all seven of my stepdads, Lars Nilsson is definitely in my top three (and mainly because he brought Penelope with him). He's a one-hit wonder for the song *A Viking Raid on the Dance Floor*.

The marriage only lasted six months, but our friendship has remained as solid as if we were real sisters who actually like each other. Penelope has been by my side starting in our awkward teenage years—mine made bad by the ever-popular combination of braces and glasses, hers because she was already six feet tall at fourteen. We nursed each other through our first real heartbreaks and cheered each other on for our first real job interviews. She was there every step of the way when I started the business. A lot of the sweat equity put into transforming the old mechanic shop into an uber-cool retail space was hers. She held me while I cried when The Dirtbag ran off and was there the next night to make me daiquiris and rage with me when I found out the employee pay cheques bounced because he had not only stolen my all-time favourite board (a Retro Noserider longboard), but he had stolen all the money in the business account as well. Penn has made multiple offers for me to move in with her and her boyfriend, Eddie, but there's no way I'm going to be a beaver dam. They've got a good thing going, and the last thing they need is a sad third person homesteading on their sofa. Besides, the money I'd save on rent won't even touch what I owe.

I walk inside the pub, the delightfully cool air hitting me at the same time that I spot Penelope. She's dressed in a bright green tank top and an equally loud bohemian skirt, and the sight of her makes me happy. A lot of women Penn's height try to make themselves small, but not Penn. She owns her six foot-two inches and is unapologetic about the space she occupies in this world. If you ask me, more women could take a page out of her book.

Penn looks up from her phone and gives me a sympathetic look. Standing, she says, "Bring it in, girl."

I hug her tightly, allowing myself to soak in all the compassion. I forwarded the bank email to her as soon as it arrived this afternoon, and she immediately sent back that *Monsters, Inc.* gif of the little girl getting a hug from that big blue furry monster. Penelope is my people. We pull back and sit down at the round wooden table. In a few minutes, our trivia teammates will arrive, and we'll get focused on the game, so we're going to have to talk fast.

"Shitty luck," Penn says. She still has a slight Swedish accent, which people usually find hard to place on account of her having raven black hair. When you say someone's from Sweden, an image of a blonde comes to mind. But as it turns out, they have people with all sorts of hair colours there, just like most countries. Who knew?

She shakes her head. "I totally thought that sisterly solidarity thing might work."

"I know, right? It sounded so good." I chew on my bottom lip, thinking back to the email exchange. I knew the chance that Mary McNally would suddenly change her mind and reverse the foreclosure was slim, but I had to try.

"As if she couldn't give you more time," Penn says with a scowl. "Like seriously, if we women can't stick together, what is this world going to turn into?"

"I don't know, Penn. Makes me worried for the future of humanity," I say, tongue-in-cheek. I glance around the room of The Turtle's Head Pub, my eyes landing on a man sitting alone at a table in the back corner. Hello, Mr. Handsome. Chestnut brown hair, broad shoulders, muscular physique under his t-shirt, and there's something thoughtful about the expression on his face as he watches the cricket match on the TV mounted on the wall. If I weren't in dire financial distress, I'd be batting my eyelashes at that. But my situation is dire, so no flirting for me.

Oh, and also, I've vowed to never trust a man again, so I guess there's that. I keep forgetting that one. Just like I better forget hot guy in the corner.

"Any word from your private dick?"

I snort out a laugh. The only silver lining about the whole thing is that we get to say private dick a lot. Shaking my head, I say, "No. Honestly, at this point, I'm starting to think she may not find him."

"Even if she did, I bet he spent all the money already."

"How could he spend that much cash in eight months?"

"On women and booze," she tells me.

My gut churns and I fight the tears threatening to spill out. "Whatever. I'm not letting that bastard take me down. I'm going to figure out a way to get the money and get my shop back. Soul Surfers is *not* over."

Penn places her hand on mine. "Oh sweetie, it might be time to

… you know … accept the fact that it might be." She quickly follows that with, "*For now*. Over for now. But you will rebuild and someday, you will own and operate the best surf shop-slash-surf school on the island."

I stare at her for a second, blinking slowly. "Penn, you can't give up on me. There's going to be a way to make this happen. We just have to find it."

"In the next three weeks?"

"Lots of time," I say with a firm nod that is becoming less convincing every time I do it. "The universe was just trying to teach me I shouldn't ever trust a man with my money again." Holding my hands in front of my face as if I'm shouting, I say, "Lesson learned, Universe, so you can give me my shop back already."

She sighs. "If only it were that easy, hey?"

"I'll figure it out," I tell her.

"I've been thinking about it, and let's say you don't get the shop back. It doesn't mean you have to give up being a surf instructor. You could go work for Surf Dudes or buy some boards and just meet people at the beach."

I shake my head, tears threatening to spill from my eyes. "It's all or nothing, Penn. I lost a hell of a lot more than a business."

The money to start up my business came from my favourite stepdad, Norm. He was an Australian pro-surfer who came for a competition and stayed when he met my mom. Of all my stepdads, he was the one who actually wanted me around. He taught me to surf, and after my mom dumped him and he moved back home, he and I remained close. Norm never had children of his own, so he left all his money to me, along with strict instructions that I was to open a surf shop or school or both. Losing the shop is like losing Norm all over again. The truth is I haven't so much as touched a surfboard since the day the bank padlocked the shop and stuck the humiliating bright yellow foreclosure notice on the door. I'm terrified that what happened is going to make me hate surfing with a passion. And if that's the case, I don't know what I'll do with my life.

"I'll find a way to get it back. I have to."

"God, I wish there was something I could do. I'm so sorry you're going through this, Lola. It's all just so unfair."

"Thanks, it really, truly is." Shrugging, I say, "But hey, at the end of the day, I've got a lot. It's only money, right?"

"You need money?" Rosy Brown, general manager extraordinaire at the resort and kick-ass teammate, asks.

I look up to see that she and her husband, Darnell, have arrived. She sits down at the table next to me. "Seriously, Lola. Do you need money?"

"No, I'm fine," I tell her.

She purses her lips at me. "You're clearly not fine. Darnell, give Lola some money," she says, slapping her husband's arm.

Darnell, who still hasn't sat down yet on account of getting distracted by the cricket match on the big screen, snaps to attention. He starts reaching for his back pocket, pulling out a wallet thick with cash. "How much?"

"Zero, I'm fine," I say firmly. "I mean, unless you've got five hundred thousand dollars in there that you don't need."

A look of understanding crosses his face. "Still haven't found The Dirtbag?"

"No sign of him anywhere." Not that finding him would get the shop back. Even if he had some of the fifty-six thousand he stole, it would be too late anyway. I need the entire amount. But at least justice would be served. Offering Darnell and Rosy a bright smile, I say, "Anyway, whatever. How's everyone feeling tonight? Like winners?"

"Yup," Rosy says with a confident nod. She glances around the room. "All the usual suspects are here so we should be able to leave victorious yet again."

Penelope grins at us. "It's almost too easy, isn't it?"

Our server, Wanda, appears next to me. "What's up, nerds?"

"Not much," Penelope says with a faux-modest shrug. "Just getting ready to win again."

Wanda takes her order pad out of her apron. "Usual? Loaded nachos for the table, pint of Grasshopper for Darnell, nine-ounce house whites for Rosy and Penn, and water with a slice of lemon for

El Cheapo?" She gives me a wink to say she's just kidding, even though she's not. I'm tempted to say she should call me El Broko, but if I say that, Darnell is going to take out his big wad of cash again, and there's no way I'm going to be able to say no twice tonight.

"Water keeps the mind sharp."

"Your mind would stay sharp even if you downed an entire bottle of tequila," Rosy tells me. Then, turning to Wanda, she says, "Same order as every week. We're not going to jinx anything by trying something new today."

A couple of minutes later, Buzz, the DJ-slash-trivia master, steps into his booth to get set up. I glance around at my team, trying to get excited. As much as I love trivia, the game has become more like another job. I cajoled these particular people into joining the team for a reason—to win. The four of us have vastly different areas of knowledge. Rosy and Darnell are in their early sixties. He's a retired postal worker who spends his days fishing. He's our sports, history, and cars person. Rosy's an expert on geography, old movies, and music. Penelope, who is an audiologist on account of loving old people, handles all things science, as well as pop culture and fashion, and I'm our literature, nature, and food girl. I'm also our resident *Clash of Crowns* expert—the greatest book series-turned-television show ever written. There are a surprisingly large number of questions about the series, since the author, Pierce Davenport, came to Santa Valentina Island to write the last book. The entire nation has adopted the series as if we all had something to do with it. He adopted us right back—marrying Emma Banks, a local chef (and one of the owners of the Paradise Bay Resort where I work my day job). I have yet to meet the man in person, but someday, I hope to. I'll make a complete ass of myself, I just know it. But it'll be glorious anyway.

Wanda drops the answer sheets off at our table, and I count them to make sure we have three—one for each round—then write our team name (Multiple Scoregasms—Penelope's idea) on the top of the sheets.

Behind me, near the back of the room, I hear a man yell, "My own brother! Shithead."

The room goes quiet and everyone turns in the man's direction. It's Mr. Handsome. He's staring up at Wanda. "Can you believe it?" he asks her, his Canadian accent coming out strong, even though he's slurring his words. "Happy freaking birthday to me, eh?"

Wanda shakes her head at him and says something I can't make out. I'm hoping she's telling him he's cut off.

Penelope leans in and lowers her voice. "Urg, that poor bastard. He's been here for hours. Apparently his fiancée left him for his brother and now they're having a baby and getting married. I guess his brother—who's a total dickhead, if you ask me—just told him today, on his birthday of all days."

Rosy makes a loud *tsk*ing sound, while I narrow my eyes at Penn. "How do you know all that?"

"I heard some women talking about him in the loo." She glances over at him. "Poor guy."

Rosy turns and stares. "Hot guy is more like it. Who would cheat on *that*?"

Darnell, who has completely accepted his wife of forty-some years' penchant for younger men, just shrugs. "Must be something wrong with him."

His words feel like a little dig, even though they're not directed at me. My thoughts must be visible on my face because Penn says, "Hey, there's nothing wrong with you. The Dirtbag is just a dirtbag. That's all there is to it."

I offer her a smile I don't mean. "Totally."

Rosy gazes shamelessly in sad, hot guy's direction. "Just look at that jaw. Mmm, mmm, mmm. And that body. He must work out."

Penelope and I exchange an amused glance, then she says, "One of the women in the bathroom said he has an amazing butt, too."

No one said that. Penn's just winding Rosy up. Rosy is a world-class bum looker. She's famous around the resort for staring at the FedEx guys in their shorts.

Rosy's eyes light up. "Really?" Craning her neck, she says, "I wonder if we can get him to stand up and turn around?"

Penn taps her lips with one finger. "We just need to come up with a good excuse."

Darnell shakes his head at us. "Do you know how mad you'd all be if I said something like that about a young woman?"

Rosy pulls a face. "We're just having some fun."

"Anyway, enough fun. We've got a game to win," I say, giving the hot, sad man one last glance. Honestly, he is stupidly handsome.

"Okay, trivia geeks," Buzz, the world's least enthusiastic trivia master, says into the microphone. "Who's ready for round one?"

A whoop of excitement fills the room.

"As always, I'll read out the instructions," he says, his face and voice completely devoid of emotion. "We'll play three rounds of twenty questions with a thirty-minute break between rounds. I'll repeat the question twice, and only twice. When the round is over, your team captain passes your answer sheet to the table to your right for them to mark it. Multiple Scoregasms, err, I mean the winning team takes home the two-hundred-dollar prize, and I can move on to playing music for the normal people who will arrive here at ten o'clock while you lot go back home to your cats and tarantulas."

A lady at the table next to us, who definitely has at least five cats, probably hairless, hisses at him.

Buzz's eyes grow wide. "Let's begin. Question one: What famous athlete lit the torch at the 2010 Winter Olympics in Vancouver, Canada?"

I look over at Darnell, who shakes his head. "Don't know that one, I'm afraid."

"Okay, let's think," Penn says. "It's got to be someone Canadian."

"WAYNE FUCKING GRETZKY!"

I turn to see that sad, hot, drunk guy is sitting up with one finger in the air and a sloppy smile on his face.

Buzz sighs deeply. "Dude, you can't shout out the answers. You'll wreck the game for all the nerds."

"Sorry, sorry," he slurs. "Won't happen again. I'm just…had a little too much to drink on account of my brother stealing my fiancée, knocking her up, and deciding to tell me on my birthday

Beach, Please

that they're getting married. It's my birthday today, by the way. I'm thirty-one."

Slack-jawed, Buzz says, "Okay. We don't need your life story. Just stop shouting out the answers."

"Won't happen again. I prolly don't know any of the other answers. I only know that one because Wayne is a friend of my parents," he says, waving his hand in front of his face for no apparent reason. He turns to the people at the table next to his and says, "I fuckin' hate hockey."

"Moving on," Buzz says. "Question two: In the *Grimm's Fairy Tales* version of Sleeping Beauty, what was Sleeping Beauty's name?"

"Wasn't it Aurora?" Penn whispers.

I shake my head. "No, that's Disney. It was—"

"BRIAR ROSE!"

I groan and shoot a glare at the Canadian train wreck.

"Seriously, dude," Buzz says. "If you don't stop, one of these people is going to sick their python on you."

"Shut up, Buzz," a guy at the back calls.

"Oh, come on, we all know at least five people in this bar have pet snakes."

Several players shift uncomfortably in their seats while Buzz points around the room at them. "Exactly. Question three: In the movie *Christine*, based on the novel of the same name by Stephen King, what make and model was the car named Christine?"

"PLYMOUTH FURY!" the guy shouts, followed by a little giggle. "Sorry. Last one. I promise."

"Yup, make that the last one or we're going to have to ask you to leave," Buzz says.

Luckily for drunk guy, he keeps his mouth shut for the next fifteen questions. Well, about the trivia answers, anyway. He spills a lot of tea about people named Caitlyn and Lawson, who are tying the knot after the baby is born so Caitlyn can get her body back. Poor bastard.

Buzz lets out a sigh. "Question twenty: Which highly toxic plant has no cure and is often mistaken for a wild parsnip?"

25

"Oh! I know this one," I whisper, wracking my brain for the answer. "It's the plant that killed Socrates."

"HEMLOCK!"

A collective groan is heard around the room and the drunk guy holds up both hands. "Sorry, sorry, sorry! I don't know why I keep doing that."

"I do," Buzz says. "It's because you're drunk."

The man nods vigorously. "Yes, that's why. I forgot to eat supper, so all the booze is going straight to my noggin." He lets out a little giggle. "Noggin. That's a fun word."

I watch him, my heart squeezing for the poor guy. I know what it's like to be abandoned by your person. It does not feel good. And he certainly hasn't made his life any easier by getting so wasted.

Wanda walks by and I flag her down. "Can you get an order of chicken pot pie for the sad guy over there?"

She stares at me from under her eyebrows. "Who's paying for that?"

"Me."

Her head snaps back. "El Cheapo is actually paying for something?"

"El Cheapo is actually El Nice-o sometimes," I answer, giving her a haughty look.

She shrugs and walks away, leaving me alone with my team. Rosy raises an eyebrow at me and gives me a 'you like him' smile. I shake my head and say, "I feel sorry for him."

"So sorry that maybe you're thinking a little pity putang is in order?" Penn asks.

"A little 'ride him and leave him smiling?'" Rosy adds.

The three of us laugh until Rosy starts wheezing while Darnell's jaw drops. "Women are so much worse than men."

"Oh yeah, we totally are," Penelope tells him. "And I'm not even sorry about it." Leaning in, she says to me, "So, how about it, Lola? Are you using a chicken pot pie to get into his pants or what?"

"No! Of course not. I just feel bad for him." Glancing back, I see Wanda has just arrived at his table. She sets the plate down and points to me.

He squints his eyes, seeming as if he's trying to get a good look at me. Then he stands, picks up the plate and walks over, using the careful, deliberate steps of someone trying to appear sober when they clearly aren't.

I smile up at him as he nears the table. I'm about to tell him there's no need to thank me, when he sets the plate down. "Look, Miss, thisisverynice of you," he slurs. "I'm totally starving, but if you think that if I eat this, it means I'll sleep with you, I won't, 'cause ... no."

Because ... no? What the hell?

3

A Canadian's Guide to Making a Horrible Impression...

Aidan

Whoops. I should not have said that. She's angry. Her cheeks are almost as red as the rims on her glasses and she's giving me a death glare, not that I blame her.

"I don't want to sleep with you! That's a pity pot pie," she tells me, her voice unnecessarily loud.

"Oh, okay then. Thanks you very much." Suddenly feeling sheepish, I rub the back of my neck. "Shit, I don't know why I said that. You and your friends were staring at me a lot, then the food, and I just didn't want you to get the wrong idea. Not that you're not attractive, because you're ... super pretty. You've got that whole stern librarian thing going on with the glasses and..." *Stop it. Stop now.* "That was inappropriate. I—thanks for the feel, the mood..." Dammit. "Letme try that again. The meal. There got it."

"Okay, yup. It's fine," she says, staring at me like I'm a total nut, which seems like a reasonable response, based on how I've been acting this evening. "I wasn't looking at you because I want to get you into bed. It was because you've been talking quite loudly about your situation."

Beach, Please

Wincing, I say, "TMZ, eh?"

"What?"

"Not, not TMZ, TMJ?"

"Do you mean TMI?"

I attempt to snap my fingers but miss. "That's the one. TMI. I'm not normally an open book. I'm closed. A closed book. It's just … been a very bad day."

The older woman at the table pats my forearm. "No need to apologize. You poor thing, you." She turns to the man next to her. "Darnell, get the poor man a chair."

Darnell hops up, gets a chair from the table next to theirs and gestures for me to sit. "Darnell Brown. The bossy one is my wife, Rosy."

I hold out my hand and we shake. "Aidan Clarke. The woman missing from my side is going to have my brother's baby. A girl. Isn't that wonderful?"

"We heard," Darnell says, scrunching up his face. "That's got to hurt."

"Nah, I'm fine," I tell them, flopping into the chair. "I definitely didn't move five thousand miles away from them to escape the pain." Turning to the younger women, I smile. "And you are?"

The one next to the one I insulted, who might be the tallest woman I've ever seen, says, "I'm Penelope Nilsson. She's Lola Gordon. We're ex-step-sisters who have become besties."

"I'm too drunk to follow that, but 's'nice to meet you, Penelope," I say, then turn to Lola. "Lola, L-O-L-A, Lola…" I sing.

Lola gives me a half-hearted smile and nod.

"You prolly hear that a lot," I say.

"A few times, yeah," she answers.

Boy, she's cute. Like, really, *really* cute. Somewhere in my drunken haze, I decide I want to impress the pants off this woman. Well, not literally. Unless she wanted me to, that is. What was that thing I think about falling in love again? Oh right, that it's the worst idea ever. But we don't have to fall in love. Maybe just into bed. "So Lola, here's the thing," I slur, holding up one finger because that seems like a serious person thing to do. "Are you from around here?"

"Yes."

"Darn. I don't date locals."

She raises one eyebrow.

"That makes sense in my head. I'm not normally this drunk. Actually, I'm not normally drunk at all. Stone cold." There's a word missing there but for the life of me I can't think of what it is.

"Oh, okay," Lola says, but I'm not entirely sure she believes me.

Rosy pats my hand. "You should eat. Soak up a little of that booze."

"Good plan, Rosy," I say with a grin in her direction. I pick up the fork and dig into the slice of pie, then look back at Lola. "You must hate that song, right? People must always be singing it to you and asking if you love to drink cherry cola."

"I don't hate it. It's a good tune, but it does get a little old after a while," Lola says.

"Especially when people sing that bit about her looking like a woman but talking like a man," Penelope adds.

"Oh, I bet." Turning to Lola, I say, "You don't talk like a man, by the way. You have a nice woman voice. I like it."

Lola seems to be fighting the urge to laugh, and I'm pretty sure it would be at me, not with me.

"I'm making an ass of myself," I say.

"Oh, no!" Rosy says.

"Not at all," Darnell tells me.

Lola nods. "A little bit, yes."

Pointing at her, I close one eye so there's just one of her. "Honesty. Thank you."

"How long has it been since … you found out?" Penelope asks.

Glancing at my Gaiman watch, I say, "About four hours and seventeen minutes, give or take."

Rosy *tsks* and shakes her head. "Terrible. Just terrible."

"No, I mean, how long since you and your fiancée broke up?"

"Oh, six months, four days, and twenty-two hours."

"Give or take," Lola says.

"I'm a firm believer in giving accurate information," I tell her. "Unlike the woman I thought I was going to spend the rest of my life with."

"And your brother," Penelope adds.

"Your own brother," Rosy says, rubbing my hand. "Poor, poor man. Eat up, Aidan."

Penelope says, "Aidan, I just feel so bad that you're alone on your birthday. Where's the rest of your family?"

"Back home in Canada," I tell her, shoveling a bite into my mouth without testing for heat. *Hot! That's way too hot!* I let my tongue hang out and try to blow cold air across it, but it's not working. "Hot, hot," I say, my words coming out muffled.

"Here, have Lola's water," Penelope says, sliding the glass to me.

I douse the flames and manage to swallow. "Thank you. That did *not* feel good."

"You okay?" Rosy asks, rubbing my back. And the way she's rubbing it makes me wonder if it's maybe a little more than a sympathy rub.

Can't be, right? Her husband is sitting on the other side of me.

"I'm fine, thanks. Or, I will be, anyway. Not sure how long it takes to get over something like this."

"Burning your mouth?" Rosy asks. "It should feel better in a few hours."

"No, I meant having the loveofmylife leave me for my brother."

"Lola can relate," Penelope tells me. "She and her boyfriend had a surf shop together until he stole all the money and skipped town."

"Oh, ouch," I say, wincing.

Lola raises one eyebrow at Penelope. "Seriously?"

"What? I was just trying to make Aidan feel better."

"By telling him about the most humiliating moment of my life?"

"No judgment here," I tell Lola. Tapping my chest with my fingertips, I say, "I feel you. I feel you, dawg."

Did I just call her dawg?

"Thanks. For what it's worth, I hope they have a colicky baby who keeps them awake for a solid year."

I grin at the thought. "That would be oddly satisfying."

"Oh! And the lack of sleep causes them to turn on each other, and they wind up divorced and miserable," Penelope says.

"Yes, *that*." I point at her and grin, but then my smile fades. "Although I don't really want them to end up divorced. Not now that there's a child involved. Especially a colicky one."

"Aww." Penelope touches her hand to her chest. "You're so sweet. How could *anyone* cheat on you?"

"It's cause I'mboring," I tell her, my words slurring together.

"No, you're not!" Rosy, who has no idea whether I'm boring or not, says.

"Compared to my brothers, I am. I'm an IT guy. Well, I was, anyway."

"That's not boring," Penelope tells me.

"Would you like me to tell you everything there is to know about bank cybersecurity?"

She wrinkles up her nose. "Err…"

"Exactly. That's why I'm a boat captain now. I bought a catamaran and I take tourists out on three-hour snorkeling trips," I tell her before breaking into song. "A three-hour tour!" I giggle a little, then shake my head. "But as great as my new life is, there's no way I can compete with my brothers."

"I'm sure you're every bit as great as them," Penelope says.

"Newp, afraid not. All four of them are hockey superstars. My parents were too. My dad played for the Calgary Cougars for years, and now two of my brothers play for them. My mom was on the Canadian Women's Olympic team," I tell them.

"And you didn't make it?" Rosy asks.

"I never got that far. Turns out, when you strap knives to my feet, I have no coordination whatsoever."

"Oh, how sad," Rosy says, tearing up a bit.

"Wait. Did you say your last name is Clarke?" Darnell asks.

I nod, my heart sinking to be seated next to someone who I now realize is a hockey fan.

"Wow, I didn't know there was a fifth brother."

"Most people don't," I say, my cheeks heating up a little. I pick at the chicken pot pie with my fork, letting a little steam escape. "Anyway, it doesn't matter. I moved here to get away from ... all that, and 'til today, I was doing a pretty decent job of it. But I'll be fine. Tomorrow, I'll shake it off and keep going."

"Good for you," Lola says with a firm nod. "No sense dwelling in the past."

"Exactly," I tell her.

Gosh, she's pretty. Those certainly are huge, brown eyes behind those red-rimmed glasses. And that is one very kissable mouth. I should stop staring like this or she's going to call the bouncer over to have me removed. Besides, no good has ever come from me staring at a woman like this. Even when that woman did seem to be staring back.

―――

"I love your bus!" I say as I follow Penelope up the steps. "I can't believe this is yours. I've seen it around town and always thought it was super cool."

"Thanks," Lola tells me, getting into the driver's seat.

I plant myself on the seat behind hers. "And you can drive this beast?"

"Yup."

"Surfing and driving buses and owning businesses. You're one impressive person, Lola," I tell her. "Kind, too, to offer to see me home safely. And pretty. Very pretty, even with the glasses."

Doh! Come on, brain, come up with better stuff to say than that.

Lola glances back at Penelope, who's in the seat next to mine, and the two burst out laughing at my sloppy attempt at being charming. Looking at me in the rearview mirror, she says, "Thanks."

"That came out wrong," I tell them. "I should stop talking."

"No, it's fine," Lola says. "You're good."

She starts up the engine, and after listening to all the sounds it's making, I start to wonder if this old bus will actually be able to move, but a few seconds later, we're barreling down the road toward my place. I stare out the window for a bit, watching the buildings whiz by, then for no reason whatsoever, I stand up and slide the window down and feel the breeze on my face. "WHOOOHOOO!" I shout into the wind. "I'm on a bus with two lovely ladies!"

Some people on the sidewalk snicker and I offer them a sloppy grin. "I love the air here," I announce. "It's so…smells nice. Not like stupidCalgary, where it's dry and doesn't smellatall. Do you ladies love the air here so much, you just breathe it in?"

"Umm, yeah, I guess so," Penelope says.

"It's great, but I need you to sit down, Aidan, or I'll have to pull over," Lola tells me.

"Oh sure, sorry," I answer, planting my butt on the seat. "Say, would you wanna go hit a club or something? Dance the night away and forget our troubles?"

"As much as I'd love to, I have to be at work at six," Lola says.

"I also have to be up early," Penn tells me.

If I weren't so numb with booze, I'd be disappointed. "S'okay. It's prolly for the best anyway. I'm a terrible dancer, so it would only show you I've got no moves." I glance out the window, then look at Penelope. "Did I say that out loud?"

"The bit about not having any moves?"

"Yeah, that."

"You did."

"Damn. I only meant to *think it* with my inside voice." I lean over and whisper to her, "I like your sister friend. If I weren't planning to be alone for the rest of my life, I'd definitely be asking for her number."

Penelope leans in and says, "I'm pretty sure she can hear you."

"Is my whisper voice not working?"

"About as well as your inside voice."

I snort out a laugh at myself. "When I sober up, I'm going to be sooooooo embarrassed."

"Don't worry about it. We've all had nights like this," Lola says.

"Thanks, you're both so nice." Leaning back, I slouch and rest my head on the seatback, then close my eyes.

What seems like a couple of seconds later, the bus pulls to a stop and everything goes quiet.

"Aidan, we're at your place," Penelope says, tapping me on the shoulder.

I jolt to sitting upright. "Already? That was fast."

"You kind of passed out there for a few minutes," Lola tells me.

"Oh geez, I am *not* gonna feel so good in the morning, am I?"

"Probably not," she says, pulling on the handle to open the door.

I get up and stumble down the steps, then bounce back up. Turning to them, I salute. "Thanks for the ride, ladies!"

They both follow me off the bus. Lola gives me a concerned look. "I think we should make sure you get inside before we leave."

"Nah, I'mfine," I tell her, holding up the key. I weave my way up the sidewalk, then up the four steps to my front door. "Yup, got it from here," I slur as I fumble with the lock on my front door.

My companions wait patiently while I try to get my eyes to focus on the lock. "Just have to remember how keys work."

I back up and look at the house number. "Twenty-four, yup, that's right." Holding up a key, I sway a little as I stare at it. "That's the mail key," I tell them.

"Maybe try a different one," Penelope suggests.

"Good idea," I answer with a sloppy grin.

Lola takes the keys from me. "Why don't I give it a try?"

Glancing at Penelope, I say, "Better idea."

A moment later, I stumble into my front entrance and kick off my shoes. The pair follow me inside. "I'm going to leave the keys on your credenza," Lola says.

"Perfect. Do you guys wanna drink? An herbal tea or anything?"

"No, we have to go," Penelope tells me, following me into the living room. "You sure you're going to be okay?"

Spinning around, I say, "Yup. Absolutely great. I'm gonna sleep it off and move on with my life."

"This is a nice place. Very… tidy," Lola says, walking over to the wall of windows. "You must have quite the view."

"S'gorgeous," I answer, flopping onto the couch and laying my head down. "I love it here."

I close my eyes. "You sure I can't get you something? I could cook a frozen pizza or maybe fire up the grill and make some steaks?"

"We're fine, thanks," Lola answers.

"Okay," I say, yawning.

I feel a blanket covering me up and a second later I hear her voice close to my head. "I put a garbage can right here in case you need it."

"Try to sleep on your side," Penelope tells me.

"Side sleep, got it," I mumble.

"Good night, Aidan. We'll let ourselves out."

"You sure I can't make you some toast?" I mutter.

I hear them say good night and tell me that they're letting themselves out, and my final thought before I drift off to sleep is that I haven't felt this cared for in a very long time.

4

Cyber-stalking, Ice Cream Feasts, and Opportunities of a Lifetime…

Lola

ONE OF THE many joys of owning the surf shop was that we didn't open until nine in the morning, so although I was always busy, I got to sleep until at least seven-thirty every day. Unlike now, when I'm up at the butt crack of dawn so I can be ready to answer room service calls by six.

Also, I was doing stuff I *loved* every day. The Dirtbag and I took turns working in the store and running the surf lessons. I'd either be at the shop with the overhead doors open to let the sun and salt air in while I helped people find what they needed, or I'd be out in the waves enjoying the incredibly gratifying experience of seeing someone get up on the board for their very first time, knowing I helped make that happen. The joy on their faces, even if they were only up for a few seconds before they lost their balance, was exhilarating. A little piece of heaven you take home with you.

Room service calls, not so much.

I'm currently on with the least decisive woman on the planet, who wants 'a little something to hold her over while she waits for her husband to wake up.'

"Umm… I don't know, do you recommend the oatmeal?" She sighs as though this is the most important decision she'll ever make. "It's not too mushy, is it?"

Of course it's bloody well mushy. It's oatmeal! "I quite like it," I tell her, while I pick up my mobile phone and open Google and search: Clarke brothers, hockey, Canada.

Huh, they're all hot. Even the parents. I scroll through images of them even though I know I shouldn't. First, because I'm at work, and second, because I'm never going to see the guy again, and even if I did, I'm not exactly up for love. Maybe a quick roll in the hay, though. Although the guy is a hot mess, so…

"But do you like mushy oatmeal? Because I like mine a little more textured."

More textured? What does that even mean? "Honestly, with enough brown sugar, I'll eat just about anything," I say, trying to sound helpful even though my answer could not be more vague.

"I can't have sugar. Hmm… Maybe I should just go down to the buffet without my husband. I could leave a note."

Yes, for God's sake, do that. "The buffet is certainly a wonderful option. That way you can see the oatmeal before you decide. It shouldn't be too busy yet, so you can probably snag a lovely poolside table."

I come across a photo of all five brothers dressed in tuxedos, arms around each other as they grin at the camera. They share the same dark hair, the muscular build, the huge smiles with straight white teeth. One of them has a scar across his eyebrow and looks to be a little older than the others, but he's still every bit as good-looking. I zoom in on their faces, wondering which of these men is Lawson the Betrayer (as Aidan called him last night).

The woman on the phone is still nattering away, something about her nightgown and makeup. When she stops talking, I say, "Right, so the oatmeal then? I could send up a plate of fruit as well."

"What kind of fruit?"

Stay calm, Lola. Don't snap at the needy lady. "It's a lovely blend of honeydew, papaya, purple grapes, and strawberries, sprinkled with shaved coconut."

"And are the strawberries fresh? There's nothing worse than a strawberry that's about to go off."

Doing my best to soften the edge in my voice, I say, "Yes, of course the strawberries are fresh. All the food we serve is fresh, both through room service and the buffets." Hint, hint.

She laughs. "Of course it is. How silly of me." I hear a male voice in the background. "You know what? My husband's up now. I think we'll go down to the buffet after all."

"Wonderful," I tell her. "Have a lovely day."

I hang up and open an article in the *Toronto Tattler* titled "Hockey's Royal Family Scandal—The Forgotten Clarke Brother Gets Forgotten by Fiancée," but before I can read the first line, I get another call.

"Room service, Lola speaking, how can I help you this morning?"

"Lola? Like the song?" the man asks.

"Yup," I say, my voice raising an octave. "What can I get you today?"

"Hmm. I'm not quite decided yet. How's the oatmeal?"

I lift my glasses and rub the bridge of my nose. "Terrific. Just the right texture."

I get so busy that it's late evening before I have time to read the article. I'm at home in my basement suite apartment. I should probably tidy up instead of reading, but it'll only get messy again. Besides, I'm exhausted. I was out a lot later than I planned last night, and I've just finished working on my bookkeeping side-gig. Time to curl up on my couch under a cozy blanket.

The reporter managed to dig up a lot of details on Aidan's three-year relationship with sports physiotherapist Caitlyn Whitehall. Instagram posts of the two of them together doing 'in love' sorts of things are shown, followed by photos of her with his brother. By the end of it, my heart feels like it's been cracked open. If I thought love dealt me a bad hand, it's nothing compared to what Aidan's been through.

Also, yum, because he can pull off all sorts of looks—tuxedo, T-shirt and shorts, and especially no shirt and shorts. I scroll back to a photo of him with his brothers at their parents' oceanfront cabin on Vancouver Island. But not because they're all shirtless. I'm not a pervert. It's because he looks so happy holding up his beer, and there's something comforting about seeing him that way. Okay, it's also on account of the no shirt thing.

Oh my God, Lola, stop cyber-stalking Aidan Clarke. You don't want a man, remember? Men equal heartache and possible bankruptcy. Although he doesn't seem like the type to steal all your stuff and disappear. But he *did* say that whole thing about 'because no' when he thought I was trying to get him into bed. Even if I was stupid enough to put myself back out there, he's definitely not ready for any type of relationship. The guy's been gutted. Like, yesterday. I stare at the picture for another second (okay, a solid minute) before closing the article.

"Nope, he's not for you," I mutter. "You need a miracle, and you're not going to find one sitting here ogling some hot hockey family."

I open Google and type in, "How to make five hundred thousand dollars in three weeks," but before I press search, a video about a HUGE *CLASH OF CROWNS* ANNOUNCEMENT catches my eye. I press play on the video and watch as the NBO logo appears on the screen, then it cuts to Grammy-nominated actor Destiny Poulsen, from the original *Clash of Crowns* series, smiling at the camera. "Hello! I'm Destiny Poulsen. You may know me as Oona, the warrior princess from the *Clash of Crowns* series. I'm here to make a huge announcement on behalf of NBO. Unless you've been living under a rock, you already know that the prequel series, *Blood of Dragons*, is nearly here! Season one of the show *and* Pierce Davenport's highly-anticipated first novel in the series, *Clan Wars*, will be dropping at midnight exactly one month from the time of the posting of this video. It's the first time in history that both the book and television show will come out at the exact same moment.

"This is a huge deal, people, and to celebrate this epic event, NBO will be hiding five crowns that look just like this one," she says,

Beach, Please

holding up an ornate medieval-style gold crown. "Each one will be hidden in key locations around the globe, including Ireland, Slovenia, Greenland, Morocco, and the Benavente Islands. As of the airing of this video, we've posted a single picture of each crown in the location where they'll be hidden to whet your appetite. And in exactly eight days—next Friday, March 24th—we'll post the first clue to each crown, so listen carefully, because I'm about to give you details you need to know," she says, setting the crown on a black velvet crown holder thingy. "A cash prize comes with each crown. The first one to be found will snag one lucky winner—or team—a cool million dollars. The second one is worth five hundred thousand. The third, four hundred thousand, the fourth will be worth three hundred thousand, and the fifth winner will walk away with two hundred thousand dollars!

"Can you believe it? Those are life-changing prizes!" She grins into the camera. "In order to win, you'll need not only a mode of transportation that will work in the given area, but you'll also need in-depth knowledge of *both* the books and the TV series. The clues are *hard*, so only the biggest Crownheads have a shot at the cash. In fact, being a Crownhead won't be enough. You'll also need first-hand knowledge of the geographical area. Searching on Google is not going to cut it. Go to NBO.com slash *Blood of Dragons Hidden Crowns* to find out more about the contest rules. And get yourself ready for an epic adventure of a lifetime!"

Destiny picks up the crown and places it on her head while a few bars of the theme song for *Clash of Crowns* plays, then the video ends.

My heart pounds as I click the link and I scroll until I get to the location of the crowns. My ears weren't deceiving me. They're going to hide a freaking crown somewhere here on the Benavente Islands and I'm going to be the one to find it!

A few minutes later, I pull up in front of Penelope's condo building. Glancing up, I see that the light is still on, so I rush to the front door and buzz an annoying amount of times, too excited to remember my door buzzing manners.

"Hey Lola, everything okay?" Eddie says into the speaker.

"How'd you know it was me?"

"I saw Bessy."

"Right. Can you let me up? Something hugely massively amazing happened!"

"Awesome!" He buzzes me up and I sprint up the stairs to their third-floor condo, sucking wind by the time I get to their already-opened door.

Eddie's sitting on the couch playing *Call of Duty*. Without glancing at me, he says, "I'm right in the middle of a battle. Penn's just getting out of the shower. She should be out in a second."

"Sure, sure," I say, pacing while I wait for her to appear.

A few seconds later, she comes hurrying down the hall in a robe, her hair wrapped in a towel. "What's going on?"

"This!" I tell her, thrusting my phone at her.

She takes it and watches the video, with me standing next to her, my eyes glued to the screen.

When it's over, I grin at her. "This is it! This is my golden ticket, Penn!"

She opens her mouth, then shuts it. "I mean, it's exciting, but isn't it a bit of a long shot?"

"Is it?" I ask, walking over to her cupboard and taking out three bowls. We don't have to talk about it. We're going to have ice cream sundaes because that's what we do when we have something big to talk about. "It's literally a contest made for me personally. I'm a huge Crownhead and one of the crowns is hidden *right here*! It's destined to go on this head," I tell her, pointing to myself.

"Well, I mean, it's not hidden right here. It's *somewhere* on *one* of the islands," she says, rooting around in her freezer for a carton of ice cream.

"Babe, do you want a sundae?" Penn asks Eddie.

"Affirmative," he says.

"Do you think he's answering me or saying that to one of his teammates?" she asks.

I get out some chocolate sauce in a squeeze bottle, while Penn grabs a can of whipped cream and a jar of maraschino cherries. "Let's just make him one. If he doesn't want it, we can split it."

"Good call," she says, scooping the ice cream into the bowls.

"Give us a celebratory amount of ice cream because there's *no way* I'm *not* finding that crown and getting my shop back," I tell her.

She doesn't answer which means she doesn't agree.

"What? You don't think I can do it?"

"Of course I think you can do it. It's just that…well, do you know how many islands there are, if you include all the tiny uninhabited ones?"

"No. Do you?"

"No," she admits. "But it's a lot."

"Can't be that many. Eddie, how many islands are part of the Benaventes?" I ask.

He tilts his controller and opens fire on someone on the opposing team. "I don't know. A hundred and thirty-two, give or take."

She gives me a pointed look.

"Who cares? I'll know what the clues mean which will make it easy peasy."

"I mean, I suppose you might find it."

"I will find it. *Will*," I say, shaking the can of whipped cream.

"You heard her, the clues are hard."

"Penn, how many times have I missed a *Clash of Crowns* question at trivia night?"

"Never."

"Exactly."

I spray the whipped cream on top of the ice cream, then Penn pours the chocolate sauce on while I scoop out a couple of cherries from the jar for each of us, skipping Eddie's bowl on account of him hating cherries.

Penn takes Eddie his sundae, then we sit down at the table and I scoop a bite with the perfect ratio of ice cream-to-whipped cream-to-chocolate sauce. I pop it in my mouth and let the flavors do their thing. *Mmm…* "This is my chance to get back the life I'm supposed to have."

"Can you imagine if you win?" she asks, taking a giant bite. With her mouth still full, she says, "You can march right into that bank and plop the cash on that awful Mary McNally's desk and say, 'Suck it, be-otch.'"

"Eeek!" I squeal. I swipe the screen on my phone, then bring up the contest rules. The two of us read through them while we eat our sundaes. Immediate disqualification for: breaking the law, trespassing on private property, threatening or physically harming other treasure hunters, impacting environmentally sensitive areas negatively…

The list goes on and on and I scroll through the legal stuff without reading it. I'm not going to do anything illegal.

Eddie gets up from the couch and walks over, standing behind us while he eats. "Says there you need either a helicopter or a boat."

Penelope gasps. "Aidan's got a boat!"

"Who's Aidan?"

"That sad guy from last night, remember?"

"Oh right. The drunk dude."

My pulse picks up a bit and I concentrate extra hard on the screen, hoping Penn won't notice that my face is heating up. Trying to sound casual, I say, "Right. I totally forgot he has a boat."

When I finally look at her, she raises one eyebrow at me and grins. "You like him."

"Do not."

"Do so. I can tell by how hard you're pretending you forgot all about him."

"I did forget about him. I've got bigger fish to fry here, Penn."

"So if I look at your search history, I'm not going to find his name in there?"

Grabbing my phone off the table, I say, "Nope, you won't."

Eddie bursts out laughing. "Did you see how fast she did that?"

"You totally Googled him," Penn laughs.

My face flames. "Okay, but only because his life is such a trainwreck. Not that mine isn't. But, anyway, whatever. I looked him up, but not because I want to marry him or something. The guy's a mess. Besides, I'm done with men, remember?"

"The more you ramble, the less convincing you are," Penn says. Glancing up at Eddie, she says, "She's rambling, right, babe?"

Beach, Please

"Definitely rambling. You like him."

"He's handsome, I'll give him that. But seriously, no thanks. Not interested. Too busy trying to save my surf shop to even think about romance." I scrape the bottom of the bowl even though all the 'gettable' ice cream has been gotten, unless I want to start licking, and I'm not an animal. Well, if Eddie weren't here…

I open the menu on the contest site and click on 'Benavente Islands.'

The page loads, showing a photo of a crown sitting in a cave.

"Oh! Yes!" I say.

"You know this particular cave?" she asks, oozing skepticism.

I pull a face. "No, but at least this narrows it down."

Looking down at my phone, she says, "Siri, how many caves are there on the Benavente Islands?"

Siri answers with, "According to Wikipedia, there are six hundred forty-eight caves scattered around the Benavente Islands, most of which are located on the big island."

"That's a lot of caves."

I nod, my optimism starting to wane. Penn must be able to tell because she shakes her head. "You know what? You're right. You can do this, Lola. This could be the answer to your prayers. You should go for it."

"Do you think so? It doesn't sound crazy?"

"It does sound crazy, and you should totally try anyway. What have you got to lose?"

I jump up. "Exactly. I've got *nothing* left to lose." As soon as I say it, I realize how depressingly true that is. My shoulders drop and I say, "Literally nothing."

Then I remind myself I have a shot at something amazing, so no time to wallow. I put my bowl in the sink and grab my purse. "I gotta go!"

"Where are you going?"

I yank open the door and step out into the hall, then turn back. "To Aidan's to beg him to give me a ride."

The look on her face tells me her mind went to a very dirty place. "Not that kind of ride. Pervert."

"If he's offering, you should take both!" she calls as the door closes behind me.

I let out a loud laugh while I hurry to the stairs.

A few moments later, I start up Bessy's engine and we rumble down the road, my heart in my throat. How the hell am I going to ask a total stranger for this type of favour? It could take *days* to find the right cave and there's no way I can afford to pay him for that kind of time.

Oh, what if he doesn't even remember me? He was so drunk last night, it's possible the whole evening will be a total blank for him. Also, he might be a completely different person when he's sober. He could be a total dick. He might be all, "Why would I help you? I don't even know you. Besides, I've got my own problems, Four Eyes."

But he really didn't seem like that type of guy last night. He seemed very sweet. The way he didn't want his brother and his ex to get a divorce now that there's a baby involved? That's a guy who'll give a girl in need a lift. We'll strike a deal—something fair for both of us. I don't want charity. I'm a very serious businesswoman fighting to get her business back, and this time I'm going to do it all on my own. No partner. No inheritance. Just me figuring it out for myself. That way I know I can trust the owner because she'll never let me down.

But first, I need to find a boat, whether it's Aidan's or someone else's. Because that money is my very best shot at getting my life back. Only it'll be so much better this time because I won't be relying on a lying, thieving dirtbag.

5

Hangovers, Good Brothers, and Mothers on a Mission

Aidan

It's late in the evening and my hangover is still here, reminding me why I don't drink. Good thing today's clients were two families with children ranging in age from five to twelve, so at least there was a lot of shrieking all day in addition to the waves and the hot sun. By four o'clock, I was tempted to go find Stogie Stew and hand him the keys.

I've been on the couch for the past three hours now watching golf, on account of Formula One being far too loud for me today. The truth is, I've been trying to distract myself from the periodic bouts of humiliation that hit when my brain unlocks a new memory of last night. God, I was a total moron. Seriously pathetic. I can never, *ever* go back to The Turtle's Head again. Well, maybe in disguise. No. Not even then.

My mind keeps wandering back to those kind people who fed me and took me home. Penelope and Lovely Lola. I get a full-body cringe as I remember telling her I wouldn't sleep with her. Then that whole thing about her being a sexy librarian. Urgh! And the bit about her being sexy even with glasses? And the whispering about liking her? I am never coming back from that. Ever.

With any luck, I can avoid her for the rest of my life. She'll be easy to spot, what with the bus and all. When I see her coming, I can just turn and go the other way to save myself the embarrassment. Earlier this evening, I Googled her because I knew there was something bad that had happened to her but I couldn't remember what. I didn't remember her last name, but a quick search of Lola, surf, and San Felipe gave me the goods. I read an article about how her stepdad had left her the money to start her own surf business and how her ex took off with all the money in the account. Apparently the guy disappeared into thin air. The authorities put out a warrant but they haven't found him and now her shop is in default on the loan. Poor Lola. And I thought I had it bad. At least I didn't lose my livelihood when I got screwed over.

My phone rings and I see my brother Bennett's face on the screen. I mute the TV and answer the phone. "Hey, Bennett."

"Oh good, you're alive."

"Why wouldn't I be?"

"Mom hasn't heard from you since Lawson told you about the baby so she's worried sick about you," he says, adding, "On a side note, I gave him royal shit for telling you on your birthday."

"Thanks."

"I got your back, bro," he says. "In fact, if we weren't on the same team, I'd have cut him off the moment I found out."

"I appreciate that."

"Wanna know something else? I haven't even passed him the puck once this season."

I burst out laughing. "Are you serious?"

"Hell yeah, I am. Why do you think he hasn't scored?"

"Is that why? Did you know he actually had the nerve to complain about it to me?"

"Moron."

"Right? As if I care how many points he gets."

"Twelve," Bennett tells me.

"Twelve? That's it?!"

Beach, Please

"Yup," he says, laughing some more. "That'll teach him to break the bro code."

"Not that it matters now," I say. "He's madly in love with Cait and they're planning to spend their lives together."

"Yeah, well, still. He's gotta pay for what he did."

I chuckle a little. "Thanks, Ben."

"Now, back to Mom, because there's some shit you need to know," he says, his voice growing serious.

"Right, our mother who spoke with me only yesterday, yet is somehow in a panic about my safety."

"She figured you'd call her right away to talk about it, and when you didn't, she started imagining all sorts of awful scenarios."

"Dead in a ditch?" I ask.

"Obviously."

"Why always the ditch?"

"Who knows, but you should have called because now Mom and Dad are hopping on a plane to find you."

My stomach drops and I close my eyes. The last thing I want to do right now is deal with my parents. "What? When?"

"Tomorrow morning. I know they want to surprise you, but I figured you'd rather have a heads up."

"Wait, let me get this straight. They're so worried that they decided a big surprise was in order?"

"I think they want to catch you doing … whatever it is they think you're doing that isn't good for you."

"Like what? They'll find me with a needle in my arm or something?"

"That may have been mentioned at one point," he says, sounding far too amused.

"I'm not… Jesus. I'm fine."

"Are you?"

"Yes," I snap.

"Okay, relax. I'm just asking," he says. "We're all kind of worried about you. You just up and left without any warning."

"Yeah, well, I needed to get away, but trust me, now that I'm here, I'm totally fine."

"Still trying to hook up with tourists?"

"There's a little of that from time to time," I say. "In fact, yesterday I had a boatful of single women." I don't mention that they're only single because they're widows. "Honestly, Ben, I'm living the good life here."

"Okay…"

"Seriously. I've never been happier."

"You're going to have to *really* sell that when Mom and Dad get there."

"Why?" I ask, my Spidey Senses tingling.

"Because they're planning to buy a place there."

"What?!"

"Yup. Mom can't stand being so far away from you, especially with you being so alone in the world," he says. "But don't worry because they'll only be there, like, six months a year."

Six months a year of my mother pressuring me to find someone new and get married? Nope. Not doing that. "Are you messing with me, Ben? Because I swear to God—"

"I wish I was. They're all packed. They arrive tomorrow evening at six," he tells me. "And do you want to hear the best part?"

"No."

"I wouldn't want to hear it either, but trust me, you need to know this."

My gut tightens a little more. "What?"

"They rented the Airbnb next door to you." He bursts out laughing while my mouth hangs open. "They're going to spend the next week being your neighbours."

"Are you fucking kidding me?"

"Nope," he says, still chuckling. "Apparently they didn't want to invade your space, but they wanted to be somewhere where they can keep an eye on you."

"They know I'm an adult, right?"

"Honestly, I'm not even sure," he says. "But I do know if they like the Airbnb, they're going to see if it's for sale."

Shit. Shit. Shit. "And they'll offer way above asking just to make this happen."

Beach, Please

"Yup. You know Mom. When she gets an idea in her head…"

"There's no stopping her. Son of a…"

"Yeah, well, hopefully I've given you enough time to get out ahead of this thing. I better run. I've got an early practice."

"Okay. Thanks for calling," I tell him, even though no part of me is feeling grateful at the moment.

"Yup. Let's do it more often. Good luck with the 'rents!"

"Thanks," I say, all sarcasm.

I hang up and flop back onto the couch. What the hell am I going to do now? I've worked very hard to cultivate a nice, quiet life of being totally alone, and they're going to completely ruin that. Besides, it's not like we have anything in common. If they actually buy a place here, we'll spend half the year staring awkwardly at each other over dinner, which is the last thing I want to do. Actually, that's only the second-to-last thing I want to do. The very last thing is for my mom to start showing up with nice girls she meets at the grocery store and suggesting we go for a nice ice cream date. And she will be relentless about finding me someone. Relentless. She treats matchmaking for her sons as if it's an Olympic sport, and as someone who actually made it to the Olympics, the woman knows how to achieve her goals.

I get up and pour myself a bowl of ripple potato chips and get some garlic dip out of the fridge.

Think, Aidan, think. How do you stop the world's most determined woman and the man who loves her from buying the house next door?

If I'm them, I'd want to know my son has a bunch of good friends who have his back. Which I don't. I have zero friends here, which is completely on purpose. I dip a chip, then pop it in my mouth and chew while I think. A bunch of good friends, or maybe just one really great girlfriend? Maybe if they think I've fallen in love with someone, they'll go back to Canada and I can keep my life of blissful solitude. Only I don't have a girlfriend. I wonder if the old lady with the walker from yesterday is free this week.

Dammit. A sense of desperation comes over me. Where the hell am I going to find someone to pretend to be my girlfriend by tomorrow? One thing's certain, I sure as shit won't find one here.

Grabbing my keys, I hurry to the front door. I yank it open, only to see Lola from last night standing on the step smiling up at me, with a slightly wild look in her eyes.

"Hi Aidan. I'm sorry to just … show up at your house like this. I didn't know how else to get ahold of you. I have a time-sensitive business proposal for you, and if you say yes, it could be … well, extremely lucrative."

Stepping aside, I say, "Come on in."

6

Shit's About to Get Weird...

Lola

I FOLLOW HIM INSIDE, butterflies swarming my insides. He seems annoyed. There's a tense energy about him that wasn't there last night. Maybe he *is* a jerk.

Okay, Lola, he let you in. That's got to mean you have a chance here. Don't come right out with the details. Warm him up with a little small talk first. Then ease him into the crazy.

He leads me through the living room to the kitchen, where the patio doors are open, letting in the warm breeze. "Can I get you a drink?" he asks. "I'm sticking with water tonight for obvious reasons, but I've got beer if you want one."

"Water would be perfect," I tell him, watching as he reaches up and opens the cupboard to get a glass down, the muscles in his arm flexing in a way that I can't seem to ignore. "How are you feeling today?"

He glances over his shoulder at me with a grimace. "I've definitely felt better. I haven't been that drunk since … well, I can't actually remember when."

"Is that because it's been so long or because you were too drunk to remember?" I ask with a little grin to let him know I'm teasing.

He sets the water on the white marble island, then leans against the counter on the opposite side of the kitchen. "The first one. I'm honestly not much of a drinker. And can I just say I'm completely embarrassed about last night? I'm probably never going back to The Turtle's Head again."

"Oh, don't worry about it. You were fine," I tell him, fighting a smile. "Everyone loved you there."

He shakes his head. "I made a total ass of myself. I've literally been having full-body cringes all day as the evening comes back to me bit by bit." Rubbing the back of his neck, he adds, "And I think I owe you an apology. Well, more than one, actually. I distinctly remember accusing you of wanting to sleep with me, and then later saying something about liking you…"

Okay, so he's not a jerk. Maybe I do have a shot at getting him to help me. My cheeks warm at the memory of him 'whispering' to Penn about me on the bus. "Don't worry about it. I didn't take offense. Well, not to the bit about you hypothetically asking for my number, you know, if you weren't through with relationships forever. But you already apologized for accusing me of trying to get you into bed, so consider it forgotten. Although, talk about mixed messages."

He winces again, and good lord, how does someone look so sexy when they're just wincing? Maybe I should just hire a water taxi to take me to look for the crown. I'd drain my bank account and max my credit cards, but it might be the smarter option because I have a feeling that spending too much time with Aidan is going to be bad for my 'no men ever again' promise.

"Well, anyway, thank you for being so kind last night. Feeding me and giving me a lift home and unlocking the door for me when I forgot how keys work," he says. "I honestly don't know where I would have ended up if it weren't for you. Probably in a gutter outside the pub."

I chuckle a little, then say, "It was nothing."

"No, it was something. I was falling apart and you were kind when you could have just pretended not to notice." He stares into my eyes just a second too long. Clearing his throat, he says, "But, you came here to talk business, so let's do that."

Oh God, I *did* come to talk business, but now that I'm here, I don't know what to say. Heart pounding. Palms sweaty. "Do you think we could sit outside?" I ask, stalling for more time to think about how to frame this whole thing.

"Sure," he says, pushing off the counter and picking up his glass of water.

I start for the patio doors with him following closely behind me. I can't help but hope my butt looks perky in these cargo pants before reminding myself that a) they're too baggy to show my bottom, and b) he's probably not looking. He's too much of a gentleman. Besides, he's clearly not interested. And neither am I, so there's that.

When we get out onto the covered deck, Aidan flicks on the string of lights that hangs from the soffits above us, and we settle ourselves at a round table.

"This is really nice," I tell him, glancing around to take in my surroundings. The sound of the waves lapping against the shore both calms me a little and reminds me why I'm doing this. It's so I can get back what I lost—days spent in the ocean, earning a good living and loving what I do.

"Thanks, I love it here," he tells me, staring out into the night. "It's very peaceful."

"I believe it. I live in a basement suite with a view of my landlord's Buick. Well, and some shrubs, so…"

He smiles at me. "So, not exactly your forever home, eh?"

"I hope not." I take a sip of water. Then, suddenly realizing how thirsty I am, I gulp down the entire glass in one go.

Aidan's eyes are wide when I look at him. "Can I get you another water?"

"I'm good, thanks," I tell him, wiping my lips with my fingers. "I'm nervous actually."

"Why?"

"Because we don't know each other at all and I'm about to ask you for a giant favour."

He narrows his eyes a little. "I thought you said it was a lucrative business proposal."

"Well, it could be, but it's a long shot, to be honest."

"How long?"

"I don't know how to quantify it, but like, *pretty* long. Maybe even a hundred."

His lips quirk up into a grin. "A hundred, eh? That does sound like a long shot."

"Yeah, it could be. But if it pans out, wow. It'll be amazing."

"Lucrative."

"Very," I say with a firm nod.

When he doesn't immediately say yes to the thing I want him to do that I haven't told him about yet, I chew on my bottom lip for a second, then say, "And obviously you can say no if you want. You're not in any way obligated to help me out."

The right side of his mouth curves up. "Are you giving me permission to say no?"

"No, I mean, obviously, you don't need my permission to say no to me. I just said that so you won't feel bad if you do turn me down. What with you being Canadian and all."

"You figure Canadians have a hard time saying no?"

Nodding, I say, "I meet a lot of Canadians at the hotel and you're all so nice."

"We're nice but we do know how to say no."

"Really?" *Damn.*

He nods, then lets a tiny grin escape. "We do it politely. Usually accompanied by an apology."

"Oh, well, that would be the polite way to do it."

"I think so," he says. "Now, do you want to tell me about this deal or should we keep talking about the quirks of being Canadian?"

"Right, the deal," I say, wondering if I arch my back and stick my tatas out, if it would help get me the yes I need. *No, Lola, you are not going to resort to using your feminine wiles.* "So, here's the thing about the deal... Umm, before I tell you what it is, can I give you a little background so you'll understand why this whole thing is so important to me?"

"Sure."

"I'm not sure if you remember Penelope telling you that I had a surf shop and that my ex took off with all the money in our business account…"

"I do recall that. I'm really sorry that happened to you," he says, his expression doing something to my insides. "That's a shitty deal."

"He also took my favourite surfboard."

"Bastard."

"Right? Like seriously, why my personal favourite, when we had an entire shop full of them?"

"He sounds sadistic."

"I think he might be. He did a great impression of a compassionate, caring human being, and he did an *amazing* job pretending to be in love with me, but the whole time, this completely different person was there, lurking just under the surface."

"That's the worst, isn't it?" Aidan asks.

"Yeah, it really is."

"Like, why pretend? If you're not into someone, just damn well be honest and move on, without stealing money and surfboards."

I nod emphatically. This is good. We're getting somewhere. "Or starting up with your person's brother behind his back."

"Or that."

"Anyway, in three weeks, the shop and all the inventory are going to be auctioned off, and everything I worked so hard for will be…" I make a poofing sound and mime an explosion. "…Gone. I've been working my ass off to try to come up with the cash, but it hasn't been even close to enough. And tonight, the perfect opportunity just … dropped from the sky."

A look of surprise crosses his face. "That doesn't happen often."

"No, it doesn't, which is why I have to go for it."

"So, what's the opportunity?"

"Here, why don't I show it to you?" I ask, pulling my phone out of my pocket and finding the video. I press play and slide my phone over to Aidan, then wait while he watches it, my stomach twisting in knots. His expression is totally neutral, and I can't even begin to guess what he's thinking. Probably something like, 'This woman is nuts. There's no way this is going to work. How do I get her out of here without her throwing herself on the floor and clinging to me like a baby sloth? Sloths have incredible grip strength so it would be hard to shake her. And it'll also be super embarrassing for both of us. Mostly her.'

When the video finishes, he hands my phone back. "I can see why you figure it's about a hundred on the scale of long shots."

Nodding, I do my best to appear confident. "I know, but I'm one of the world's biggest Crownheads. I've read the books and rewatched the series an embarrassing number of times."

His eyes light up with amusement. "Like, how many?"

"Can I *not* say?" I ask, my cheeks heating up.

"If you want to convince me, you're probably better off telling me."

I close my eyes and wrinkle up my nose. "Six times for the books and fifteen times for the TV series."

His jaw drops, then he chuckles. "Wow, that is a *lot* of times."

"I know, but it's seriously the greatest series ever written. Are you a fan?"

Shaking his head, he says, "I've never seen it or read the books."

"Well, they're amazing."

"Apparently," he teases. "So you need a boat."

Okay, here we go. "Starting next Friday. It might just be one day, like day one we find it and done. Or could take a few days. Maybe even a week, I don't know." I swallow hard, then force myself to keep going. "I can't afford to rent your boat for that much time, so I'm hoping you'd be willing to take a chance that we'll find the crown and we can split the winnings. I mean, I can't afford to give you half on account of needing so much to get my shop back. I was thinking maybe ten percent? If we find the first crown, that would be a cool hundred thousand in your pocket."

"And if we don't find one, I get nothing."

"Yeah, not ideal, I know. But I promise you, I'm honestly an expert and I *know* I can solve the clues."

Beach, Please

He shrugs. "That may be the case, but there's no way of knowing if there's someone else out there who can solve them quicker."

"That's why the plan requires you to be a bit of a gambler."

He sits back in his chair and doesn't say anything, which causes me to panic a little. I keep talking before he can say no. "*Or* if you're not a gambler, we could set up a payment plan. It might take me a long time to pay you back, but I promise I will." I chew on my lip again, then say, "I'm not going to lie. It would be a really, really long time, and I don't know if you're okay to be out that kind of cash for like, a *long time*, but if so, I will—"

He holds up one hand. "No, that option doesn't sound good for either of us. I imagine the last thing you need is more debt."

"True." My heart sinks. He's definitely going to say no, which means I'm going to have to find someone else before the first clue is dropped. "Look, I have a feeling that this whole thing is going to go fast once it starts. All five crowns might be snapped up on day one. What I'm asking for is a few hours or maybe a couple of days of your time and gas. I'm sure to rent out your boat for that long would be more than I can swing right now, but would you be willing to do it for a discount? Just for your costs? I know it's a big ask for a total stranger and that you have no reason to say yes to it, but I also truly believe that we can find a solution that will work for both of us here. Maybe I could work it off cleaning your boat or answering phones. There's got to be *something* I can do for you that you need."

He stares at me long enough for me to squirm in my seat a little, then he says, "Actually, there is something, but it's a bit … weird."

7

No Good Can Come from Two Desperate People Hatching a Plan...

Aidan

HER RIGHT EYEBROW SHOOTS UP. She definitely thinks it's a sex thing. "Weird how?"

"Not like that," I tell her. "Believe me, that's the last thing on my mind."

"Okay, good, because that's the last thing on my mind too," she says. (Although the way her face is flushed right now suggests otherwise.)

"Tomorrow evening, my parents will be arriving. I guess they're so worried about me that they decided to drop everything and rent the place next door for the next week."

She wrinkles up her nose. "Oh no, did you call them last night when you were drunk?"

"No," I answer. "Apparently the fact that I *didn't* call them after my brother dropped his big bombshell on me was enough to get them on a plane."

She cringes and says, "Wow, imagine what they would've done if they'd spoken to you."

I allow a small grin to escape. "I'm guessing the police would have been called."

She grins back. "I'd say ambulance and fire too."

"Most likely." My smile fades as the reality of what's happening comes back to the forefront of my mind.

Lola's face grows serious. "Sorry. I didn't mean to offend you. You know, in case you were trying to save face or something," she says. "Although after last night, there's no point in trying to save face with me. You've already shown your soft underbelly."

My soft underbelly? So, I'm a *dog* in this analogy? I love dogs, but I do not like the comparison at all. Maybe Lola is not the woman for the job. Although, she is pretty much the only woman on the island that I know, and she's here, needing a favour from me, so she really is my best shot.

Before I respond, Lola says, "I'm sorry. I shouldn't have said that soft underbelly thing. I can tell by the look on your face that you didn't appreciate it, which I totally understand. I only meant that I can relate to what you're going through. Our situations aren't exactly the same, but the end product is—we're both alone, having been left in a very public way."

"Right, yeah. You're not wrong about the saving face thing. That is exactly what this is about," I tell her. "Not saving face with you. I get that that ship has already sailed, but with my family. I'd love to find a way to not appear to be…" *A total loser.* "Stuck. I'd much rather they believe I've moved on."

"Totally," she says, nodding emphatically. "They're probably irritating the hell out of you, asking if you're okay every time they talk to you and telling you to come back home to be around the people who love you. Like as if *that* would solve anything. Just being right there with the whole thing in your face all the time. The media reporting on them, every single person you know knowing what happened. No thank you," she says, seeming adorably upset on my behalf. "And clearly you're *not* okay. So having them show up right now is the last thing you need. Being forced to pretend you're fine when you're *so not fine*."

Exactly. How does this woman get me so well? Wait. I'm so not fine? My sense of pride kicks in and I say, "I am fine. Most days."

She shakes her head at me and places her hand over her chest. "No, you're not. You're hurting, Aidan."

"I'm actually pretty happy here on my own. Yesterday was a shock, but honestly, I'm already over it. The hangover is the worst part," I tell her. "But now, I have another problem because as it turns out, they're so concerned about my welfare that they're planning to do some house-hunting while they're here, starting with the Airbnb next door."

Lola gives me a blank look. "And that would be bad because…"

"Because I don't want my parents living next door. I like that they live back in Canada. It works for me. I'm here, living the good life, on my own, answering to no one, while they're there, all together, doing what they do without me being there not fitting in with the rest of them."

She pulls an 'aww, what a sad puppy' face, but I hold up one hand. "No, no. I'm not saying that because I want you to feel sorry for me. I accepted long ago that I have nothing in common with my family. I'm totally okay with it, honestly. I have my own interests, things I want to learn, books I want to read, while they have—"

"Each other?"

"Hockey. They have hockey," I tell her, having a sip of water. "Do you know what the best thing about living here is?"

"No hockey?"

"Exactly. And they will bring it with them. You see, my parents are nice people. They volunteer and donate big wads of cash to various causes. It wouldn't be long before they're famous all over the island for starting up some sports program for underprivileged children or their tireless efforts at some soup kitchen."

"The bastards," she says wryly.

I blink a couple of times, trying not to let my irritation show through. After all, I'm about to ask for a much bigger favour than she's asking for here. I better be nice about it. "I only mean that I like living somewhere where nobody knows who I am or who my family is. I love my privacy, and I'm not about to give that up."

A look of understanding crosses her face. "Is this the part where it gets weird?"

I nod, my pulse quickening a bit. "My best shot at preventing them from bringing the Clarke family fame with them is to convince them I have a wonderful life here, complete with…" I clear my throat. "Someone who cares about me."

She points at herself. "Someone like me?"

"Yes, that's what I was thinking." I wipe my palms down the sides of my shorts. "If I can make it seem like I have a girlfriend and that having them here would actually be less-than-ideal, I'm pretty sure I can make them go home permanently."

"So I pretend to be your girlfriend and make it look like you're super happy."

"Exactly."

"For how long?"

This sounded so much better in my head a few minutes ago, but now that I'm having to actually say it out loud to someone who is basically a total stranger, it sounds…worse. "They'll be here for a week."

"So, we swap favours? I pretend to be your girlfriend and you take me to get my crown?"

"Yes."

"What about the money?" she asks.

"You keep the money," I tell her.

"Seriously?"

"Seriously. I figure it's a fair trade. My time for yours."

"But you'll be out gas too," she says. "And that's going to add up fast."

"Trust me, when you meet my parents, you'll realize I've gotten the better end of the deal."

"What are they? Jerks or something?"

"No, they're very nice. But they're also … pushy. Especially my mother. She's going to start talking marriage and babies about five minutes after she meets you. Besides, I'm asking for a week of your time and your thing could be over in a matter of hours. And honestly, my thing has a better chance of working so you might be doing all of this for nothing."

She stares at me for a second, her eyes narrowing a little. "You don't think we're going to find the crown, do you?"

I glance out at the water, then back. "I think a lot of people are going to be out there racing for that crown, and with every person out on that water, your chances get smaller. It's not a judgment on your knowledge, it's just math."

She nods a little, looking worried, then straightens her back a little. "It's not just math. This may sound crazy, but that crown has been put out there for me to find it. It's exactly what I need to get my dream back, exactly *when* I need it. The universe has done me a solid. All I have to do is go out and get it."

I consider her words for a second. Do they sound a little nuts? Yes. But it's also the most positive way possible to look at her situation. She's not going down without a fight. "I love your optimism."

"Without hope, there's no point in living."

I let her words soak in. Although I completely disagree, I say, "I guess that's true. So, do we have a deal?"

"We have a deal. You help me. I'll help you. Done." She holds out her hand and we shake. She's got a nice, firm handshake, and the feeling of her soft skin does something to me that it shouldn't. I chalk it up to it reminding me what a woman's skin feels like and nothing more. After all, it's been a while since I've touched one of them. Well, other than all that sunscreen rubbing-in yesterday, but I refuse to count that.

When we let go, I tell my heart to slow the hell down already. This is a business deal. Well, sort of. Hers is all business, mine is personal. I stare at her for a second, wondering if my parents will buy that we're a couple. We're complete opposites. She's a cool surfer chick and I'm an IT guy doing his best impression of a boat captain. But she's also my best shot at getting through the next week without my parents moving in next door or having to hear 'you need to come home' a thousand times or having their pity faces staring at me every damn time I look up.

She stares at me for a second, making a clicking sound with her tongue, which I'm guessing is her thinking sound. "If you really want to convince them, I should probably move in."

No, thank you. The very last thing I want is someone invading my space. "I don't think that's necessary."

"You don't? I mean, you want this to work, right?"

"Obviously."

"And what's going to make it both seem more like a permanent situation plus feel more awkward than if you've got a live-in girlfriend who's got nothing more on her mind than getting you all to herself?"

My temperature goes up at the thought but I keep a straight face. Then I glance out at the water and realize what this is about. "You just want to live here for a week, don't you?"

"Can you blame me?" she asks. "Buick. Shrubs." Pointing in the direction of the water, she says, "Beach."

God, she's fun. She's also right. Having her live here will be far more convincing. "Okay. It's not a bad idea, but we should set up some ground rules."

She lets a small smile escape. "Obviously no sex."

"Obviously. And no using my razor."

"Eww. Never."

"I have a guest room, so that'll be where you sleep. You don't floss your teeth in bed, do you?"

"Are these things your ex used to do, because if so, I'm not at all sure why you weren't the one to end things."

"I'll take that as a no."

"Yes, it's a no. I should run," Lola says, standing and picking up her glass. "I have to work at six and I'll have a lot of packing to do when I get home."

"Just throw some clothes in a bag. And a toothbrush."

I get up and follow her inside, trying not to let myself glance at her bottom. After all, I like to think I'm a gentleman. Whoops, I peeked. Nuts. Her pants are too baggy to actually get a good look, but I'm pretty sure under all that fabric is a very perky behind.

"…make it look like a woman lives here."

Dammit. She's been talking this whole time. "Sorry?"

She pulls the front door open and turns to me. "Decorations? There's no way anyone would believe a woman lives here."

"Oh, right," I say, looking around my sparse living space. "But don't overdo it. Just a couple of pillows, maybe a few photos of yourself."

She grins at me, and it's not an expression I find particularly comforting. "Leave it to me. By the time they show up, it's going to look very much like I've been here the whole time."

She steps outside, then turns to me. "Oh, any allergies or foods you hate so much you couldn't choke them down no matter what?"

"What?"

"I should know these things if your parents are going to believe any of this."

"Umm…ice cream."

She stares at me as if I just told her I eat kittens for breakfast. "What? Did you say you hate ice cream?"

"Yeah, I know it's weird."

"Is this on account of it having the word ice in it? Because there's no actual ice in ice cream. Unless you count the little crystallized bits if you leave it in the freezer too long, but I don't because they're not there when they make it," she says.

I narrow my eyes, momentarily confused. "How did you know I hate ice?" Before she can answer, I realize I must have told her last night. Hell, I probably told about a hundred people that.

"You may have mentioned it," she says. "I didn't think you were serious about it."

Folding my arms, I stare down at her for a second. "Is this a deal-breaker for you? The ice cream thing?"

"Ice cream is life. It's the one thing that has gotten me through these last few months. Well, that and Penn," she says. "So if this weren't a business thing, yeah."

"Wow, you must really love ice cream," I say with a grin. "Good thing we're only pretending to be a couple."

She nods, looking far too serious for the topic at hand. "It's probably for the best, yeah. I can fake-love someone who hates ice cream for a few days, but beyond that…I couldn't do it."

There's something about that statement that doesn't quite sit right with me. I suppose it's a sense of rejection, even though she's only fake-rejecting me, and for a very frivolous reason, I might add. I smile anyway. "Good to know. I'll see you tomorrow."

"Yes, you will. And with any luck, in under two weeks, I'll be a million dollars richer!" She turns and rushes down the steps.

When she's halfway down the sidewalk, I call, "Think of all the ice cream you can buy!"

She spins around and says, "So. Much. Ice cream."

I laugh, then close the door and watch through the window as she climbs onto her bus. Who is this strange-yet-wonderful woman? She's clearly filled with compassion, fueled by adventure, and is a straight-up optimist in spite of the crappy turn her life has taken. She might be a little out-there—the whole thing about the universe giving her exactly what she needs exactly when she needs it doesn't exactly follow logic. I mean, there are probably hundreds of people out there tonight believing that crown is meant for them. Thousands even. And if I had to guess, I'd say every one of them needs a million bucks to solve whatever problems they've got going on. The money won't solve mine, but I sure hope we find it so she can get her shop back.

I wander around my living room for a bit, feeling suddenly restless. I should be upset after finding out about my parents coming, but somehow I'm not. Am I annoyed? Yes. But I'm also low-key excited to be able to pull one over on them and get them off my back, hopefully forever. And that's all thanks to Lola showing up literally at the exact right moment. If I were Lola, I'd think it was the universe doing me a favour, when in reality, it was just a random coincidence. Nonetheless, we can help each other.

I flick off the lights and walk down the hall to my bedroom, thinking about Lola, and what she's been through. As I climb into bed, I resolve to help her in any way I can. Lola's a good person. If anyone should be able to live their dream, it's her.

8

Potted Plants and Pushy Best Friends Who Make You Think Things You Don't Want to Think...

Lola

You up?

> Yup! Been waiting to find out what happened.

He's in!

> REALLY?! That's awesome! So, are you going to split the money with him or what?

No, I get to keep the money.

> What?! He doesn't want any money?

Nope.

> What does he want?

He needs me to be his fake girlfriend.

Beach, Please

My phone rings and I pick it up immediately, glad that The Dirtbag isn't here, because if he were, I'd have to get out of bed to take this call on account of not wanting to keep him up.

"What do you mean, fake girlfriend?"

"Just what it sounds like," I tell her, then fill her in on how Aidan's parents are so worried about him living here all alone that they're coming to shop for a house, then give her a quick run-down of our plan. Penn is silent while I talk which means she does not approve. I wrap it up with, "Look, I know this is nuts, but this is my best chance at righting everything that is wrong with my life. Just think, Penn, in a couple of weeks, Soul Surfers could be back open for business again."

"Yeah, I get why you're doing it. But there are so many things that could go wrong with your plan."

"Like what?" I ask, even though I actually don't want to hear it.

"Well, first of all, what if he's a creep who's just getting you to move in so he can peep at you when you're in the shower or something?"

"You met the guy, Penn. He's not a peeper. Besides, moving in was my idea."

She pauses, then says, "Why would you do that?"

"Two reasons: First, because it'll make his parents think it's a permanent situation so they'll be far less likely to move here. And second, because I could really use a week in an oceanfront cottage."

"Ah, I see," she says. "Do you think you might bring a surfboard while you're there? Maybe dip your toes in the water, hang ten-style?"

The thought of it makes my heart squeeze. "No. The waves aren't good at his beach."

We both know it's an excuse, but thankfully Penelope doesn't call me on it. Instead, she says, "You'll get back to it when you're ready, right?"

"When I've got my shop back."

"Oh, Lola, even if it doesn't happen, surfing is part of you," she says, her voice gentle. "You can't just let that die because of The Dirtbag."

"I won't. Seriously, I won't. I'm just not feeling it yet," I tell her.

"Okay, I'll leave it alone for now."

"I appreciate that. I've got bigger fish to fry right now, like figuring out how to make it look like I live at Aidan's and brushing up on my *Clash of Crowns* knowledge."

"Right. I do have one question."

"Is it about how this isn't exactly fair, since I'm going to walk away with a million bucks and he's only getting a pretend girlfriend for a few days, because I've already thought of that, and I agree. I'm planning to offer him ten percent anyway. Like a serious, don't-take-no-for-an-answer offer when all is said and done."

"That's very nice of you, but that wasn't my question," Penn says.

"Oh, well, what is it?"

"How are you going to pretend to be a couple when you don't know anything about each other?"

"I know stuff about him."

"Oh yeah, like what?"

"He hates ice cream," I say sheepishly. "All right, you may have a point, but I guess we'll just have to wing it."

"You're just going to wing it with a total stranger?"

"Yup," I say, my voice going up an octave as it occurs to me how hard that might get. "You know what? I'll be fine. We'll have a couple of hours before they get there tomorrow to interview each other. I'll just memorize his answers and wing the rest."

"You'll memorize everything you would normally know if you were in a long-term committed relationship?"

"Hello? Trivia queen here who is more than capable of remembering facts," I say, even though her questions are making my stomach somewhat queasy. "Anyway, I should go. I'm going to pack before bed so I can go straight to Aidan's after work tomorrow."

"Right. I'll let you go," Penn says. "Good luck tomorrow."

"Thanks! I won't need it though. I have a very good feeling about this."

"Good luck anyway," she tells me, and I know she thinks I've totally gone off the deep end now. "And who knows? Maybe you and Aidan will wind up falling in love and by the end of the week, you won't just be a fake couple."

"Not going to happen."

"Why not?" she asks, then quickly follows that with, "I mean, I get it that The Dirtbag did a real number on you and Aidan's brother really did a number on him, but if you'd both open yourselves up to the possibility, I think you'd make a very cute couple."

"I'm hanging up now."

"Okay, too soon. I get it. But someday, you'll be ready to find someone, and wouldn't it be awful if you had already met Mr. Right, but you turned him down because of what Mr. Wrong did?"

"Why are you even talking about this right now? I have to pack, move in with Aidan, then find a crown, get my shop back and start my surf school back up. The last thing I need is a man. A man is how I wound up in this situation."

"Sorry, I don't know. It's just that he's super cute and the two of you seemed to be kind of sweet together last night."

"He was hammered and I was trying to be nice."

"I know, but there was a total vibe."

"Yes, alcohol vapours coming from his pores."

"He said he liked you."

"Oh my God, Penn. The guy was so wasted, he would have gone home with a potted fern if it showed any interest."

"A potted fern?"

"I happened to be looking at mine when I said that," I tell her. "Should I bring the fern?"

"Definitely."

"Anyway, the point is, there's no chance for romance between Aidan and me. Is he handsome? Yes, I'll give him that. And he seems nice enough in that boring Canadian guy sort of way, but trust me, tonight when I saw him, he did not give off that sort of vibe at all."

"That's too bad, because I think you two could be good for each other," she says. "He's so sweet. Remember what he said about not wanting his awful brother and his horrible ex to divorce now that there was a child involved? He's one of the good ones."

I don't tell her I had the exact same thought on account of it only encouraging her. "The Dirtbag knew what to say to seem like one of the good ones too."

"No, this was different. It was how he actually thinks, because there's no way a guy that drunk could pretend to be someone he's not. Aidan Clarke is a good one."

I sigh, beyond frustrated with this conversation. "He may be, but I promise you, Penn, he and I are not going to happen. End of story."

She makes a little pouty *hmph* noise, then says, "Never say never."

"I'm hanging up for real this time."

"Love you."

"Back at you. Talk to you tomorrow."

I end the call, then hurry around my place, stuffing throw pillows and blankets into garbage bags. I make a pile by the door of all the things I'm going to take and by the end, I'm glad I have a bus as my mode of transport. The entire time, I mutter away to myself about Penelope being a total busybody and how annoying it is that everyone in relationships wants all their single friends to be in them too. By the time I crawl into bed, it's well after midnight.

I yawn, feeling some of my irritation drain from my body. I know she just wants me to be as happy as she is, but yeesh, enough already. I can be every bit as happy as she is *on my own*, thank you very much. In fact, I am happy. Or I will be when I get back what is rightfully mine.

I close my eyes and wait for sleep to come, only it doesn't. Instead, my brain swirls with thoughts of possible places the crown might be, and strategies for how to get there first. But most of all, it swirls with thoughts of Aidan Clarke, his broad shoulders and big smile. Dammit, Penn. Why'd you have to make my mind go there?

9

This Invasion Was Brought to You by Target Home Decor...

Aidan

I woke this morning completely conflicted about what I'm doing. There's a small measure of guilt at the fact that we're going to be bold-face lying to the people who brought me into this world. Small because, let's face it, I'm only doing this out of necessity. My mom will *never* let up until she sees me happily settled down with a woman. There's also a certain amount of irony in having a woman *move in* with me for a week so I can get back to my life of solitude. But mainly, I'm worried about the fact that this is not a failsafe plan. *So* many things could go wrong with this. We barely know each other. How are we supposed to make it seem plausible that we're an actual couple? What if my parents figure out we're just pretending and it only serves to make them *more sure* I need them to live here? Or if they hate her and decide Lola is all wrong for me so they move here permanently to be here for me when we break up?

All the ways I come up with that this might fail lead to my parents waving to me from their back deck and shouting, "Howdy, neighbour! Is dinner tonight at your place or ours?"

I shut off the shower and towel off, checking the time again.

According to her text, Lola is going to be here in exactly four minutes. I've been giving my house a deep cleaning for the past three hours, which pretty much hasn't happened since I moved in. Although I keep my place tidy, it was bachelor clean, not cohabitating clean. So now the baseboards, light switches, and ceiling fans have all been wiped, my bookshelves dusted, and my cutlery drawer de-crumbed.

I pull on some jeans and a T-shirt, then hang my towel and shut off the bathroom light. I'm just walking into the living room when I hear the doorbell. My stomach flips. We're actually doing this. Although I suppose if things don't go well over the next couple of hours and we figure out that it won't work, I can call the whole thing off. Well, my part anyway. I'll still take her to find the crown. As I pull the door open, the knowledge that I can always change my mind helps calm me down a little.

"Hi, honey, I'm home," Lola says. Or at least, I think it's Lola. I'm staring at a large potted fern with legs.

I reach out and take it from her. "Wow. You brought a plant?"

"Not just one," she says with a huge grin.

I set it down, expecting her to follow me inside, but she doesn't. Instead, I see she's already walking back to her bus. "Come on, we've got a lot to do and very little time."

I hurry out to the bus, and when I climb aboard, I see the first several rows of seats are stuffed with boxes, overflowing garbage bags, a lot of plants, and some suitcases. "You know this is only for a few days, right?"

"Yup," she says, tossing a garbage bag at me. "But we've got to make it look authentic."

"Okay, so long as you know this isn't permanent."

She gives me a glare while she picks up a suitcase. "Don't flatter yourself."

"I'm not. I'm flattering my beachside cottage."

"Oh right," she says, looking a little sheepish. "Either way, no need to worry. I promise I'll move out the second your parents leave. Now, let's get to it. We've only got a couple of hours until they get here and we have a ton of unpacking to do, plus I need to find out everything there is to know about you, starting with, what's your favourite food?"

"Steak and potatoes with a side of fried mushrooms," I say, stepping off the bus.

"Potatoes, how? Baked? Fried?"

"Mashed with lots of butter."

We walk back to the house with our arms loaded, and I find myself impressed with how fast she can move with those short legs. I have a long stride and I'm having trouble keeping up with her. "What about you? Favourite food other than ice cream?"

"Gnocchi with clam sauce, but let's concentrate on you."

"Why?"

"Because they know you, so I can't just make shit up."

I set the bag down in the living room and turn to go back outside. "So, are you giving me permission to make shit up about you?"

"In the interest of time, yes."

I give her a broad grin. "Well, this could be fun."

She stops walking and narrows her eyes at me. "Within reason. You can make stuff up about me within reason."

We start moving again and I say, "So, I can't say you used to be a stripper, for example?"

Hopping back on the bus, she says, "Not if you don't want me to tell them that we met when you were getting a lap dance from my good friend Chastity."

"Fair enough."

We make another five trips back and forth while she grills me.

"Favourite show?"

"*Star Trek*, but not the original. *The Next Generation*."

"The one with Captain Picard?"

"Yes."

"Solid choice. Favourite book?"

"*Airborne* by Kenneth Oppel."

"Favourite sport?"

"To watch or play?"

"Both."

"Formula One to watch, and a tie between jogging and weight training to play."

"Literally none of those things are sports."

"A good argument can be made for Formula One."

"So, no sport for you?"

"Correct. I prefer solitary physical pursuits."

She raises one eyebrow. "That doesn't bode well for our sex life."

"Our sex life is just fine, thank you."

Shutting the front door with her foot, she says, "Just fine? That doesn't sound very exciting at all."

My face heats up a little while I set the last box on the floor. "You know what I mean."

She stares up at me with a look in her eyes that makes me feel a little hot under the collar. "What *are* you like in bed?"

"I don't think my parents will want that information."

"It'll give me an idea about our vibe. Are we wild? Loud? Can't keep our hands off each other? Or more … intimate and cuddly."

Oh. My. God. I'm getting all sorts of images I shouldn't be and I find myself wanting to give her an answer she'll want to hear. "Can't we be both depending on the day?"

"Ooh, good one, yes," she says, yanking open a garbage bag to reveal several fluffy pillows in yellows, peaches, and pinks. She starts setting them up on my light brown leather couch, doing a karate chop on the top of each one to create an indent. Next comes off-white faux fur throw blankets that get draped on the couch and my favourite armchair.

"That's my chair."

She looks up at me. "And?"

"And I don't want a blanket on my chair."

"Relax. You'll love it," she says, leaving it where it is and opening another bag. "It's very cozy."

"I don't like cozy."

"That's ridiculous. Who doesn't like cozy?"

"Me," I say, yanking it off my chair and folding it up. I set it on the couch, only to have her pick it up and do that weird draping thing across the corner of the other armchair.

"There. Better?"

"I guess."

"Put the tallest plants in the corners, and the smaller ones next to your media console," she says, pulling candles out of a box.

"Candles?"

"Do you have something against candles?" Lola asks, setting up not one, not two, but *three* candles on my coffee table.

"You're literally breathing in burning wax. That can't be good for you."

"So we won't light them," she says.

I watch as she picks up my PS5 controllers and places them in a basket she brought. "Hey, I don't want those in a basket. I use them all the time."

Rolling her eyes, she says, "So take them out of the basket when you need them. They look better hidden."

She stands back and admires her handiwork, then mutters something about this space definitely needing an area rug.

"I draw the line at rugs. We're not renovating here."

"Relax, we don't have time to go shopping," she says, opening a tall box and pulling out a large, framed painting. "It would really pull the room together, though."

She pulls a hammer and a small clear container of picture hangers out of the box.

"*Art*work?"

"Of course. No woman lives in a place with bare walls."

"Nope. I draw the line at artwork."

She purses her lips and raises one eyebrow at me, then says, "Do you want them to believe this or not?"

"Obviously, but do we really need to make holes in the walls to do it?"

"Yes, Aidan. Yes, we do," she says, thrusting the hammer at me. "Your dad won't notice but there is no way your mom is going to be fooled into thinking we've been living together for months without me hanging some art."

I take the hammer, but say, "I actually think she won't notice."

Walking over to the wall, she holds the painting up, then moves it to the left a little and nods. "Right here."

"No way. I'm not hanging that up."

"Why not?"

"First of all, it's ugly. I don't even know what it is."

"It's an abstract and the colours will definitely give the room the cheerful lift it needs."

"Cozy *and* cheerful? Forget it. I much prefer the stoic vibe I've got going."

"Oh my God, are you going to complain about everything?"

"No, but this is ridiculous. You're turning my man cave into a Pottery Barn showroom."

"Which is exactly what you need in order to give the illusion you're here living your best life with the woman of your dreams," Lola says firmly. "Now, are you going to put the hook in the wall, or am I?"

"Fine, I'll do it."

"Good."

An hour later, I have a bead of sweat running down my back. I've hung what feels like dozens of mirrors and framed pieces of art (even though Lola says it's really only ten in total), made room in my closet for her clothes and cleaned out two drawers in the bathroom for her stuff (in case my parents are the type to snoop, which they totally are). My bedroom is filled with candles, my bed is basically hiding under a mountain of pillows that will take me half the night to remove so I can get in to go to sleep, and my bathroom counter space is now covered in vials, jars and bottles, brushes, and hair accessories. As I stare at it, I realize how very much I don't miss living with a woman.

My brain is exhausted from answering a barrage of questions—everything from my earliest memory (getting hit in the face with a floor hockey puck) to what I was voted most likely to do in my high school grad yearbook (die a virgin, hardy har har) to my biggest pet peeve (throw pillows everywhere).

We pack up the suitcases, boxes, and bags and return them to the bus, then Lola says, "Okay, now as far as my situation goes, I

Beach, Please

don't want to tell your parents about The Dirtbag or me losing my shop." She's trying to sound business-like but I can tell it's upsetting for her even to mention it.

"Why not?" I ask gently. "None of that is your fault."

Shrugging, she says, "I'm the one who trusted him. Besides, it'll make me sound unstable and the last thing you want them to think is that I'm not a safe bet."

"Okay, how do we explain Bessy?" I ask, glancing at the enormous logo that reads Soul Surfers Surf School.

"Let's say I bought her off a friend who had a surf school and that I'm planning to start my own soon."

"Sure," I tell her. "That sounds plausible. What do we say you do for a living?"

"Let's stick to the truth on that. I work at the resort taking room service calls from six a.m. 'til two, then do bookkeeping for three to four hours in the afternoons and evenings."

"I didn't know you did bookkeeping."

She nods. "I have eight clients. I started a few months ago when I was trying to scrape together enough cash to get my shop back. Oh, and on Thursdays I play pub trivia which pays my gas bill every month."

I stare down at her for a second, realizing how hard she must have to work to keep everything going. "You must be so tired."

"I'm twenty-eight. Now's the time to work hard," she says, starting back toward the house. "We should get back inside. I'd like to take a quick shower before your parents get here."

"Sure." I glance at my watch and my heart speeds up. "They're probably getting off the plane by now so we should have about half an hour until they 'surprise' us."

Once we're back in the house, she looks around. "We're ready. Now all we have to do is make sure we seem surprised."

"And in love," I remind her.

"That too," she says, looking up at me.

God, she's pretty. "I think we can manage that."

"For your sake, we better hope so."

10

And He Thinks His Mom is Pushy...

Lola

OH MY GOD, they're here. I had just gotten out of the shower and wrapped a towel around myself when I heard the doorbell ring. I stare at myself in the bathroom mirror, feeling totally panicky while I listen to Aidan (who I can tell is totally overacting even though his voice is muffled through the door).

"Mom! Dad! What are you doing here?"

They say something back that I can't hear—probably something about being worried about him or wanting to surprise him or some such. Then he says, "Come on in! I can't believe you're here!"

Take it down a notch, buddy. You're not playing to the back of the Sydney Opera House.

Okay, how do I play this? Obviously, I pretend to believe we're alone. And as per our conversation earlier, my role is the hot-to-trot, wants-sex-all-the-freaking-time live-in girlfriend. As awkward as this is going to be, it really is the best way to send them packing.

Without overthinking it (or thinking about it at all, to be honest), I swing the door open and walk out into the living room with the

Beach, Please

oversized towel wrapped around me. "Babe, have you seen my ph—"

I stop talking when my eyes land on his parents and let my mouth drop.

Aidan's eyes bulge out of his head (as do his parents') and he hurries over to me. "Lola, my parents are here! They've come all the way from Canada to surprise me."

His dad sets his gaze on the floor, looking completely embarrassed while his mom stares right at me with her eyes wide. Aidan wraps an arm around my shoulder.

Ooh, that feels nice.

He grins at them. "Lola, this is my mom and dad, Ginnie and Miles. Mom, Dad, meet Lola, my girlfriend."

Ginnie breaks out into a huge smile. "Girlfriend? Why didn't you tell us you had a girlfriend?!"

She rushes over and… oh, is she…? Yes, she is. She's hugging me, even though I'm dressed only in a towel. Well, I have undies on too, but she doesn't know that. Boy is this a tight hug. She must be crazy excited that Aidan's got a girlfriend.

I hug her back with one arm, while holding up my towel with my other hand. "Nice to meet you, Mrs. Clarke."

She pulls back. "Call me Ginnie, please." Grinning up at Aidan, she says, "Well she's just beautiful." Turning back to me she says, "Look at you. Even with wet hair and not a stitch of clothing on, you're gorgeous." Back to Aidan. "Aidan, why on earth haven't you mentioned her to us?"

I look up at him and feign being hurt. "You haven't told your parents about me?"

Aidan's face turns bright red, but I give him a quick smile, then wink at his mom. "Just kidding. I knew he hadn't told you and I'm cool with it."

"You are?"

"Yup." I reach up and pinch his chin playfully. "Aidan's got very good reasons for everything he does. Don't you, babe?" I ask, leaning up for a kiss.

He gives me the world's stiffest, fastest kiss, then says, "That

I do."

"You should tell them then," I say.

He gives me a hard look, then turns to them. "Well, I didn't want you to get your hopes up. It's only been three months."

Ginnie's face falls and she looks like she might cry. "Oh my sweet boy, are you worried she's going to leave you too?"

He stiffens a little and I decide to field that question for him. You know, give him his gas money's worth. "Of course I'm not going to leave him. Aidan's the best guy I've ever known. But he had to be sure about me before he'd introduce me to his family."

His dad nods. "Is this because you're worried she'll leave you for one of your other brothers? Because I'd say that chances of that are not all that good."

Not all that good? What the hell?

"No, Dad. Obviously I don't think Lola's going to pull a Cait."

"And the other boys aren't going to pull a Lawson either," his mom says. "They're all furious with him."

"As they should be," I say, hitching up my towel a little.

Aidan looks down at my towel, then says, "Umm, do you want to go get dressed, hon?"

I let out a little laugh. "Oh right. I almost forgot." Glancing at the island, I say, "Oh, there's my phone. I was worried I forgot it at work. I'll just go get dressed then."

I hurry out of the room, which has gone completely silent. When I'm halfway down the hall, I hear his dad say, "And here your mom has been so worried about you being lonely."

I quickly throw on a tank top, a light cardigan, and some jeans. When I come back out, I find them all standing on the deck staring out at the ocean.

"This is some view, son," his dad says. "The pictures you sent don't do it justice."

I join them outside and wrap my arms around Aidan's waist. "Honestly this view is half the reason I agreed to move in."

We all laugh and I give him a little squeeze. "Just kidding, babe. I'd have moved in with you even if we lived in some crappy basement suite with only a single shrub to look at."

"Aww, she's so sweet," his mom says, clutching her heart. "Miles, isn't she sweet?"

"So sweet," he agrees. "Lola, I'm so sorry to barge in on you guys like this. I thought we should call, but Ginnie loves surprising people."

"I do. I just love surprises," she says. "I hope you don't mind us intruding on you two love birds."

"Not at all," I tell her. "I'm thrilled to get a chance to meet the people who raised my favourite guy here. How long can you stay?"

"They're here for a week, but they're not staying with us," Aidan says.

I do my best to look both surprised and disappointed. "What? *No*, you should definitely stay with us."

Aidan tightens his grip on my hip a little in what I'm guessing is a 'don't push it' gesture. "The good news is they're staying right next door."

Ginnie nods with an open-mouthed smile. "Uh-huh! Can you believe it? The place next door was available."

"No way! Really?" I ask.

"Yes way," she says.

"Well, next time you *have* to stay with us," I tell her. "We've got an empty guest room just waiting for Aidan's family."

"You do?" his dad asks.

I look up at Aidan with a raised eyebrow. "Babe, did you not tell your family about the guest room? I told you to invite them."

"It must have slipped my mind," he says, narrowing his eyes slightly at me.

"Oh, come on," his dad says. "You didn't tell us on purpose so no one would invade your little love nest."

Love nest? Any money says Aidan will hate having his 'man cave' called a love nest. He grins at them and says, "You caught me, Dad. We're still in that honeymoon phase."

His dad says, "Ha!" and slaps him on the shoulder. "I knew it."

"I just can't believe you have a girlfriend!" his mom says again.

"Well, now you know." He drops a kiss on my head, then says, "I absolutely have a girlfriend."

I absolutely have a girlfriend? Who says that?

"You look so happy!" Ginnie explains, wrapping her arms around her husband's waist. "Doesn't he look happy, Miles?"

"Yes, he looks very happy."

Ginnie tears up a bit. "I'm just *so* happy that you're happy. This whole time I've been picturing you out here, totally alone with sad, bare walls and one chair, and here you are in a lovely, homey place with a lovely girl."

"Oh Ginnie, believe me, the place was pretty bare when I got here." About two hours ago.

"Hey, I had a couch and two chairs, thank you very much," he says.

"But that was it," I tell them with an 'isn't he silly' laugh. "Anyway, are you two hungry? We were just about to make some dinner."

Miles shakes his head. "Oh no, we couldn't invite ourselves for supper. Not after surprising you like this."

"Nonsense," I say. "We've got plenty of food." I hope.

"Well, if you're sure…" his dad says.

"We wouldn't have it any other way," I answer, letting go of Aidan. "You hang out with your parents. I'll make supper."

"No, I'll help."

"Babe, I've got it," I tell him. "You visit."

"Okay, I'll come in in a minute to grab some drinks."

Crap. Why did I offer to cook? I have no idea what food he's got in the fridge. If any. I also don't have the first clue where anything is in the kitchen. I walk inside, sliding the patio door closed, then hurry over to the fridge and open it.

Huh, surprisingly well stocked. There are fresh tilapia fillets, all the fixings to make salad and loads of fruit. I check in the walk-in pantry and see it's also filled with all sorts of healthy food. I grab a package of tortilla shells, then check to see if he has what I need to make fish taco sauce. Yup. Mayo, sour cream, lime, and sriracha. Pulling the tilapia out of the fridge, I get to work preparing it for the grill.

I'm just drizzling the fish with some olive oil when Aidan comes

Beach, Please

in. He closes the door behind him and says, "A towel? You decided to meet them in a towel?"

I shrug. "I thought it would make me seem authentically surprised."

"Of course, because who in their right mind would come out in only a towel?" he asks.

"Exactly," I tell him. "Did you come in here to scold me, because that's the last thing I need right now. I'm trying to prepare a nice meal for my future in-laws."

"No, I came in to see if you needed help, but while we're on the subject, you can lay off the whole babe thing. And you probably don't need to touch me so much."

"Why? Do you think I'm making them too uncomfortable?" I ask. "Because I'm trying to make them *just* uncomfortable enough that they won't want to shop for houses."

"They're fine, but you're making *me* uncomfortable."

Raising one eyebrow, I say, "Dude, I'm just doing what you asked me to do. Pretending I'm in love with you."

"Yeah, well, it would help if you didn't … smell so good. What kind of perfume is that? It's distracting."

My cheeks warm up a bit, knowing that I'm clearly having some sort of effect on him. "I'm not wearing perfume."

He stares at me for a second, looking dumbfounded. "Well, shit. Maybe just try to keep your distance a little. My mind is getting all mixed up."

I stifle a smile. "Do you think your parents will like fish tacos?"

"Yeah, they're not picky," he says, opening the fridge and grabbing out a bottle of white wine.

"Perfect," I say, pointing to the tray of tilapia. "Do you mind grilling that while I prep the sauce and make a salad?"

"Sure." He takes down four wine glasses, pours one for me, then picks up the bottle and the other three glasses. Walking to the door, he says, "I'll go fire up the grill."

"Thanks, babe."

"How does this feel so much like a real relationship?" he mutters before he slides the door open.

I chuckle to myself while I slice the lime and squeeze it into a glass bowl.

An hour later, we've eaten dinner, polished off two bottles of wine, and are sitting back on the deck watching the sunset.

"That was delicious," Ginnie says again. "Thank you so much for your hospitality, Lola. A lot of women wouldn't be so gracious about us just showing up like this."

"Come on now, Ginnie," Miles says. "It's not kind to compare."

"What? Did you think I meant Caitlyn?" Ginnie asks innocently.

Miles purses his lips at her. "Clearly."

"Oh no, I just meant generally-speaking," she says. Then she mutters, "Although the woman does hate a pop-by."

Nodding, Miles says, "True. She hates it."

I glance at Aidan to see how he's doing with his ex being brought up. He smirks at me. "Not Lola. Lola's a real people person."

I grin at them. "It's true. I love people."

"You must love working at the resort then," his dad says.

Aidan cuts in with, "I told them about all your jobs."

"You sound very industrious, young lady," Ginnie tells me.

"Oh, I'm trying."

"What Lola really wants to do is open her own surf school. In fact, she's halfway there. She's already got the bus."

"Is that your bus parked out front?" Miles asks.

I nod. "Yup."

"It's so fun! I love the colors and the logo," Ginnie adds.

Aidan smiles at me. "Lola bought it from a friend who was shutting down and moving back to the U.S."

"Yeah, I may have jumped the gun on getting the bus first, but it felt like an opportunity not to miss and I'm hoping to get things going soon."

"As soon as a few weeks from now," Aidan says, wrapping his hand over mine. "She's an amazing surf instructor."

Beach, Please

His mom's eyes light up. "Maybe you can teach us how to surf while we're here!"

"Oh no, I don't…" I start, then trail off because I'm not going to tell them that the idea of getting on a surfboard is like shards of glass to my heart.

"Yeah, hon," Aidan says. "You should totally teach my parents. They'd love it."

"We really would," his mom says, looking totally excited. "I've always wanted to learn."

I turn to Aidan and give him a look that says no freaking way. "I don't know, *babe*. I'm *super* out of practice. I actually haven't taught anyone for quite a while and I'd hate to take your parents out when I'm so rusty."

Unfortunately he doesn't pick up on my vibe, so he places his hand on mine and gives it a squeeze. "Hon, you've been surfing your whole life. You'll get right back into it, I promise." He turns to his parents. "Plus it'll give you and my parents some time to get to know each other."

Through gritted teeth, I say, "Uh-huh."

"How about on your next day off?" he asks.

Plastering on a smile, I say, "Sure thing. It's best to go in the morning when you're starting out. The waves are a little tamer in the early part of the day."

"That sounds terrific," Miles says.

"When's your next day off?" Ginnie asks.

"Wednesday."

"Wednesday it is, then," she says with a big grin. "Now, onto more important things. How did you two meet?"

"At the pub," Aidan says, smiling at me.

"Yup, at the pub." Feeling irritated at having been roped into surfing when I'm not ready, I add, "Poor Aidan was still struggling with that situation with his brother and his ex, so he was absolutely hammered. I bought him a slice of chicken pot pie to help soak up the booze."

His mom puts both hands over her heart. "Oh, you sweet, sweet girl." Then she turns to Aidan. "I knew you were in more pain than you let on."

"It was just one bad day," he says, shooting me a glare. "But it was so long ago I hardly remember it."

I give his parents a cutesy smile. "He hardly remembers it because he was so drunk."

We all laugh, including Aidan, only his laugh comes out in a loud, aggressive way.

"Anyway, my friend and I drove him home and made sure he got inside safely. He was such a darling. Even though he was so inebriated he kept offering to make food for us. Can you imagine?"

"That's my boy," Ginnie says. "He really is one of the good ones. That business with Caitlyn was nasty. We want you to know we're not at all happy about what she and Lawson did."

His dad sighs and glances at the table. "No, we're not, but we're going to have to accept the situation now that there's a baby involved."

Aidan clears his throat. "Yup. There's no undoing that."

"But honestly," Ginnie says. "Now that I see you with Lola, I know things have worked out exactly the way they should have. Lola's perfect for you. Such a better fit than Cait."

I beam at her. "In what way?"

"Well, for starters, she's just not that outgoing and you are an absolute delight. I can tell you're the type who'll make sure this one gets out of the house once in a while."

"True, I'm always dragging him places."

"She is," Aidan says. "In fact, we've got a trip planned in six days, but I suppose we'll have to cancel that now that you're here."

"You'll do no such thing!" Ginnie says. "We didn't want to disrupt your life. We came to make sure that you're all right. You two go off on your trip. That'll be our last day here anyway."

"Okay, we'll think about it."

"Don't think about it. Do it," his dad says before letting out a loud yawn. "Oh, I am wiped. I think the heat is getting to me."

"Is it always this hot?" his mom asks.

Aidan's eyes light up. "Oh, it's usually much warmer. This is sweater weather for Lola."

Miles wipes his forehead with a napkin. "Well, not for me."

"We should go back to the rental and turn up the air conditioner." Ginnie stands. "And let you two love birds get on with your evening."

I run my fingertip down Aidan's jaw and give him a sultry look. "I won't say no to that. I just can't get enough of this guy."

"Oh, my," his mom says. "We should skedaddle then."

We stand and gather up the plates and all walk inside together. Then Aidan and I walk them over to the front door.

His dad turns to us and gives Aidan a hard look. "You know, son, I'm a little irked that you didn't tell us about Lola here. Your mom has been worried sick about you, and here you are as happy as a clam."

"Sorry, guys. If I had realized how worried you were, I would have definitely said something."

Ginnie reaches up and pats him on the cheek. "I know you would have. You're such a good boy." She gives him a big hug, then gives me one too, which I find much less awkward after some wine and having clothes on.

"We'll see you tomorrow," she says.

"Looking forward to it," I tell her.

His dad opens the door and they meander down the steps and onto the sidewalk. Aidan drapes an arm over my shoulder casually. I put my hand on his and he lifts mine to his lips, as though it's the most natural thing in the world. A little thrill runs through me as I feel his lips brush against my skin.

"Goodnight, Mom and Dad. Hope you have a great sleep."

"I will now that I know how well you're doing," his mom says. "Goodnight! So nice to meet you, Lola!"

We watch them walk across the lawn to the house next door, then as soon as they're gone, he takes his arm off me like I'm on fire. We step inside and he closes the door, and the whole surfing thing comes back to me. I level him with a dirty look. "Seriously? Volunteering me to teach them how to surf?"

11

Illogical, Messy, Angry Females...

Aidan

"What? I thought you wanted to be a surf instructor," I tell her. "How about you telling them our humiliating origin story?"

"What's wrong with that? I thought it would sound cute," she answers, walking over to the kitchen. "Besides, it's one less lie to have to remember."

I follow her to the kitchen (that is a complete mess after her having made one meal) and start scraping the leftover food into the compost bucket. "What's wrong with it is that I look like a pathetic jackass in that story and the whole idea behind this is for them to believe I'm doing well."

She opens the dishwasher and starts loading it. "Sure, but they don't know it was two days ago. They think that was when you first moved here."

I watch as she puts the plates in the wrong spots, my irritation growing. "But that's not the point. The point is that we could've easily skipped the part about me getting so wasted I couldn't get myself home."

Next, she puts the forks and knives in *one* cutlery holder. "You can't put them all in together like that."

"What?" she asks, straightening up.

"The knives have to go in their own section of the cutlery holder."

"Why? They're all getting washed in the same water," she says, adding some spoons to the mix.

I reach down and pull the knives out. "The knives need to be alone because they're made from a different steel alloy. They get spots when you mix them."

"Wow, someone's anal."

"I'm not anal. I'm just not a barnyard animal," I mutter.

"Excuse me? A barnyard animal?" she says, wiping her hands on a dish towel. "Do it yourself. I need to study for the contest."

Letting out a big sigh, I say, "I'm sorry I said that. I didn't mean it. I'm just upset about you making me look bad."

"Well, you *should* be sorry," she says, glaring at me. "And you know what? It would be nice if you could focus on all the things I did right instead of the one thing I messed up."

"Like wandering around half-naked in front of my parents?" I ask. Okay, I know I'm being rude, but for reasons I can't quite pin down right now, I'm beyond irritated with her and I know it's about more than just her telling them how we met.

"Oh my God, could you drop it already? It was a *big* towel. It's not like I gave them an eyeful of side boob or something!" she says, walking toward the hallway. She turns and says, "In fact, they saw a lot less of me than they will when I'm teaching them to surf against my will!"

"What is your *problem* with that?"

"My problem is I don't want to do it, okay? And you just … strong-armed me into it when I was clearly giving you *the look*," she says, imitating herself giving me a wide-eyed expression.

"I'm supposed to know what that face means?"

"Yes!" she shouts. "This is the universal 'end this now' face, made popular by mothers around the world."

With that, she spins on her heel and stalks to the bathroom. I follow her, too annoyed to let it go. "How is it that you're so desperate to get your surf school back that you're living here with me, but you don't want to actually give any surf lessons?"

She yanks open the top drawer, grabs my toothpaste, then angrily squeezes some onto her toothbrush. Tossing the container on the counter without putting the lid on, she jams the toothbrush into her mouth. Her words come out muffled as she says, "It's complicated. I'd rather not get into it right now if you don't mind."

I twitch a little at the sight of my toothpaste tossed so carelessly on the counter, then pick it up and screw the lid back on. Putting it back in the drawer, I say, "There. That's how you put away toothpaste."

"I know! I figured I'd put it away barnyard animal-style since I'm already being accused of it."

"I already apologized for that," I tell her calmly. "And I *am* sorry, it wasn't called for."

"You're damn right it wasn't." She spits the toothpaste into the sink. "Especially after I cooked such a nice meal for your parents and was trying to clean up."

"But to be fair, you had just called me anal which I don't recall you apologizing for."

"But you *were* being anal. Who cares about some spots on their knives?"

"I do!"

"Uh-huh, could that be because you're a bit… anal?" She pours some water into the glass and swishes, then spits again.

I stare down at all the jars of creams and makeup brushes, feeling my anger level rise a little more. "Wow, this evening has been a perfect reminder of why I'm going to stay single forever."

"Is that supposed to hurt my feelings? The anal guy who likes making decisions for me doesn't want to make this permanent?" she asks, angrily pumping some sort of liquid onto a round cotton pad. She starts scrubbing her eyelids with it in a way that makes me wince. "Oh no! I'm so upset now. I was hoping we'd fall in love and have lots of anal kids."

"You know what?" I say, my tone curt. *Don't say it. Do not say that we should forget the whole thing. You need her as much as she needs you.* "I think we should call it a night. We can sort this out when we're both feeling more calm."

I turn to leave the bathroom, only to hear her mutter, "Or after you take that giant stick out of your ass."

I stiffen, then walk away, telling myself it's not worth it.

It's true what they say: you really don't know a person until you live with them.

12

Unforgivable Girl Talk...

Lola

"You said that?" Penelope asks.

She and I are on the phone getting caught up while Aidan is out on his boat with his parents for the day. As soon as I got home from work, I threw on my bikini and am currently lounging on his deck in the sun. I just spent the last ten minutes going over the argument Aidan and I had the night his parents got here. "Yeah, I'm not sure if he heard me because he was already leaving the bathroom, but he may have."

"So, I guess I was wrong about you two making a great couple."

"Dead wrong. We'd kill each other if we had to live together for more than a week," I tell her. "Here, he seemed so nice, but good lord did he ever change as soon as I moved in. What a control freak."

"I mean, he's not wrong about the knives."

"Are you serious right now?" I ask.

"I'm just saying…"

"Well, don't. After three days with Mr. Clean, I'm all stocked up on irritation."

"I take it things haven't gotten much better since the first night?"

"Not a bit. Luckily, I'm gone before he gets up in the morning so I don't have to start my day dealing with his crap. But he leaves me these little notes all over the place: 'please wash out the blender immediately after use,' and 'does that hot stick in the bathroom have an auto shutoff mode, because I burned myself on it hours after you left for work.'"

"Oh. Oh dear."

"Yup. It's not great. We play nice in front of his parents, which is super weird, because we're all touchy-feely and he's so sweet the whole time that I almost start to forget what a jerk he is, but as soon as they leave, the wall goes back up and we go our separate ways. I've been going directly to my room to rewatch *Clash of Crowns* and take notes."

"What does he do?"

"Plays video games, and I think he reads. I saw some sci-fi book on the kitchen table."

"Aww, so he's a nerd like Eddie," she says, sounding all annoyingly dreamy.

"Not like Eddie at all. Eddie would never call you a barnyard animal."

"He might if I had just called him anal."

I let out a long sigh and cover my face with a towel, not wanting to burn. "Penn, come on, I called you so you could be on my side."

"Sorry, I am."

"Thank you," I say, even though she has yet to prove she's on my side. I let out a groan. "And tomorrow's Wednesday which means I'm supposed to take them out surfing. I might just fake an injury or something. It's not like teaching them to surf was part of our deal."

"Are they awful or something?"

"No, they're actually pretty amazing. They're funny and nice and all sorts of grateful. In fact, if it weren't for their son being such a jerk, I'd want to marry him just to have them as my in-laws."

"They're that great?"

"Yup. You'd love them," I say. "No wonder his ex upgraded to a different brother. She probably couldn't stand the thought of losing his parents."

I hear a light cough near me and I yank off the towel to see Aidan standing there. *Oh shit.*

Raising his eyebrows, he says, "I just thought I'd let you know I'm home. My parents are at the rental if you want to go hang out with them."

He turns and walks back inside, leaving me to panic. Sitting up quickly, I whisper, "He just got home and he definitely heard me say that."

"Oh shit," Penn says. "That was harsh."

"Oh my God, I feel so bad," I say, tears springing to my eyes. "That was like, the worst thing I could have said."

"Yeah, talk about salt on a wound."

I peek in the window and see him sitting in his favourite chair. "There's no coming back from that, is there?"

"Not really."

My gut churns. "I better go apologize."

"Good luck."

"Thanks."

"Text me to let me know how it goes."

"Will do. See you."

I hang up and pull my t-shirt and shorts on over my bikini, then take a deep breath before I walk into the house. Oh, God, how could I screw this up so badly? I literally said the meanest thing anyone could say to him. I wouldn't blame him if he hates me forever.

13

Blurred Lines...

Aidan

WORST. Week. Ever. This was a terrible idea from the start and I never should have suggested it to Lola. To be fair, I couldn't have guessed things would turn out this badly. She seemed so nice and normal when I met her—buying me supper and driving me home. And when she came over to ask me to help her find the crown? Generally very normal. Well, except for what she was asking me to do. It's a total long shot, but I get why she needs to take it. But she seemed great. Cute, even.

How was I supposed to know she'd get all mad about the whole surf lesson thing? The woman wants to be a surf instructor, for God's sake. Also, the whole whipping through my house like a cyclone thing? Not cool. Especially when I burned my hand on the straightener the other morning. Who leaves something like that plugged in? And this morning there was a bunch of her hair stuck to the shower wall. How did it get there? Was she rubbing her head against the wall?

I'd never say this out loud, but my barnyard animal analogy wasn't exactly inaccurate. I know it's only a few days, so I should've just sucked it up and said nothing. But there's just something so irritating about her having taken over every corner of my house. It's suffocating, irritating, and just plain rude.

And now to come home after a long day on the boat with my parents, who, I'll be honest, are exhausting, only to hear her say Cait *upgraded* me for a different brother to keep my parents? Wow. Just wow. That stung. Also, it's a ridiculous thing to say. She doesn't even know them. They've been putting their best foot forward (or feet, I guess) the entire time. They've barely even mentioned hockey or ranching, which are usually their only two topics of conversation. Who got a hat trick last night? (Who cares?) Or what happened when the latest calf was about to be born breech and the vet had to be called? (Honestly, what happened is too disgusting to repeat.)

My mom has also been playing it cool, which makes nothing but sense. She's not about to start pressuring us to get married and have a bunch of babies when they've only just found out about Lola. She's been so great actually, she's almost lulled *me* into a false sense of security and I know the woman. It's coming. It's just a matter of time.

If our whole plan wasn't working so well, I'd be packing Lola's crap for her at this very moment instead of playing golf on my PlayStation. As it is, my parents have no clue that the entire thing is just made up. They've totally bought the act. In fact, they're thrilled that I found 'the one.' They went on and on about how wonderful she is today when we were out on the ocean. *Such a better fit than you and Cait. So much more in common with each other, both of you wanting to make a living in the great outdoors, providing experiences for people. The way she looks at you. Her eyes just light up when you walk in the room.*

There hasn't been one mention of buying a place here. They've done some exploring when I've been busy at work, but they haven't gone house-hunting. So, yeah, I need to make this work, no matter how much Lola and I can't stand each other.

The crazy thing is when we're around my parents and being nice to each other, it actually *feels* good, which is insane because we couldn't be more wrong for each other. But somehow the scent of her, the softness of her skin, the sound of her laugh … gets to me.

And I don't even want to think about how hard it is to fall asleep knowing she's in the other room. I keep remembering what she looked like in that damn towel and the whole thing is driving me nuts. I wasn't lying that first night when I told her it was doing my head in, because it totally is. I don't want to want her, and yet, when she's got her arms around me or I'm holding her hand, it's all right there in that moment. Something real. Or more accurately, a total illusion that is somehow managing to fool even me. There's no actual way that any of this is real—not with someone who just called Lawson the Betrayer 'an upgrade.'

Thank God my parents have decided to stay at the rental this evening. There's no way I could've handled another evening of the babe and hon show tonight. I need a break. A real break from all the chitchat and stories about me when I was a kid. And mainly I need a break from her. With any luck, she'll spend the entire evening in her room preparing for the search for the crown. Urgh, the search for the crown. The last thing I want to do is get on a boat with the woman after all this. As tempting as it is to tell her to find another ride, I'm going to stick to my word. I just hope she actually can solve the clue as fast as she thinks she can so we can be out and back in under a day. I cannot wait to say *adios* to her for good.

I hear the patio door slide open and my heart thumps. She's probably coming to apologize. No thanks. Not interested.

Yup. She's standing next to me, clearly waiting for me to look up at her. Well, go ahead and wait because I'm very busy lining up this putt.

"Aidan, I just wanted to apologize," Lola says. "I didn't mean what I said."

I keep my eyes trained on the television while I take a practice swing. "Oh, you meant it. You just didn't mean for me to hear it."

"I didn't… I just… It was awful of me and it's not true. I'm sure your brother isn't in any way an upgrade. Not that you can upgrade a human, like we're all hotel rooms or something. And obviously I know she didn't start sleeping with your brother because she loves your parents. That would be a bit nutty." She pauses, then says, "I'm making it worse, aren't I?"

I putt and miss. "A little bit, yeah."

"I'm really sorry."

"Okay."

She stands there while I sink the next shot and wait for the game to load up the next hole. I'm hoping she'll just take the hint that I don't want to talk because I definitely do not want to talk.

I take a couple of practice swings, then, just as I'm taking the shot, she says, "Do you think we should talk maybe?"

The shot goes way off to the right and I grunt a little. "About what? You apologized, I said okay. I'd say that's over."

"I don't know. I just don't like how tense it's been between us and I was wondering if maybe it's bothering you too."

"Not enough to call my bestie and make fun of you."

Out of the corner of my eye, I see her nod. "That's fair. And you're right. I should have come to you to talk about what's bugging me."

"I didn't say you should have come to me. If this were a real relationship, yes. But it's not. I'd just appreciate you not dissing me behind my back." My next shot goes straight into the water. *This. This is why I love being alone.*

"Okay, well maybe this isn't the best time for us to talk anyway. Your parents are probably on their way over any minute, right? Should I make some supper?"

"They're not coming over," I tell her. "They're both tired from being out on the boat all day. Oh, and they're leaving a day early because we're going on our trip." They're going to L.A. to watch my brother Wilder play, but I don't bother telling her that because the less I have to say to her, the better.

"Okay, I hope they're not upset about it."

"On the contrary, they're thrilled that I'm leading such a full life with a woman who's so obviously in love with me." I lay on the sarcasm thick like peanut butter.

Lola lets out a small sigh and I make the mistake of looking up, only to see her biting her lip. "All right, well, maybe I'll go out for a few hours. Give you some time to yourself."

"Sounds delightful."

I continue playing while she gathers up her phone, purse, and keys. She opens the front door and says, "I really am sorry."

Then she leaves before I can say anything. Not that I have anything to say anyway.

The next several hours are spent blissfully alone. I play three rounds of golf, listen to loud music, and eat what I want, when I want—with no mess left in the kitchen. Although, I was too lazy to make myself something good. I just slapped together a couple of peanut butter and jelly sandwiches, and had a huge bowl of potato chips, all of which are making me feel kind of gross right now.

By nine o'clock, I've had enough of playing video games. By ten, I'm starting to worry. What if she was so upset, she got in an accident? Or she's so over this whole thing that she doesn't come back? That would totally screw things up for me. I only have to make it through three more days with my parents believing I'm in a happy, long-term relationship. If she disappears, they're going to know we had a huge fight, which doesn't exactly say stable and committed.

I shut off the PS5 and wander over to the window just in time to see her pull up in front of the house. My pulse picks up and I know I have to fix this. I need her as much as she needs me. At least until Friday. Then we can go our separate ways.

I hurry over to the coffee table and grab my book, then settle myself on the couch and open it up so it looks like I've been enjoying my alone time instead of worrying.

When she walks in, I give her a nod. "Hey, how was your evening?"

"Fine." She shuts the door behind her. "I just went home and made a sandwich. Hung out on the couch all evening."

I almost smile at the fact that we've been doing the exact same thing.

She fiddles with her keys a little, then says, "Look, I know I screwed up and that you'll probably hate me forever, and that's fine. I'm a big girl. I can own up to my mistakes. But like it or not, we're stuck together for a few more days here. Then we're going to be out on your boat looking for the crown. I'm just hoping we can find a way to make it more pleasant for both of us."

I shut my book and say, "I don't hate you, and yes, it would be nice if we could find a way to get along."

She sits down on the couch and curls up so she's facing me. "I don't know how things went so far off the rails the first night, but they really did."

"Yeah, I came to your room that night and knocked because I wanted to apologize, but you didn't answer. There was a light on so I figured you didn't want to talk. Since then, I've been waiting for you to approach me."

"Really?" she asks, looking genuinely surprised. "I was probably watching *Clash of Crowns*. I've been wearing my earbuds so I won't keep you up."

"Okay, well that explains that." I let out a long sigh. "I'm sorry I was rude to you. I think it all felt like too much. The redecorating and the cuddly cutesy stuff and then I was embarrassed and I turned into a total jackass about it."

"Yeah, you kind of did."

"But you weren't such a peach yourself. If you ask me, you got unreasonably mad about the surfing thing."

She gives me a conciliatory nod. "You're right. You had no way of knowing that would upset me."

"I really didn't. I mean, how could I possibly know you'd be mad about that?"

"You couldn't." She sighs. "The thing is, I haven't been on a surfboard since The Dirtbag left me."

My head snaps back. "You haven't?"

She bites her bottom lip, looking very vulnerable. "I haven't even touched one, to be honest. I think about it a lot. And there have been moments I've been tempted to just rush out and go hit the waves, especially on a day like today, when the swells are big and the sky is blue. But then when it comes down to it, it just … hurts too much."

My heart squeezes, knowing exactly what that feels like. "That makes perfect sense."

"It does?"

"Yeah, I think that was part of why seeing all your stuff everywhere has been getting to me. It's because it reminds me of what it's like to live with a woman."

"The good parts?" she asks.

I offer her a playful grin, needing to lighten the moment. "No, the annoying parts. You're super messy."

We both start to laugh, and it feels good for a moment. So good that I'm suddenly reminded how dangerous this whole thing could be. I let my smile fade. "But, yeah, it reminded me of something I don't want to remember."

We're both quiet for a minute, then she says, "Being dumped is the worst, no?"

"So, *so* bad," I tell her. "Which is why I'm never doing any of that again."

"I hear you."

"I know it would kill my parents to hear me say this, but I honestly am through with relationships. I actually *like* living on my own and having full control over my toothpaste cap and having spotless knives. If anything, these last few days have confirmed that for me."

She screws up her face for a second. "I feel like I should be offended, but in the interest of keeping the peace, I think I'll just say you're welcome."

"Thanks," I say wryly. "So, listen, if you're not up for taking my parents tomorrow morning, we can make some excuse. It's fine."

"Thanks. I appreciate that."

I stare at her for a moment, hating like hell that she's letting him ruin surfing for her. "But can I just say, if you're avoiding doing something you absolutely love because of some asshole who clearly doesn't give a shit about you, that's a little..."

"Dumb?"

Yes. "Counter-intuitive, maybe?"

"Self-protection is intuitive," she says in a neutral tone.

If she was at all defensive right now, I'd back off, but I think she needs to hear this. "Are you sure? You're letting him take away something that was an integral part of your life. So much so that you're still driving that old bus around town and you're willing to live with a total control freak just at the off-chance of getting your business back."

She stiffens a little. "It's not an off-chance. It's a very good chance."

I narrow my eyes and keep my tone light. "What was it on your scale of long shots? One hundred?"

"Something like that," she says with a small chuckle.

"So, it's a bit of a long shot."

"What's your point?"

"My point is that you're giving him way too much power over you."

"I am not," she says, her cheeks colouring. Letting out a long sigh, she says, "Look, I know it might not make sense to you, but somehow I feel like if I can get my shop back, it won't hurt to get back on a surfboard. I'm scared that if I try now, I'm just going to fall apart. And other than a few days when the whole thing first went down, I haven't let myself fall apart. I've stayed focused on my goal. I'm scared that if I open the floodgates…"

"That you'll really freaking fall apart?"

"Yeah, that."

"Do you think you will?"

"I don't know. I might."

"So, you fall apart. You can pick yourself back up again."

She groans and tucks her head against the couch. "But what if I get out there with your parents and I get all emotional? What do I tell them?"

"I could come with you guys. Take the lesson, too. That way if you give me this look…" I give her the wide-eyed look she gave me her first night here. "I'll run interference until you feel better."

She chuckles a little, then bites her lip again, looking so worried that I decide to back off. "If you're not ready, Lola, it's okay. I'll just tell my parents you got called into work or something." I pause, then add, "But if you think you can do it, imagine the relief you'll feel once you rip off that Band-Aid."

She stares up at the ceiling fan as it slowly spins above her. Then she looks at me with a determined expression. "Okay, I'll do it."

"You sure?"

"Yeah." She nods a few times and smiles. "You're right. I have given him way too much power over me. And that has to stop."

I smile, feeling oddly proud. "Good for you."

She smiles and narrows her eyes at me. "So, are we friends now?"

I grin back. "I hope so. In fact, I think once we get all your girlie crap out of here, we could probably be good friends."

Laughing, she says, "Trust me, it'll be a relief for me too. Although I will miss the view."

14

Dude...

Lola

TEXT CONVERSATION WITH PENN...

> So? Is it WWIII over there?

No. We made up.

> What sort of making up? Eyebrow raises (jk)

The talking kind. We both apologized and agreed to be friends.

> Well, that's boring. I'm happy for you though.

Thanks. And you'll be glad to know I AM going to take his parents surfing tomorrow. Aidan's coming too.

> REALLY???!!!

Yup.

> Happy dancing over here!

> Hopefully I'll be happy after the fact. Right now, the thought of it is still terrifying. What if I hate it now and I always will and it's all because of TD?

> You won't.

> How can you be sure?

> Because you were a surfer when you were 6. And 7. And 17. And 27. And it's all you've ever really loved to do, other than hang out with me and read. It may not be in your DNA but it might as well be. Surfing is as much a part of you as music is for my dad. Can you imagine him if he couldn't play synthesizer?

> He'd be miserable.

> Exactly. You're going to fall back in love with it the minute you get out there. I know it in my bones.

> God, I hope you're right.

> I guess we'll find out tomorrow…

———

Blerg. This was a horrible idea. Why did I ever let Aidan talk me into this? Actually, if I'm throwing around some blame, this is also on Penn. She did her share of the hard sell on getting me to get back to surfing. I'm terrified. I mean, what if I forgot everything I knew? What if I can't explain what I used to know anymore? What if I suck at this? What if I hate it?

Okay, calm down, Lola. Calm down. Think of the positives. On the plus side, since my talk with Aidan last night, things have been a lot less tense. I made a point of tidying up my stuff and putting the cap back on the toothpaste and he hasn't written me any nasty notes today, so there's a win right there.

I've got Ginnie, Miles, and Aidan all loaded on the bus. Even though it's only nine in the morning, the lack of air conditioning is doing in the parents, who are dressed in long-sleeved swim shirts and shorts. I just heard Miles tell Aidan that he's 'sweating his balls off,' so that's an image I don't need.

I'm just pulling up in front of my main competitor's shop—*Surf Dudes*—and am about to go inside to rent the boards, since mine have been locked up by the bank. This is not a thought I'm relishing. Not that they're not nice dudes, it's just ... super humiliating. The surfing community on the island isn't exactly huge, and *everyone* knows what happened.

I take up three spots in their lot, then cut the engine and open the door. *Okay, Lola, pretend you're happy to be doing this. Maybe it'll lead to actually enjoying it.* Smiling back at my passengers, I put on a tour guide voice and say, "First stop, Surf Dudes to rent the boards."

As Ginnie and Miles scramble to get off the bus, Ginnie says, "Do you think they have air conditioning in there?"

Aidan hangs back a bit and waits for me. "You okay?"

"Yeah," I tell him. "As far as humiliation scales go, this will rank at about a ninety ... four, but I'll be fine."

"Do you want to wait here and I'll go rent the boards?"

I shake my head. "They're good dudes. Besides, I'm sure they already know I'm here."

"Bessy really is a conspicuous ride, isn't she?" he asks.

"So much so."

Just before we walk in, I stop. "Listen, Carl, the head dude, is a little, well, have you ever seen *Fast Times at Ridgemont High*?"

"Yup."

"Remember Sean Penn?"

"Yup."

"Now that I've put that in your mind, do your best not to laugh," I tell him as I pull open the door.

When we step inside the shop, Carl, who hails from California, shouts, "There she is! Lola .... L-O-L-A, LOLA!"

He saunters over and holds his arms out. "Bring it in, girl. It's been wayyyyy too long."

I give him a hug and all my embarrassment melts instantly.

Carl's a good surf dude. He also smells of weed and B.O., so I make it a quick hug.

When we pull back, he swipes his long blond hair out of his face. "Sorry about what happened to you. When I found out, I was like, dude, no! Charlie was like, dude, yeah, we'll get more business, and I was all, dude, that's not how I want to get new customers."

I bite my lip to stop myself from laughing, and manage to say, "Thanks. That means a lot, Carl."

"No problem. So, what can I do for you?"

"We're here to rent some boards actually."

"Seriously? Where are your boards?"

"Gone."

His head snaps back. "Gone? Shit, that blows."

"Yeah, it super blows," I say, then realize that Aidan's parents are standing right next to me with expectant looks on their faces. "Carl, this is Ginnie and Miles. I'm taking them out for some lessons today, along with…" I crane my neck and spot Aidan who's over by the far wall looking at some wetsuits. Based on how his body is shaking, he's laughing uncontrollably while trying not to be noticed. "Aidan, their son."

Ginnie holds out her hand. "My son is her boyfriend," she says, and I'm not sure if she's proud or territorial, but either way, it's odd. "They live together."

Aidan, who seems to have pulled it together, walks over and gives Carl a head nod. "Hey."

Carl holds out his hand. "Carl. Nice to meet you."

They shake and Aidan says, "Nice to meet you too. Lola's told me a lot about you."

"All good, I hope."

"Oh yeah." Grinning down at me, Aidan says, "She told me you were a good dude."

"Noice!" Carl says, holding his hand to Aidan for knuckles. "Lola's a good dude too. So, boards for all four of you?"

I nod and my stomach clenches. "Yup. Four please, for the day."

Pointing to my companions, Carl says, "First timers?"

"Yup."

"Let's get you kitted up with some newbie boards."

"Awesome."

Forty-five minutes later, we're pulling up to Long Beach with four surfboards secured to the top of the bus. I climb up the ladder at the back and start untying the boards while Aidan and his parents stand ready to take them from me.

"Gosh, you're a brave one," Ginnie says to me.

"Oh, this is totally safe," I tell her, blushing a little at the compliment.

"Nope, you're brave. Own it," she tells me.

Why couldn't she have been my mom?

A few minutes later, we're all on the beach with the boards on the sand. I'm standing with my back to the ocean while they're all facing me and waiting for me to say something brilliant. My heart pounds and I feel my palms go clammy. "Okay, let's do this."

"Excellent," Miles says.

My stomach lurches a little, so I say, "How about we go for a quick dip to cool off first?"

"Perfect," Ginnie says.

She and Miles rush down to the water, while I pull off my t-shirt and shorts, leaving me in a modest, fake-in-law-appropriate two-piece. Aidan tugs his shirt off too, revealing what I feared was under it the whole damn time. An amazing physique. Dammit. Why couldn't he be covered in scales? I definitely don't need friends who have that going on.

"You okay?" he asks. "You look nervous."

I snap out of my ogling and say, "That's because I am." Glancing at his chest again, I say, "But, this is good. I need to do this." *Am I talking about him or surfing right now?*

"And more importantly, you *can* do this."

Can I really?

Oh, Lola, down, girl, down. It's just a man without a shirt on. You've seen hundreds of them.

"You ready to fall back in love?" Aidan asks.

"What? Okay." Is it getting crazy hot out here? I suddenly feel feverish. "But I thought you didn't believe in love."

He points to the water with his thumb. "With surfing."

"Right… Oh yeah. Totally."

He starts toward the ocean and I follow a few steps behind feeling like a total idiot. Although I suppose I'd rather feel all hot and bothered and kind of foolish than be a blubbering mess right now. I tell myself this is nothing. I can do this. It's just surfing.

Only it's not just surfing. This is so much more. It's the first step of me getting my life back. The second my toes touch the water, I feel like I'm finally home. Tears fill my eyes and I forget all about not being emotional because this…is…everything.

I take a giant breath, then let it out as I wade out into the warm, clear blue water. When I'm in up to my thighs, I reach out and dive just under the surface, letting the ocean soothe my soul. When I pop back up, I turn around and see Aidan staring at me, slack-jawed with an expression that does something extra nice to my lady bits. *What? That's not supposed to happen.*

The four of us spend the next few minutes wading in the water and chatting, then Miles says, "So, should we do this?"

"Yup. Let's go." We make our way back to the shore with me slightly behind Aidan again, and dammit, if I'm not salivating over his muscular back.

Focus, Lola. Focus. You're supposed to be teaching these people something. Oh right, surfing.

When we reach the boards again, I say, "Okay, so the first step in learning how to surf is to choose the right beach. You'll notice there are no rocks or other impediments here, just nice, soft sand. Also, these aren't the biggest waves, but they're just the right size for beginners. Anything more and it's a lot harder to get up on your board in the first place, which is about half the battle."

I glance over to my left and see a couple of young men watching us. They're holding surfboards and based on their Speedos, I'm going to guess they're from either France or Italy. I turn back to Aidan and his parents and keep going. "The second step is to know where to lay on your board when you're paddling out. Each board is a little different so when we get out in the water, I'll help you find the sweet spot so that the nose of the board isn't tipped too far up toward the sky or aimed down into the water. Once we get out there, we'll play with that little bit to figure it out. Before I teach you how to pop up and stand, we'll take our boards out, just into waist-deep water, and practice riding the waves back to shore while we're laying down. That way you can get a feel for how to catch the waves which will make it much easier when it's time to actually stand up. Let's make sure our leg straps are done up because we are definitely going to fall off out there and we don't want to be chasing our boards all over the Caribbean."

I smile at my students, my confidence starting to return. "Any questions?"

"Sounds simple enough so far," Ginnie says.

"Excellent. Let's go."

We all pick up our boards and walk out into the water, this time with his parents trailing behind a bit. Out of the corner of my eye, I see the two guys walking into the water about twenty yards down the beach from us. This happens all the time, so I know what's going on. They clearly want free surf lessons.

Aidan notices them too. "I think you have a couple of fans." There's an odd quality to his voice. Something I haven't heard before. It's the way he said fans, like it's a dirty word. Huh. Interesting.

"Happens all the time," I say vaguely.

"I bet it does." Yup, he sounds jealous.

I grin over at him. "Does it bother you?"

"No, obviously not," he says, sounding defensive. "I just think it's a little rude is all. They're practically salivating."

"Eh, it's all good," I tell him with a shrug.

"Really?" he asks. "You don't mind?"

"Not a bit," I say, stopping now that we're in up to our waists.

The men stop too, about twenty yards down the shoreline from us.

Aidan scoffs. "This is ridiculous. They're actually following you. I'm going to say something. They can't just ogle you like that."

Okay, time to shut this down. He's just turning toward them

when I grab his arm. I lower my voice and say, "They don't want me. They want free surf lessons."

He blinks a couple of times, then glances back at them. "Are you sure?"

"One hundred percent."

"Oh, so *this* is what happens all the time. Not men ogling you."

I chuckle a little, then says, "Yes, Aidan. They want me for my knowledge."

His parents have caught up with us, so I get back to teaching. I show them how to grip the sides of the board and I lay down, my heart fluttering with happiness as my body touches the board for the first time. It's not my Retro Noserider, but it's great anyway.

We spend the next half hour or so doing this, as I talk to them about how to spot the foamy waves, how to paddle with their hands cupped, and how to kick their feet. The two guys are still following along, watching and copying us without trying to look like they're copying us.

"Jean-Pierre, like this?" one of them asks his friend, kicking his feet wildly.

"Yes, I think so," his friend says.

I chuckle, then call over to him. "You don't need to move your legs so much. Small kicks."

He smiles at me and tries it again with more success this time.

I give him a quick thumbs up. "Better."

"Thanks!"

We head back onto the beach and take a quick break to drink some cold drinks I brought, then I make an outline of our surfboards in the sand and draw a line down the center of each one. Our new companions, who have been hanging out in the water, quickly rush to the shore and make outlines of their boards too.

Miles, who seems a little put out that they're horning in on their lesson, says, "Hey fellas, she's a *professional* instructor, so I hope you're planning to pay her."

Jean-Pierre looks shocked. "Oh no, Hugo and I are just doing our own practice over here."

"Oh, come on. Nobody's going to believe that," Miles says.

Hugo grins sheepishly. "Okay, you caught us. We want to learn. How much is the lesson?"

I shake my head. "Don't worry about it. This one's on me."

"You should charge them," Aidan says. "Your time and knowledge has value."

"And I also don't have waivers for them to sign. No waivers, no cash," I tell him.

"Oh, smart," he says.

I give him a wink. "Not my first time." I smile at my growing class. "Okay, now I'm going to teach you how to pop up. We'll try it first on the sand because if you're practicing on the board when it's out of the water, you might crack it, and trying this for the first time *in* the water is just plain frustrating."

I lie down in the center of my outline and show them how you do a gentle backbend to get yourself started. Hugo mutters under his breath, "Oh, very nice!"

Aidan lets out a low growl and I stop for a second and grin at him. "Did you just growl?"

"No."

"He did," his mom says with a laugh. "That guy said 'very nice' and he growled."

Miles bursts out laughing too. "Possessive much?"

Hugo looks worried. "Sorry, I didn't mean anything by that. I only meant to remark on your good form."

Aidan glares at him. "Maybe don't remark on her good form, okay, buddy?"

His parents both try to stifle their amusement but fail miserably while I lie on my imaginary board with my mouth hanging open. If this is part of the act, he should be up for an Oscar.

I shake my head and decide to get back to the task at hand. Using my hands to push off, I show them how to lift their bodies and plant their feet in the center of the board. We practice this for a while and then, when I think they've all got it, I ask if they're ready to give it a shot out in the water.

The next hour is pure bliss for me as we joke and laugh our way through the lesson. My new students seem to be getting it too, and although I focus my attention on Aidan and his parents, I offer them a few tips as we go. Nobody takes themselves too seriously, and they all manage to get up at least twice, which is pretty impressive, especially for people Miles and Ginnie's age. When the lesson is over, I stay out and surf a bit on my own, catching a few waves and showing off a little with some snaps. I finish off with a roundhouse cutback that ends in applause as I ride the board almost all the way to shore.

I pick it up and walk over to Aidan, then lay it down and collapse onto the sand next to him, my entire body humming with happiness under the warmth of the sun. It's not just because I never lost my love for surfing. It's because today, I've made a huge leap forward in getting over a very bad man.

Aidan turns his head in my direction. "How was that?" he asks in a low tone.

"Incredible," I say, grinning at him.

"Good. I'm glad."

"Aww, you two look so sweet," Ginnie says. "I need to get a picture of you together."

We both sit up and Aidan puts his arm around me, pulling me in. I rest my head on his shoulder and smile, my heart pounding and my stomach fluttering for some strange reason. I don't want either of those things to happen. Yes, he's hot, but he's also a fussy neat freak and we have absolutely no future together.

"You two are going to have the most beautiful children," she says, still holding the phone up.

My face flames at that thought and I can't help but feel a tug of guilt for lying to them like this.

"Did you get the shot, mom?" Aidan asks.

"Nuts," Ginnie says. "The camera was aimed at me the whole time. One second."

"Sorry about this," Aidan murmurs.

"It's fine, really," I say, even though it's not fine because the longer our bodies are pressed together like this, the more I'm enjoying it. If I'm not careful, I'm going to wind up feeling very confused about what we're actually doing here, and with us about to spend who knows how long alone together on his boat, I definitely can't afford to be getting confused. I remind myself that he's solidly anti-relationship. I remind myself we have nothing in common. I remind myself that the last thing I need right now is a man. And yet, the smell of his skin and the feeling of his arm around me is suggesting otherwise…

15

This is Not a Real Date. I Repeat. Not a Real Date...

Aidan

WE MADE IT. Well, almost. My parents are leaving late this afternoon. First, they're taking us for a big crab lunch to thank Lola for the surf lessons. One last meal of pretending, then they head straight to the airport and we come back here so Lola can move out. Tomorrow morning, we take off to find the crown, and with any luck by tomorrow night, we'll be free and clear of each other.

My urgency to have this over with isn't because I'm still bitter about what she said. In fact, it's quite the opposite. The last couple of days have been surprisingly great with her. So great that I need a night alone to rid myself of all these feelings I've been having.

I sit in the living room waiting for Lola to finish getting ready. The restaurant we're going to is pretty swanky so I'm in a button-down shirt and a pair of slacks. I'm actually wearing socks and shoes, which I haven't done since I moved here. So far, I'm not loving it. Checking the time, I see it's only a minute until we have to leave, and I'm starting to get pre-annoyed that she's not ready yet.

A second later, she comes walking into the room, and whatever irritation I had dissolves. She's got her hair down in soft curls and she's wearing a short flowy halter dress that shows off her toned arms and legs. My jaw drops and it takes me longer than it should to pick it up. Dammit. She definitely saw that. I can tell by her grin.

"What do you think? Will this do for the restaurant?" she asks.

"You look … yeah, perfect," I say, sounding like a complete moron.

I stand up and find myself wanting to walk over to her, instead of to the door. She smiles up at me. "Thanks. It's been a while since I got dressed up for anything, so I'm feeling a little self-conscious about it."

My eyes drift down the length of her again and back up. "You've got nothing to feel self-conscious about. Believe me." Oh God, now I'm ogling her. Clearing my throat, I say, "We should go."

The drive to the restaurant feels first-date awkward, which is crazy because this isn't a first date. We've been living together (and driving each other insane) for days already. We've both let it all hang out, too. I didn't hide my sci-fi books or stop playing video games like I did when I was first with Cait. I didn't pretend to be breezy about the mess factor either, which I did when Cait moved in. I've been myself to a fault. And so has she—leaving her stuff (including the wall hair) all over.

But for some reason, there's a shift in the energy between us. It started yesterday when we were at the beach for the surf lesson. Something changed.

"Have you been to this place before?" I ask as we pull into The Stoned Crab parking lot.

"No, but I hear it's amazing."

I park and see my parents have already arrived. They're standing on the sidewalk in front of the restaurant watching us. Lola reaches for the door handle, but I say, "Wait there, okay?"

I get out and quickly make my way around to her side, then open the door for her and hold out my hand.

She takes it, blushing a little as she gets out of the truck. "What a gentleman."

"Gotta make it look good, right?" I ask.

Her face falls a little, then she smiles up at me. "Right. Of course."

"Look at you two," his mom says. "Gorgeous. Miles, aren't they gorgeous?"

"Yup, they're a good-looking couple."

I slip my hand into hers and we follow my parents into the restaurant. I don't let her hand go as we're led through to the patio overlooking the harbour. Instead, I hold it firmly, feeling oddly proud as the restaurant patrons smile up at us when we walk by.

When we get to our table, I pull her chair out for her, then wait while she sits down.

My mom beams at us. "We taught him well, didn't we, Miles?"

"Yes, dear. We taught him well," he says with a roll of his eyes.

The server comes by with waters for the table and we order some appetizers—seared scallops and herb and garlic bread. After she leaves, my mom holds up her phone. "Let's get another picture."

I wrap my arm around Lola's shoulder, and we hold our cheeks together and smile while my mom gets a few shots. When she's done, she smiles at her phone. "Oh, those are nice. I'll send you these so you can frame one. I noticed you don't have any photos of the two of you in your house."

"We'll have to fix that, won't we?" Lola asks me before giving me a quick kiss on the lips.

My heart starts to pound a little harder even though I give it strict orders not to do that. "Yup, right away," I say, knowing that in a couple of hours, this will all be over.

"Now, we need to figure out when we're going to see you again," Mom says. "Dad and I want you both to come for Christmas."

Shit.

When neither of us answers right away, my dad says, "Look, we know it'll be awkward with Lawson and Cait there, but we're hoping it'll be a chance to put all that business behind us."

Mom quickly adds, "But we don't want to pressure you. We just thought that since you're clearly over Cait and you're so happy that it might be possible for you to come home for a visit."

My dad nods at what my mom is saying. "It doesn't have to be

Christmas though. We know you'll probably be busy since it'll be prime tourist season and all."

"But sometime soon," my mom says. "We want Lola to meet our parents and your brothers." She grins at Lola. "They're all going to love you." Then she looks slightly panicked. "But not too much. Just the normal amount."

Lola chuckles. "I knew what you meant."

"So, what do you say? Will you come?" Mom asks. "It's so beautiful there in the winter. We're only an hour from some of the world's best skiing."

"It's true," Dad tells her. "Amazing conditions."

"All right," I say. "Thank you for the invitation. We'll certainly try."

"Good, because meeting the family is the next logical step before you two get married," Mom says, staring down at her menu.

Ah, here she is. The mother I knew was lurking inside this fun, breezy woman all week.

My dad sighs. "Ginnie, we agreed we weren't going to do this."

"What? I'm not pressuring them."

"Yes, you are."

"Am not. Kids, do you feel pressured?"

Lola says, "No," at the same time that I say, "A little bit."

Both my parents turn to each other and say, "See?"

Thankfully, the server stops at the table with the appetizers and takes our order for the main course, a seafood platter for four. When the for arrives, we take a minute to plate up and have a few bites of the buttery bread and the scallops while I scramble to think of a way to play this. Why didn't I anticipate them talking about the next time they'll see us? *Stupid, Aidan. So stupid.*

"Look, I'm not trying to pressure you. I know it's early days and all," my mom says. "But the thing is, neither of you is getting any younger here and you're clearly perfect for each other. I've never seen Aidan this happy."

"Ginnie, seriously," Dad says.

"What? I just want Aidan to be happy, Miles. Don't you?"

"Obviously, I do. I just—"

Beach, Please

"Then let me talk." She looks at Lola. "I've never seen my son so happy, not even when he was with Cait. He didn't look at her the way he looks at you. He certainly didn't growl when another man noticed her."

My face flames with embarrassment. "Okay, come on. Let's not pretend that being jealous is a virtue."

"Obviously, it's not," Mom says. "But the fact that you've got those protective feelings for her is telling." She looks at Lola. "Can I be completely honest with you, Lola?"

"I think you already have been," I say, not liking where this is going.

Mom gives me a dirty look, then says, "This will come as a shock to you, I'm sure, but Miles and I came here to house hunt. We've just been so worried about him that we decided he needed us to be close by."

Oh God no. Please don't tell me when you were out exploring that you were actually buying a house.

Mom looks at me. "Relax, we didn't buy anything. We realized that you're doing well here."

"Really well," Dad says. "You've built an amazing life for yourself here. You've got the boat and Lola and your house. You don't need us, which is a good thing because it's too frigging hot here."

Thank God. "I have," I say, taking Lola's hand and giving it a squeeze. "Thanks to this lady right here."

Lola squeezes my hand back. "You two are honestly the best parents. To consider moving here like that. Not a lot of parents would do that."

Her voice is a little sad and I can tell she must mean that her own parents wouldn't consider doing something like that. I lift her hand to my lips and give her a kiss, hoping to take some of the sadness away. She looks up at me and her eyes glisten.

"See? That," my mom says, pointing at our hands locked together. "You never did that kind of thing with Cait."

"Okay, Mom, I'm sure Lola doesn't want to talk about Cait."

"It's okay," Lola says. "Especially when we're talking about how much better we are together."

"All right, I'm not going to say anything else. I promised your father I'd keep my big mouth shut," Mom says. "But I'll just say this: you belong together. What the two of you have going on is the real thing. Don't let it go."

"That was … something," Lola says as soon as we get in the truck.

We've just hugged my parents goodbye. They're on the way to the airport to return the rental car and fly to L.A. and we're heading back to my place to de-Lola my house.

"Yeah," I say. "I feel a bit shellshocked actually."

"She must have really been holding back all week."

"Big time," I say, pulling out onto the road.

"Huh." Lola nods. "I finally get it."

"Get what?"

"Why you needed me. The woman is persistent."

"Right?" I grin over at her, glad that she gets it.

"Even though I know this is a sham, I was about five seconds away from buying a plane ticket to Calgary for Christmas," she says. "In fact, I still might."

I chuckle. "Thank you, Lola. It's been a weird and difficult week in a lot of ways and I really appreciate you sticking it out with me."

"Happy to help."

Two hours later, all of her stuff is loaded on the bus. She's patched the holes in the walls with some sort of putty she brought and has promised to come back and sand them down soon so it'll look like she was never there.

We're both quiet as I walk with her out to Bessy, carrying the fern. "Okay, see you tomorrow morning for the big race?"

"Yup. Nine a.m. sharp at the pier?" she asks.

"I'll be there." I glance at her lips, then back up to her eyes. This feels like a moment for a kiss, even though it is so obviously not a moment for a kiss.

She takes the plant, our fingers brushing and sending a jolt of excitement through me. She disappears behind the plant, and I can't help but think about when she showed up at my house six days ago. It feels like a lifetime ago. Hurrying up the steps, she sets the plant down and gives me a salute. "Enjoy having your house back."

"I will," I say. "Have a great night."

She's about to close the door when I say, "Would you like me to follow you to your place so I can help you unload all of this?"

"Oh, no. That's very sweet of you, but I've got it covered."

"You sure?"

"Positive." She grins down at me, then says, "See you tomorrow for part two of our deal."

"The adventurous part."

"Yup!" she says before closing the door.

Okay, Aidan, go back inside now. You're starting to seem pathetic.

Nope. Apparently, I'm just going to stand here until she pulls away.

She gives me a slightly confused look, waves, and then leaves. As soon as I get inside, I look around, shocked at how bare it all seems to me now. *Huh. Maybe I'll buy a couple of pillows or a fern or something.*

I flop down onto my armchair and turn on the TV, feeling completely unsettled even though I should be thrilled. We did it. We managed to fool my parents. I'm back to being gloriously alone. So why do I feel so miserable?

16

Never Let Your Lady Bits Take Over Your Brain...

Lola

Okay, Lola, time to study.
Now.
Go!
Do it.

YOU CANCELED on your trivia team tonight so you could study and booked two of your vacation days to find the crown, so you better damn well study. So far, I've put everything away, had a shower, talked on the phone with Penn about the last couple of days, using words like incredible (to describe the surfing), nice (to describe how things have been going with Aidan), and exciting (to describe what's about to happen). Before we hung up, she made me promise to check in with her every hour tomorrow to let her know how it's going. Luckily Penn didn't push me on how I'm feeling about Aidan now because if she had, I totally would have admitted I have never been so confused about anything in my life.

I want him. I hate him. I like him. I want him even more. He's infuriating, sweet, sensitive, kind, picky, uptight, and sexy all at the same time. He makes me laugh. He makes me think. He makes me feel brave and beautiful.

I open the final book in the series, *Fire of Knights*, and thumb through it, hoping that skimming the pages will refresh my memory. It might, too, if I could focus for more than five seconds. Instead, my stupid brain keeps going back to that moment at lunch today when Aidan kissed my knuckles. As much as I keep telling myself it was all for show, deep down in my bones, I know it wasn't. He could tell I was thinking about my own parents and feeling sad, and he wanted to make me feel better. Just like I could tell he actually meant it when he said I looked perfect. It's not like anyone was there to hear it. It was just the two of us. Perfect. That was the word he used. He could've said 'nice,' or 'great,' or even 'pretty.' That would have worked too. But he didn't. He said perfect. And the look on his face when he said it was the type a guy gives you right before he makes a move that causes you to be very late getting wherever you're going.

But none of that matters, because we've firmly established that this isn't a real relationship *and* that a relationship is not on the table. Period. End of discussion. And I'm happy about that. Even if it were an option, not getting involved with him is the right choice. It's smart. Logical. It's what's going to happen anyway, so I better damn well stop thinking about him and his stupid soft lips on my skin and how handsome he is when he's all dressed up and how hot he is when he's in nothing but some swim trunks and how thoughtful he was when he asked me if I wanted him to follow me home and help me unpack. That wasn't for show, was it?

Oh God, I better get back to studying so tomorrow morning I can solve the clue immediately and we can part ways before I fall completely head-over-heels in love with a guy who is all wrong for me (and doesn't want me anyway).

Focus, Lola, focus, because thinking about Aidan Clarke's muscular body is not going to get you a crown tomorrow. And that's the one thing you do need...

It's already hot out by the time I pull into the parking lot of the pier. I park next to Aidan, then grab my backpack stuffed with the *Clash of Crowns* novels and all the notes I've been making, and the cooler with the food I packed for the day—two thick hero sandwiches with ham and turkey slices, cheese, tomatoes, lettuce, and lots of mayo, a plastic container of cut-up fruit, one with hummus, one filled with cut-up carrots, cucumbers, and red peppers, a bag of barbecue-flavoured chips, and some brownies. All prepared in my own kitchen so he didn't have to see the mess.

I'm going to be all business today. No more flirting or touching or wanting him to touch me. Just super-focused Lola going after her million-dollar prize. I climb off Bessy and offer Aidan a polite smile. "Good morning."

"Morning," he says, pocketing his keys and walking over to me. He takes the cooler bag out of my hand, his fingers accidentally brushing against mine. *Hmm, that felt nice. Nope. No, it didn't.*

He smiles down at me and my heart flutters a bit. "You ready to win a million dollars?"

"I am," I say as we walk side-by-side toward the boats. "Super ready. I'm totally focused."

"Good stuff."

When we step onto the pier, it bobs a little under our weight and I feel a bit of excitement building. "I brought all my *Clash of Crowns* books with me, and a notepad. My phone's all charged up so I can look things up online too," I say, my words quick. "I think we should stay at the pier until I've solved the clue. No sense in wasting gas until we know where we're going."

"Smart thinking," he says, stopping in front of a big white catamaran with the name *Zelda* painted on the side. He bows a little and says, "Your ride, milady."

Am I blushing? Dammit, I am. That won't do. I take hold of the rail, then climb aboard. "This is such a nice catamaran. I love the slide."

"I thought it would add a sense of fun," he says.

"Totally does." I walk around the deck a bit. "Oh! And you've got one of those net thingies for people to lay out on. Nice."

"It's actually called a trampoline, which seems odd since you can't bounce on it."

"Can't or shouldn't?" I ask, raising one eyebrow.

"Can't. No give whatsoever."

"You tried it?"

Glancing up at the sky, he gives me a sheepish grin. "I may have."

I laugh, getting a mental image of what happened. "And how did it turn out?"

"Both my legs buckled and I wound up on my knees."

Covering my mouth, I laugh some more.

"You're wishing you had been here to see it, aren't you?"

"Kind of, yeah, but even just imagining it is pretty good." *Am I flirting? I am, aren't I? Stop that, Lola!*

I walk over to the table and set my backpack down.

"Why don't you get yourself all set up and I'll unpack the cooler into the fridge."

"Sounds great."

As soon as he disappears into the cabin, I let out a groan. "Pull it together, girl."

A group of four people walk past, talking loudly as they make their way to a nearby boat. My heart sinks. They're definitely on the quest for the crown. One of them is even wearing a cape.

When Aidan comes back, I look up at him, feeling panicked. I gesture for him to come over, then whisper, "More people showed up while you were inside."

He looks around, then says, "They could be fishermen."

I shake my head. "They didn't look like fishermen to me."

"How can you tell?"

"Too excited."

"People who love to fish find it very exciting," he tells me, and I know he's trying to calm my nerves.

"Also too nerdy. One of them was actually wearing a cape."

"Gotcha," he says, glancing at my stack of fantasy books.

"Oh, I get it. 'Too nerdy' says the huge Crownhead whose idea of fun is pub trivia."

He laughs, then says, "But at least you're not the cape-wearing type."

"Says the cybersecurity geek."

"Hey, I'm a former cybersecurity geek," he answers, gesturing around at the catamaran.

"Oh right, sorry. Totally different," I tell him. "I won't mention your sci-fi book collection."

Come on, Lola. Stop with the flirting already. This isn't going to get you anywhere. It is fun though…

A motor on one of the boats nearby starts up and the boat slowly makes its way out of the pier. "Dammit. The cape guy was on that one. I know I said that thing about waiting until I solve the first clue, but do you think we should get going now? You know, beat the rush?"

"I don't know. Once you leave the bay and get out into open water, the internet connection is pretty sketchy."

"Good point. We're definitely going to need internet for this."

Another group of people show up and I stare at them as they hurry by. "You know what? I'm not going to worry about them. I'm going to play my own game."

"Smart plan. I mean, we knew other people would be out here."

"True. It just kind of sucks to see them," I say. "Whatever, forget them. It's almost time for the clue drop. You go stand at the wheel and be ready so we can take off as soon as I solve it."

Giving me a thumbs up, Aidan heads to the wheel and stands in position behind it, keys in hand. "I'm ready!"

"Excellent."

We wait in an awkward silence for a couple of minutes, my heart pounding in my chest. I hit refresh on the NBO website and am delighted to read the words: The Quest Has Begun.

I let out a little squealing noise. "This is it!"

I click on the clue for the Benavente Islands and read it out loud. "It is said that the Latin name Benavente means 'welcome,' from bene or 'well' and the past participle of venire, which is vente, 'to come.' So welcome to the quest for the crown. The bejeweled prize hidden somewhere on the Benavente Islands will be found by only the bravest of souls—someone whose fortitude was forged from the

Beach, Please

same fires as King Draqen's sword. But more importantly, someone who understands the secret of life is riding the highs and lows. Be careful on your journey. You don't want to suffer the same fate as Ogden."

He puts the key in the ignition, waiting for me to announce that I've solved it. But I don't. In fact, I'm drawing totally blank. "Hmph, that's... not what I was expecting."

"I take it that it's harder than you thought?"

I tap my fingertips on my chin. "I wouldn't call that a clue so much as a riddle."

"Do you want some help?"

"No, I really need to do this on my own. Not that I don't think you'd be helpful, but it's a bit of a pride thing for me."

"Say no more, I totally get it."

The third boat leaves just as another group of people arrive. They get on a motor-sailor and take off immediately. *No! No more people!*

"Don't worry. They totally had a fishing vibe," he tells me, even though they are definitely out here looking for the crown.

"Think, Lola. Think," I mutter. "So obviously the bit about King Draqen's sword is the key. I think." I take book one off the table and start to flip through it.

Over the next hour, more boats leave while Aidan waits patiently at the wheel for me to solve the clue (looking ridiculously handsome, by the way. Rosy would die if she saw his butt right now). *Never mind that! God, Lola, you suck.*

I'm sweating now, even though I haven't moved anything other than my hands. "This is *so* hard."

Aidan sits down across from me, and says, "I know you want to do this on your own, and I totally believe that you're one-hundred-percent capable of doing just that, but I'd like to help."

I look up from my notebook. "Yeah, thanks. It might help to bounce my ideas off someone."

"Sure. I'm here for you."

Oh God, don't say that. That's something the guy you fall in love with would say...

17

Teamwork Makes the Dream Work...

Aidan

Uh-oh, what's that look she's giving me? She looks sort of dreamy for a second. Thankfully, she snaps out of it and stares down at her notepad. "King Draqen's sword was forged in the deathless flames of Mount Mokuša, named for a slavic goddess of life. So we need to find a cave with the word deathless, immortal, eternal, or maybe some form of the word Mokuša."

None of those words mean anything, but I pull out my phone anyway. "Okay, I'll start searching."

When I strike out with the word Mokuša, I go straight to some *Clash of Crowns* forums and start lurking, hoping that some cyber-sleuths are online sharing theories about where the crowns are hidden. I wind up going down a rabbit hole, reading through a heated debate over whether some character named Oona should have been named the true queen of someplace called Qadeathas, which I'm assuming is the setting of the story.

Six hours later, we still haven't figured it out, despite our best efforts. We're still docked, and even though I know Lola is doing her

Beach, Please

best to stay positive, I can tell she's getting a little more panicky by the minute.

We choose one part of the clue to examine, only to strike out and start questioning how the other teams could have solved it so fast. "If they figured it out *at all*," I tell her, for the tenth time. "They might just be going at this blind. Maybe they made a list of caves and are just checking them off one-by-one."

"Do you think we should try that?" she asks.

"There are over six hundred caves, so no. You'll get it. How about we have some lunch and rest your mind for a few minutes?"

"No time. You eat though."

"Sure," I say, going into the galley. My phone pings and I look down, only to see someone on the Crownheads For Life forum has posted: 1ST CROWN FOUND.

"Shit," I mutter, opening the link. It starts a news video.

I watch as the anchor sits behind the desk, a serious expression on his face.

"Good morning, I'm Giles Bigley at the ANN Newsdesk. Today's top story—after only six hours, the first of NBO's crowns has been found in Greenland, and hence, the million-dollar prize has been claimed, but not everyone is happy for the big winner. Eccentric biomedical billionaire Dick Napper took the first crown at four a.m. Greenwich Mean Time. After putting together a team of forty-six members including spelunkers, cave-divers, drone pilots, cartographers, and a former executive at Google Maps, Dr. Napper set his sights on Greenland, hedging his bets on the fewest people searching in that location due to the remoteness and small population. It was a bet that paid off, because just hours after the first clue was dropped, the crown was found in the Valley of a Thousand Flowers at the base of the Kiattut Glacier. The valley was famously used in the *Clash of Crowns* series as the home of Mehesi the Immortal, the witch who foretold that Lucaemor and Oona would become rulers of the five kingdoms of Qadeathas."

Giles looks off the set, then says, "What? I know the show."

The video feed cuts to show Dick Napper, a man in his fifties dressed in Patagonia's Climbers line. He whips off his wool beanie, lifts the crown off the pedestal, and places it on his shaved head. Two people dressed in period costumes from the series approach him and bend the knee, then proclaim him the true king of Qadeathas.

Raising his arms above his head, he looks directly into the camera and shouts, "Yeah! Suck it, world! I'm the true king! Me! Dick Napper!"

The footage cuts to a group of people standing on a street in the city of Qaqortoq, Greenland. They're dressed for adventure and are clearly disappointed. A woman in an orange puffer jacket shakes her head. "Not fair. Not fair at all. NBO didn't intend for some billionaire to swoop in and steal the crown. It was meant for true Crownheads."

The man next to her nods emphatically. "Agreed. Ridiculous. What does he need another million dollars for?"

"He doesn't," she says.

"Exactly. They should have crowned him the true king of the asshats."

The video cuts back to Giles Bigley. "There you have it, folks. History has been made. There are still four crowns to be found with the biggest bounty left at a cool half-million dollars. No word yet on whether Dick Napper's team will be moving on to another location, but rumour has it that his private jet is scheduled to land in Ireland, which is a crown location. Could it be that he intends to find all five crowns? Stay tuned to find out," Giles says. "Coming up next, is Jax Body Spray causing an estrogen spike in young males? Some experts believe it might be."

"Shit," I mutter again, glancing out the window at Lola. As much as I know she needs to know this, the extra pressure isn't exactly going to help her think clearly. Deciding to hold off for now, I pocket my phone and get out a couple of Cokes and the hero sandwiches. Walking back out onto the deck, I set one of each in front of her. "Here, fuel your brain."

"Thanks," she says with a grateful smile. "You know, I was thinking, what if the stuff about the sword is just a red herring and we should really be focusing on the name Benavente?"

"Okay, that sounds good. Switch gears and see where it gets you, right?" I take a big bite of the sandwich. It's so delicious, I let out a moan.

"That bad or that good?" she asks.

"That good."

She grins a little, then picks up her sandwich and the two of us eat in a comfortable silence for a few minutes while she continues to flip through the notes she made.

When we're done, I say, "Damn, you make a mean sandwich, Lola."

"The secret is lots of mayo," she says without looking up from her notepad.

"That's the secret to most good food, if you ask me."

She freezes for a second, then flips to the first page. "The secret is the secret."

I narrow my eyes at her. "Maybe we need to get you into the shade. I think the sun's starting to get to you."

Shaking her head, she says, "The clue. The secret to life is to have good timing. You don't want to suffer the same fate as Ogden."

"What happened to Ogden?"

"He drowned in Lake Silvermoon."

Narrowing my eyes, I say, "Was he really far from shore or something?"

"No, he was actually on the shore at the time. Matalyx was holding his head under the water."

"Okaayy ... so don't let anyone hold your head under the water while we're out looking for the crown."

She offers me a wry smile. "Solid advice regardless of the situation."

"I'd say so." I cock my head so I can read her notes. The clue is written in big block letters. "The secret to life is to have good timing. So if you don't have good timing for this quest, you might drown?"

Snapping her fingers, Lola says, "Oh my God, that's it! That cave. The one you can only get into during low tide."

"Never heard of it."

"Yeah, they took it off TripAdvisor on account of too many

people staying inside too long and getting stranded until the next low tide," she says, grabbing her phone. "One guy even died a few years ago. Now all the touristy websites have to list it as a closed attraction."

"Would they actually hide the crown somewhere so dangerous?"

"Maybe. I mean, it's only dangerous if you go at the wrong time." Lola gasps, then drops her voice to a whisper, even though there's no one around. "It's called Caverna Luna Plateada, which, if I'm not mistaken, is going to be Spanish for Silvermoon Cave."

"Lake Silvermoon, Silvermoon Cave," I say. "I think you've got it."

She does the international gesture for lower your voice, so I whisper, "I think you've got it."

She taps on her phone for another few seconds, then offers me a huge smile. "That's got to be it. *That's* our cave."

I hold my hand up for a high five. She grins while she slaps my hand, and shouts, "Yes! We did it! Let's go!!"

Glancing at my watch, I see that it's a little after four o'clock. "Low tide is at 6:23 today. As long as that cave is within two hours of here, we can make it." I jump up and turn on my navigation system.

"How do you know the exact time for low tide?"

"What?" I ask. "I'm a captain. We have to know these things."

I tap my foot impatiently while I wait for my Humminbird Helix 5 GPS to boot up. It's a little slow, but it more than makes up for that in accuracy. I type in the name of the cave and wait a minute while it calculates the distance. Lola gets up and stands next to me.

"Ha! Two hours and two minutes," I tell her. She squeals and throws her arms around me for a big hug. She's both soft and lean at the same time, and she smells like coconut sunscreen and strawberry shampoo. Man, that feels good. Too good.

Thankfully she lets go before just how good that felt becomes obvious.

"Let's go get that crown!" I tell her.

"And more importantly, one million dollars!"

Urgh, now just doesn't feel like the right time to tell her. Not when she's so happy she just hugged me. I'll break it to her soon, but I'd really like to let her enjoy the moment. Just as I put the key in the ignition, a crack of thunder rips through the air. I look up, only to see some ominous clouds have been moving in from the west.

"Oh shit," we both say at the same time.

"Let me check what the weather office is saying." I pull my phone out, only to see a red flashing storm advisory that reads: *An unexpected thunderstorm with gale-force winds is moving in and is not expected to blow over the Benavente Islands until after ten p.m.*

Lola leans over to read the warning with me, the scent of her floating around me. "Oh, come on. Seriously?"

Her shoulders drop and she looks so upset, I just want to wrap her in my arms for a hug. I won't, but I really, really want to. Then she shakes her head and smiles as if she just shook away her disappointment. "That's okay. So long as no one else found it today, this means we're all starting from the same point tomorrow."

I stare at her for a second, surprised at her ability to bounce back like that.

She wipes around her mouth. "What? Do I have mayo on my face or something?"

Shaking my head, I say, "I'm just marveling at how you manage to stay positive."

"If you don't have hope, you don't have anything," she tells me.

I let her words sink in, thinking about how, for the last six months, I've abandoned all hope of ever finding happiness again with a woman. The pain of what happened immediately causes my chest to squeeze and reminds me that hope can be lethal. "I don't know. I think it's okay to give up on things that aren't ever going to happen."

Her head snaps back. "You don't think we'll find the crown?"

"No, that's not at all what I was thinking about just then."

Looking confused, she says, "What were you thinking about?"

"Relationships."

We stare at each other for a moment, and I can see she's hurt. For a second, I think maybe I hurt her feelings just now, but then she says, "Right, on that topic, I agree."

The thunder rips through the air again, and the wind picks up, bringing the clouds closer. I hurry back over to the table and we start packing up. Lola manages to get all her books put back in her bag while I grab the plates and Cokes. "Do you want to head back to my place and regroup?"

"Yes," she says, as we both make our way to the dock. "We need to figure out a foolproof plan to be the first ones at the cave tomorrow."

18

Getting to Know You...

Lola

"There you are! I've been waiting all day for an update," Penn says in lieu of hello.

I take a left out of the parking lot, following Aidan's pick-up. By the time we packed up, the rain was coming down hard, and now I'm dripping all over my seat. "Sorry, I've been hyper-focused."

"That's okay, I figured you were too busy adventuring," she says. "So? Tell me what happened! How'd it go? What was it like being out on the boat with Aidan all day? Is he less anal out on the open ocean? Are you wearing a crown? Please tell me I can now call you Queen Lola."

Turning up the speed on my windshield wipers, I try to ignore the horrific squealing sound they make. "Um, no to the last two questions. We never left the dock. I didn't figure out the clue until the rain blew in."

"Oh, that's gotta be disappointing."

"It's not what I was hoping would happen when I got up this morning, but it is what it is. I just have to make sure I'm extra prepared for tomorrow."

"Which I know you'll do," she says. "Now, onto more important topics. How are things going with Aidan?"

"How is that more important than me getting my shop back?"

"Because if you two don't get together, it means I was wrong, and I hate being wrong."

I take a right onto the freeway that runs along the shore. "Has it occurred to you that this may not be about you?"

"No. Should it have?" Penn laughs at herself and I join in, relieved to be thinking about something other than the clue for a minute.

"Look, we already established that we're all wrong for each other. I thought we were past that."

"Yeah, but then you guys became friends so I started to hope again."

"Well, stop hoping. The man is dead serious about living a solitary life. It's literally one of the last things he said to me before we left the pier."

"Come on, you don't believe that, do you?"

"In his case, I actually do. Everything he loves to do is something you do alone—reading, playing video games, running, lifting weights."

"Literally three of the things on that list you can do with a buddy."

"But he doesn't," I say, trying to squash whatever hope I have that maybe Penn's right about us. "And maybe he's not wrong about relationships. It's not like mine have turned out so well."

"Oh, come on. Don't let one bad apple spoil your love life."

"The Dirtbag wasn't just a bad apple. He was … like that poison apple from Snow White."

"And yet, you're not dead or… in an apple coma. You're still the fairest maiden of them all, and you're destined to find your Prince Charming any day now—if you haven't met him already."

"Penn," I say in a warning tone.

"Okay, fine, I'll leave it for now. What are you doing this evening?"

"I'm actually driving to Aidan's place."

"Really?" she says, her tone suddenly enthusiastic.

"Yes, we're going to regroup and come up with a plan for tomorrow."

"Over dinner?"

"I'm not sure. We just ate lunch an hour ago, but if I'm there long enough, I assume he'll feed me," I tell her.

"Out of curiosity, how many meals did TD make you?"

"You already know it's zero, unless you count that time he poured us each a bowl of Frosted Flakes."

"Which I don't."

I sigh. "I suppose there were signs, weren't there?"

"That he was a lousy boyfriend, yes. That he was going to rob you and disappear? No," Penn says firmly.

"I hope not because if there were and I missed them, that would cause me to question my ability to ever pick a guy for myself again," I tell her.

"You could always go on one of those matchmaker shows."

I laugh at the idea as I slow down in front of Aidan's cottage. "Just pulled up at Aidan's. I'll let you go."

"Have fun with your super-hot single friend who's about to make you dinner."

"I'm sure it'll be nice, but not in the way you're hoping."

We hang up and I grab my stuff, then rush out into the pouring rain and up the sidewalk to Aidan's house, where he's already unlocking the door.

"Need any help?" I ask as soon as I climb the steps to the covered porch.

He chuckles. "Thanks, but keys aren't as complicated as they were last week."

"Funny how that is," I say as he swings open the door.

Once we're inside, I realize I'm dripping all over his hardwood floor which he is *not* going to like. Only he doesn't seem upset. He's smiling down at me while we both wipe off our faces. There's an excitement to the moment, and I'm not sure if it's because of the adventure we're going on together or just from being caught in the rain. Whatever it is, it's fun.

"You wait here. I'll go get some towels," he says, toeing off his trainers.

I wait by the door for him, looking around at his empty house and my heart squeezes a little. Even though it was such an emotional rollercoaster (and it's only been one day since I moved out), I somehow miss being here. It really did look so much more cozy with all my stuff here. But if this is how he likes it, who am I to judge?

He comes back a minute later in a fresh white T-shirt, carrying a stack of towels. I can't help but get an image of him changing his shirt, and my mind does an immediate recall of him at the beach sans the shirt. That's a thought that'll warm a girl up fast.

"When it rains here, it really frigging rains," he says.

Taking a couple of towels from him, I feel our fingers brush against each other like they did this morning when he took the cooler bag from me. I cover my face with the towel to hide the blush in my cheeks. *Okay, down, girl. All that stuff you told Penelope is exactly true. This is not going to happen. Period.*

He scrubs his head with a towel, then hands me a faded blue sweatshirt and some light grey shorts. "I thought you might want something dry to throw on. I can pop your stuff in the dryer if you like."

"Thanks," I tell him. "I'll take you up on that."

I hurry away, wanting to peel off these wet clothes as quickly as possible. I get changed, his clothes hanging off me, yet feeling somehow cozy at the same time. The sweatshirt smells like laundry soap, but there's a hint of him on it too, and it does something to my insides. I take a big whiff, then tell myself not to do that. It's creepy and weird.

I find Aidan in the kitchen. He's got a pot on the stove and is scooping some hot chocolate powder into two mugs. Glancing up at me, he says, "I know it's not cold out, but somehow it feels like a hot chocolate moment."

"I'm in," I tell him, walking over to see what's in the pot. Milk. He's heating up milk for the hot chocolate. "I love that you're not a water-in-the-kettle hot chocolate guy."

"No way. Hot chocolate needs to be creamy."

"Creamy like ice cream?" I ask with a little grin.

"And hot, as in the opposite of ice," he says, getting out a bag of mini-marshmallows from the cupboard. He holds it up with a 'would you like some' expression. I nod and he hands it to me so I can free-pour them into my mug.

I give it back to him and he does the same, then says, "Hold your hand out."

I do what he suggested and he dumps some into my palm. "To tide you over until the hot chocolate's ready."

I pop one in my mouth and let it melt on my tongue while I watch him adjust the heat under the pot. "Who taught you to make hot chocolate?"

"My grandma," he says. "She used to babysit us a lot when my parents were busy on the ranch. In the winter, she always had hot chocolate waiting when we got off the bus from school, and if it wasn't quite cool enough to drink, she'd give us each a handful of marshmallows so we wouldn't get too eager and burn our tongues."

"She sounds wonderful."

"She was. A very special person." Aidan's tone shifts a little and even though I can tell he's trying to keep his voice steady, there's an undercurrent of emotion to it.

"How long ago did you lose her?"

"Ten years. Breast cancer."

My nose tingles a little and I feel myself tearing up a bit. "I'm sorry."

"Me too. She was actually the only person in my family who really got me," he says, slowly stirring the milk. Offering me a small smile, he adds, "It's nice to be understood."

I nod, my heart tugging a little. "Agreed. My third stepdad, Norm, was that person for me."

"Your third stepdad?"

"Yes, third of seven, actually," I tell him, having another marshmallow.

"Wow, that's a lot of stepdads."

"My mom was the original Evelyn Hugo."

"Who?"

Shaking my head, I say, "Nothing. It's a book."

"Gotcha. So that must have been hard, when he and your mom got divorced."

I nod. "I was ten at the time. He was an Australian pro-surfer who wound up here for a competition and decided to stick around for a few years. He went back after my mom told him it was over. Of all my stepdads, he was my all-time favourite. He never treated me like I was in the way, which most of them did. In fact, we kept in touch after he moved back home, right up until he passed away a couple of years ago." I squish one of the marshmallows between my fingertip and my thumb and let it bounce back up. "He actually left me all his money and a letter encouraging me to start my surf shop."

"Really?"

"Yeah. Without him, I never would've had enough cash to get a loan."

"He sounds like a special guy."

"Norm was the best. I used to wish he was my real dad so I could go live with him," I say.

"Must have been hard, having to adjust to new men in your life so often," Aidan says, his eyes set on mine. Boy, those are some beautiful blue eyes. A girl could get lost in them *foreva*.

Shrugging, I say, "It wasn't exactly stable, but it could have been a lot worse. After Norm, I learned not to get too attached. Instead, I tried to accept that they'd be around for a while, then they'd be gone. None of them were bad guys, and it was never them who left. My mom gets bored easily."

"I see. And does she live here?"

"Not at the moment. She's in Johannesburg with a super old diamond mogul."

"Married?"

"If she has her way, they will be soon," I tell him. "With any luck, before he kicks the bucket."

"Yes, I'm guessing getting married is a lot easier to do when both people are alive."

"And after our Zoom call last week, I have to say I'm not holding out much hope."

"That old?"

"I literally thought he died several times during the call."

He bursts out laughing, so I add, "But to be totally honest, I wouldn't put it past my mom to pull a *Weekend at Bernie's* wedding."

He laughs again, and I watch him, thoroughly enjoying the deep, rich sound of it. I mime her holding him with one hand and making his mouth move with the other while saying, "I do."

Unable to play it straight any longer, I start to laugh along with him. When we're done, he says, "You're really fun, you know that?"

"Aww, thanks, pal."

He shuts off the burner and pours the milk into the mugs. I take mine and stir in the powder while he does the same. Outside, the rain beats down and the wind howls as it whips around the cottage, and I follow Aidan over to the living room area where we both take a seat. I curl up in the corner of the soft leather sofa and he takes a seat on the opposite side of it.

Somehow, even though we've spent so much time together, I realize how little we actually know about each other. "So, why did you decide to move to Santa Valentina, of all places?"

He has a sip of his drink, then says, "It was a spur of the moment thing. After that whole situation with my brother, I was looking online for cheap real estate and happened to find this place. After some research on the country and the town, I decided to go for it."

"Seriously? Without ever having been here?"

"Crazy, right?" he says, shaking his head as if he can hardly believe it himself. "It's the first truly impulsive thing I've ever done."

"Grief'll do that to you."

"Yes, it will."

"Do you regret it?"

He looks at me for a second, squinting as if trying to decide. "No. I don't. I love it here. Aside from the fact that this is literally paradise, I'm trying something new with my life. My job back home was pretty stressful and what I'm doing now suits me better." He takes another sip of his drink. "To be honest, I don't think humans are meant to be at a keyboard all day every day of their lives. We're meant to be outside moving and doing things."

I take a sip of the creamy hot chocolate, letting it warm my throat on the way down, even though I'm already warm enough from our conversation. We stare at each other for a moment too long, then Aidan seems to realize it's a bad idea. He sets his mug down on the coffee table, then jumps up and walks over to his desk, returning with his laptop. "First thing we need to figure out is when low tide is tomorrow."

He sits next to me on the sofa so I can see the screen, then boots it up and searches for the tide times. "Hmm, high tide is at 6:42 a.m. and low tide is at 4:12 p.m."

"Crap. Too early or too late," I say.

"Yes, I imagine by four o'clock, your competition will all be there."

Sitting back against the sofa, I let out a sigh, trying to wrack my brain for some way to beat everyone else there.

"Is there another way in? Like, could we hike in from another part of the island?"

"Maybe," I say. "Let's look."

A quick Google search shows that there is, indeed, only one way in and out of Caverna Luna Plateada.

"Low tide it is," Aidan says. "Unless you happen to have a mini-submarine we could use."

A slow smile spreads across my face as the answer comes to me.

"What?" Aidan asks. "You *do* have a mini-submarine?"

"Nope, but I do have another way to get in before low tide." I stare at him, my heart pounding in my chest. "It's risky but it could work."

19

Bad Ideas and Big Risks...

Aidan

"Risky how?" I ask, not exactly loving the gleam in her eye.

"Umm, well, not in the risking-your-life sort of way, if that's what you're worried about," she says. "I mean, it's totally safe for an experienced scuba diver."

"I take it you're experienced?"

"I'm a certified instructor," she says with a little shrug.

"Stepdad number four?" I ask.

She grins at me. "No, my own idea. I figured I should expand my skills in case the surf lessons slowed down. Plus, I rented out the equipment at the shop, so it helps if you know how to use it."

"Makes sense," I say. "Now, tell me what the risky part is."

"Umm, well, in order to get the scuba equipment by tomorrow morning, I'm going to have to cross a line that I normally would never cross."

My left eyebrow shoots up. "Exactly what kind of line?"

"The one that separates the law-abiding citizens from the … other ones."

"You mean criminals?"

"Yes. Yes, I do," she tells me. "Which is why I'm going to have to do the next thing on my own."

"You're going to break into your own surf shop and steal it, aren't you?"

"Borrow, and how'd you guess?"

"It wasn't a huge leap," I tell her. "You couldn't scrounge it up some other way maybe?"

"Not at this hour. The rental places are all closed for the day and nobody'll be open by first light," she says. "But don't worry about it. The risk of getting caught is like, really small."

"How small?"

"Eleven," she says with a smirk.

"Eleven smalls, eh?" I ask, unable to stop myself from smiling.

"Or less." She nods firmly. "Don't tell anyone but there's no security system at the shop. The Dirtbag talked me out of installing one, for reasons that are now *so* obvious to me. The bank wasn't going to do it on account of not wanting to put another dime into the place."

"But surely they changed the locks."

"That they did. But what they don't know is that the bathroom window in the men's room has no lock. Or at least, I hope they don't know. I'll wait until, say, two a.m., when the whole world—including you—is asleep, slip in, get the equipment, and get out. Easy peasy."

I shake my head at her, dumbfounded. "Who are you?"

"A woman on a mission."

"How high is the window?" I ask, my mind already on logistics.

"Umm, like about your height, I'd say."

"Six feet?"

"About that."

"And how exactly are you going to lift the stuff out of the window and get it safely to the ground on your own?"

"I'm just winging it here, but I'm thinking ladder on the outside, stepping stool inside, and some ropes."

I give her a look. "This is a terrible idea, you know."

"Or it's genius. It's a fine line sometimes."

"No, it isn't. It's a big, thick, very visible line. What if someone sees you?"

"That's why I'm waiting until the middle of the night."

"What if you get in but can't get out and have to call the cops on yourself just to get out of there?"

"That would suck."

"Yeah, it definitely would. Let's just think of some other way." I bounce my leg up and down for a second, trying to come up with a better plan. "Oh! You work at a resort. Could you borrow the equipment from them?"

Shaking her head, she says, "They only offer snorkeling. Scuba's too much of a liability."

"Right. That's why I don't offer it." I sigh. "There's got to be some other way."

She places her hand on my knee, and my mind turns to mush while she keeps talking. "Aidan, I can do this. And more importantly, I'm *going* to do this. It's my only shot at getting my shop back. At getting back everything Norm was trying to give me. It's worth risking a little time in jail."

"Is it?" I ask, narrowing my eyes at her.

Taking her hand away, she says, "One-hundred percent, yes."

"Have you been to prison?"

"No."

"It's not nice. You won't like it."

"How do you know? Have *you* been to prison?"

"No, but I've watched *Orange is the New Black*. It did *not* look that pleasant."

She grins a little, then says, "I'm not going to get caught."

"Famous last words," I tell her.

"Oh, come on, I bet more than half of the time when people use that phrase, they don't get caught."

Folding my arms across my chest, I say, "What if you're wrong?"

"What if I'm right and I can get the equipment without getting caught?" She lifts her chin. "What if I get to the crown first and win a million dollars and on Monday, I march into the bank and pay them back and by Tuesday, I'm back to doing what I love for the rest of my life, except it's so much better than before because I'll be a twenty-eight-year-old millionaire without a dirtbag boyfriend?"

Each time she says million, my gut tightens because I haven't told her yet about the first crown being found. She must see it in my face because she narrows her eyes at me. "What?"

Well, I guess I was looking for an opening. Not actively, but in a vague sort of way. "Someone found the first crown."

Her head snaps back. "What? Who? When? Why didn't you tell me?"

"Some billionaire. A few hours ago. I found out while you were so stressed about the clue that I didn't want to make things worse."

"Oh," she says, her shoulders dropping. "A billionaire? But he doesn't need more money."

"I know. I'm sorry. I was going to tell you right after you solved it, but then you just seemed so happy I didn't want to spoil your fun. And then after that … it just didn't come up."

Lola stares at me for a minute. She opens her mouth, then closes it a couple of times. Finally, she says, "Look, if we're going to … do business together, you can't hide things from me."

"Agreed. It won't happen again."

"It better not or we can't be friends."

Holding my hands up in surrender, I say, "I promise. Only the truth from now on."

"The whole truth, even if it hurts your big, nice, Canadian boy heart to tell me."

Trying to hide my amusement at her description of me, I nod. "Cross my heart. From now on, I tell you everything, even if it's going to hurt."

Poking me in the chest with one finger, she says, "You better, or I'll call your mom and tell her we're not really a couple."

"You wouldn't."

"I would." She looks so fierce and tiny, and I know that I shouldn't find her this adorable, but I can't seem to help it. She's all of those things and more.

"Understood."

Beach, Please

"Good." Her shoulders drop and she says, "Someone found the first crown already?"

I nod, my nose wrinkling up in sympathy. "Sadly yes. But a half mil is all you need, right?"

She sighs. "Yeah. It'll more than cover what I owe."

"Okay, so we need to make sure we're the first ones to that crown tomorrow morning."

"Exactly," Lola says, standing up and walking toward the door. "Which is why I should go home. I need to pick out a cat burglar outfit."

I stand, already annoyed at what I'm about to do and totally confused as to why I'm about to do it. "I'll go with you."

She spins around. "Nope. That's a very nice offer, but I refuse to drag you into this."

"You need me, Lola."

"Do not. I'm fully capable of pulling off a little B&E on my own, thank you very much."

"With Bessy, the least discreet getaway car in the world?"

A sheepish look crosses her face. "I can take an Uber."

I open my mouth but before I can say anything, she waves her hand at me. "I just heard it myself."

"Give me your address. I'll pick you up at two."

"Fine, but you stay in the truck."

"I'm coming in and we both know it."

"No, you're not—"

I hold up one hand and she stops talking. "I'm tall. There's a much better shot at getting what we need if we work together."

She chews her bottom lip for a second, then says, "I don't feel good about this idea."

"It's not ideal, but I think you're right. It's your best shot at winning."

"Listen, if you change your mind, just text me that you're out. I can always park a few blocks away."

"And carry two scuba tanks, respirators, and all the other stuff we'll need?"

"Two sets of gear? I only need one."

"You think I'm going to let you scuba dive into a cave at high tide *alone*?"

"It's really not a problem. Besides, do you even know how to dive?"

"I wouldn't be offering if I didn't." I find it an absolutely terrifying, panic-inducing way to pass the time, but I'm not going to tell her that. "I'll pick you up at two, yes?"

She sighs. "We're back to that, are we?"

"You're getting two sets of gear. It's double the risk."

"I'll make multiple trips."

"And multiply your risk of getting caught?" Shaking my head, I say, "No. We go together. We get in and out fast, and we go get that crown."

"Okay," she says, her voice loud and slightly angry. "But if you change your mind, promise you'll say something."

"I won't."

Her eyebrows knit together. "Won't change your mind or won't promise to tell me?"

"I won't change my mind. When I make a decision, I stick with it."

"Good to know." She nods, and I can tell she's trying her best to look confident. "I'll see you then."

"Looking forward to it."

She turns to leave, then turns back. "You know what? Why don't we make it four o'clock? That way we can go straight to the dock."

"Sounds smart."

"Hopefully."

My gut tightens at the thought of what we're about to do. But there is literally no way in hell I'm letting her do this alone. She needs me and for reasons I don't understand, that matters to me. "See you at four then."

"Yes, you will."

As soon as the door closes behind her, I mutter, "I just hope to God I won't regret it."

20

Please Don't Judge Me. Sometimes a Girl's Gotta Pull a Little B&E...

Lola

2:50 A.M. I stare at myself in the bathroom mirror. I'm dressed head to toe in black, including the wool beanie. My heart is racing, I'm sweating, and I'm thirsty, even though I've been sucking back water all evening. I also have to pee again, on account of the nerves and all the water. I haven't had even one minute of sleep, but I'm not even the least bit tired. Instead, I'm wide awake in a way I never have been before. I suppose this is what it feels like when you're about to cross over the line and do something you would never, ever do.

Am I actually about to break the law? Turn into a criminal?

Yes. Yes, I am.

But at least I'm not going to take an innocent Canadian with me. I'm going to the shop an hour early so I can be back in time for Aidan to arrive. That'll mean he won't wind up in jail and/or getting deported on account of yours truly.

Gawd, this is *insane*. I wish I could talk this whole thing out with Penelope, but there's no way I can tell her what I'm doing. She'd be over here in a heartbeat, tying me to a chair until I come to my senses.

The reality is, this is my one shot to get my life back and I have to take it. If we can get to Caverna Luna Plateada first thing, I know we'll be the only ones there. I've checked online at least fifty times since I got home and no other crowns have been reported as found, which means the second one is still up for grabs.

I grab a small bag I've prepared for the occasion, lock up, and hurry down the sidewalk, my feet propelling me forward even though a voice in my head is telling me to stop this instant, go inside, climb into bed, and forget the whole thing.

Sorry, brain. Heart is winning tonight. And she needs this more than anything she's ever needed in her life.

I'm just unlocking Bessy when I hear a voice behind me. "Thought you might try to do this alone."

I nearly jump out of my shoes, then turn to see Aidan staring down at me. He's already here. Of course he is. He has also elected to wear all black, except instead of a wool beanie, he has a ball cap on.

We stare at each other for a second, then he says, "Come on. Let's go."

I open my mouth to protest, then realize it's pointless. "How long have you been here?"

"A little over an hour. I figured you'd stick to the original time."

"Smart." I follow him to his truck, muttering, "Dammit. I really didn't want to involve you in this."

"And I appreciate that, but you need my help, and it'll make it so much easier for both of us if you stop pretending you don't."

We both climb into the cab and buckle up. "This is totally insane, right?" I ask.

"Yup."

"I don't feel right about having you with me. How about you wait in the truck? That way, if the cops show up, I'll be the only one to go down for this."

"Lola, it's already decided. We're not changing the plans now," he says. "Besides, if the cops show up, they're going to notice the guy dressed like the Hamburgler in the truck outside the shop. At least if I'm in there with you, we can get in and out in half the time."

"Right, yeah," I say, swallowing hard. "Can I just say I'm so sorry in advance for roping you into this?"

"It was my decision," he says. Glancing at my lap, he says, "What's in the bag?"

"Two flashlights, a nail file, and some duct tape."

He glances at me, looking completely confused. "The flashlights I get, but the duct tape and nail file are a little less obvious for me."

"Duct tape just felt right. It's a multi-use tool."

"And the file? Are you planning to bake it into a cake in case you need to break out of jail?"

"Obviously, yeah. A girl needs to be prepared," I say. "Although what would someone actually do with a nail file?"

"Pick the lock, I guess?" he asks.

"Or I suppose it could be a weapon."

"That's true," he says, nodding thoughtfully.

"Are we actually talking about this?" I ask.

Aidan chuckles. "Apparently. I wonder if this is the stuff Bonnie and Clyde chatted about on their way to all those banks."

"Most likely, yeah."

We take a left and head down the narrow alley behind the shop. There's a brick building housing a restaurant and a dentist office to our right, and the surf shop is to our left. Aidan shuts the lights off and rolls to a stop next to the restaurant dumpster, then cuts the engine. Turning to me, he says, "Last chance to change your mind."

My heart leaps to my throat. "Let's do this."

We climb out and he gets a step ladder out of the back of his truck. I point to the bathroom window and he sets it up under it. I take a deep breath, then climb up and try the window. When it slides open, I'm not sure if I'm relieved or not. If they had fixed the lock, the decision would have been made for me. But it wasn't and so this is all on me. I didn't get myself into this mess, but I'm sure as hell going to get myself out of it. Right now. Or, theoretically, I'm about to get myself into a much, much bigger mess.

I put on my backpack, grip the window, and lift myself up, but apparently I'm not as strong as I used to be back when I was surfing every day, and I slip back onto the ladder. "Shit," I mutter.

"Here," he says. "I'll give you a boost."

"Thanks."

I start to lift myself again only to feel his big hands on my rear end. Well, hello, Aidan Clarke! I probably shouldn't be enjoying this as much as I am. I mean, honestly. It's not like he *wants* his hands on my ass. He's just trying to get this over with before we both wind up in prison. Also, I'm sure I look ridiculous struggling to climb into the window.

I get through and drop unceremoniously onto the toilet, my foot landing right in the bowl. I let out a squeal and pull my now-drenched foot out. "Perfect. That's what I needed."

Aidan's face appears in the window. "You okay?"

"Yup, but my foot's soaked," I tell him. "Pro tip: try not to land in the toilet."

"Thanks for the hint," he says, easing himself in and landing on the floor without incident.

I roll my eyes at him.

"What?" he asks.

"Show off," I say, taking off my shoe and sock, and leaving them next to the toilet. No sense in soaking the floor. After a few uneven steps, I rid myself of my other shoe.

"I was wondering if you were going to limp the whole time," he says.

"Shh!" I tell him, then tippy toe out of the bathroom by the light of the street lamp in the alley.

When we get into the main storefront, I take out the flashlights and hand him one.

"Damn," Aidan says.

"What?" I whisper, my heart pounding a little harder.

He gives me an impish grin. "I just broke a nail. You wouldn't happen to have a file in your bag, would you?"

"Oh, shut up." I purse my lips so I won't laugh. Now that we're in here, laughing feels like tempting fate. "We need to take

Beach, Please

this seriously or the B&E gods are going to make sure we get caught."

"I'm not sure that's how these things work."

I hurry over to the scuba section and start gathering what we need, starting with two big bags to put everything in. I grab the buoyancy control devices, regulators, and the tanks. Aidan has masks, snorkels, and fins on his boat, so we don't need those. When I'm sure I've got everything, I whisper, "Let's go."

He looks at me. "This is a really nice store."

I stop and let myself look around for the first time. Everything is here, exactly how I left it. Each item carefully displayed, from swimwear to surfboards to sunglasses. The area for our 'Little Surfers' with some toys for them to play with while their parents shop is waiting for our little surfers to come back. The counter I used to stand behind and take payments. The smell of neoprene and sunscreen brings back all the memories—the thrill of the first day we opened the doors, getting my first sale, loading my first class of students onto Bessy, being here long after closing for the day to clean and organize. Having a small staff to look after. Being in love. Tears fill my eyes and insist on sliding down my cheeks in thin rivers, as the grief of what I've lost comes rushing back.

I feel Aidan standing right in front of me before I see him. "You okay?"

"Yeah, great," I tell him, wiping at my cheeks.

"You're crying," he says, placing his hands on my upper arms.

"No, I'm not. That would be ridiculous," I say, sniffling. "Nobody cries when they're pulling off a robbery."

"I mean, it might not be the best time, but these things aren't always under our control."

"But they should be," I say, my voice little more than a squeak.

I feel myself being folded in for a hug.

"But they aren't," he says, his voice vibrating through my chest as I feel the warmth of his big, strong body against mine. Without thinking about it, I let my hands rest on his chest, soaking in the feeling of safety and comfort. Somehow, even though nothing is actually going well in my life right now, I feel like everything is going to be okay. I'm at my most vulnerable and he's offering me his strength exactly when I need it most.

"This has got to be hard for you. To be back in here."

"I didn't think it would be, but man, it just hit me. What I'm about to lose is a lot." I pull back a little and look up at him. "And I won't ever get this back, Aidan. It's not like surprise inheritances pop up all the time."

He offers me a small smile. "Although your mom did have a lot of husbands, so…"

I let out a laugh, grateful that he's trying to cheer me up. "True. Come on, we'd better get out of here."

We break away from each other, even though no part of me wants to. Well, except the part that wants to stay out of jail. Picking up the bags and my shoes, we rush back out the way we came, neither of us saying a word until we're safely back in the truck and on the road.

"Holy shit, we just robbed a store," he says.

"Well, technically we didn't rob it because I bought all this stuff in the first place," I say. "Also, I'm going to put everything back."

"Right. Yeah," he says. "But we did break in. We're kind of badasses."

I let out a laugh. "We're *total* badasses."

"Ha! Who's boring now, Caitlyn?" he asks.

"Not you," I tell him.

"Exactly. I'm a badass adventure-seeking rebel who plays by his own rules."

"Yeah, you are," I say, holding my hand up for a high five.

He doesn't leave me hanging, and after we clap hands, he says, "You are, too, obviously."

"Thanks," I answer, feeling adrenaline still pulsing through my veins. Well, to be honest, it's more than adrenaline. There's a whole lot of lust in the mix as well. *Oh, my God, Lola, focus already!* "Okay, let's go get that crown."

21

Big Scary Monsters and Even Worse Revelations...

Aidan

By the time we have all the scuba gear loaded on the boat, the sun is just starting to come up. It's going to be mostly dark for quite a while, but with the lights on the boat, I'll be able to see enough to get us where we're going. We've both been quiet since we left the shop. For my part, it's because I'm all mixed up about my feelings for her. It's like my entire focus in life has shifted suddenly. For the last several months, it's been about trying to avoid pain, but overnight, it's all become helping Lola get out of the mess her ex left her with. I want to protect her and take care of her, even if it does mean putting myself at risk.

It's insane. I know it is. We haven't even known each other for a month, but somehow it feels like I've always known her. I untie the catamaran and start up the engine, then slowly make my way through the pier and out into the bay. Lola curls up on a bench nearby, looking exhausted.

"Did you get any sleep last night?" I ask.

She shakes her head. "Didn't even try. You?"

"A little, but I kept waking up worried that I'd miss the alarm."

Her phone pings and when she looks down at it, her shoulders drop. "That billionaire guy found the second crown."

"Seriously?"

She nods. "It was hidden at the Cliffs of Moher."

She bites her thumbnail for a second, then says, "So, we have to get the next one. If we don't, I don't get my shop back."

My heart tugs at the thought of her losing everything. "We'll get it."

She smiles at me, but I can tell she's starting to lose faith. As soon as we're out of the pier and into the open water of the bay, I gesture for her to come take the wheel. "I need to get something."

"Sure," she says, placing her hands on the wheel. "Anything I need to know?"

"Don't crank it and we'll be fine," I tell her. "I'll be right back."

I hurry inside and down the steps to the bedroom. Gathering the duvet and a pillow, I go back onto the deck and set them up on the trampoline. When I look back at her, she's got her face scrunched up in confusion. "Are you going to sleep?"

"No, you are," I say, taking the wheel from her. "That is, if you want to. There's nothing like a nap on the water."

She smiles up at me, her eyes locking on mine. "You Canadian boys really are nice."

"Not all of us," I say. "Now, go get some rest. We'll need to be on our game when we get there."

"Okay, thanks. I probably won't sleep, but maybe it's a good idea if I close my eyes for a few minutes."

She makes her way to the trampoline and settles herself on the blanket, wrapping half of it on top of her. Her eyes close and I'm pretty sure she goes straight to sleep. Something about it makes me smile. I tell myself that it's not because I'm falling for her, and that it's just because there's something inherently satisfying about looking after someone. But deep down, I'm pretty sure that's just bullshit.

Lola is the complete opposite of Caitlyn. She's filled with compassion, whereas Caitlyn's compassion was more often than not for herself, a trait I didn't notice until it was too late. Caitlyn was beautiful in a carefully made-up, well-dressed way, whereas Lola's

Beach, Please

your cute girl next door—ponytails and yoga pants. Lola's adventurous and insanely brave. If her choice of careers didn't prove that, this morning's events certainly did.

I glance at her again, feeling butterflies taking flight in my stomach. Shit. I think I might have a crush on her. All signs point to yes.

I turn back and set my sights on the horizon, telling myself that I'm wrong. Whatever it is I'm feeling, it's likely because of the intensity of the last two days. We're working so closely together, doing things neither of us would ever normally do. We've talked and shared things on a deep level, which is just a natural byproduct of the circumstances. I'm sure it'll wear off when we're not in the middle of this anymore. Maybe we'll be friends. Maybe we'll fade out of each other's lives and never see each other again. But whatever it is I'm feeling, it'll go away sooner or later. After all, we've already established that we're all wrong for each other by testing out living together. So, whatever this is, it's temporary.

It takes two hours to get to Caverna Luna Plateada. The sun is high in the sky and it's starting to get hot. I cut the engine and drop the anchor, then walk over to Lola. "Hello sleepyhead, we're here."

Her eyes pop open and she sits up looking adorably rumpled. "Already?"

"Yup. I guess you did sleep."

She stretches a little, then scoots off the netting and gathers the bedding. "You were right. That was amazing. I don't think I've ever slept that well in my life." Looking suddenly self-conscious, Lola says, "Give me a minute. I should freshen up a bit."

She disappears into the cabin and comes back a couple of minutes later looking ready to go. "I hope you don't mind. I borrowed some mouthwash."

"Of course."

She glances around, then smiles, "Hey, no one else is here."

"I noticed."

"That either means we're first or I'm totally wrong."

"We're first," I tell her, hoping to God that's true. "Come on. The only thing left to do is win."

As soon as we're in our gear, we both drop off the side of the boat backwards, plunging into the warm water. I follow her as we make our way to the cave. The opening is barely visible because of the high tide, but I know based on reviews we've read about it, we'll have to swim another hundred meters inside the cave before we reach the ledge. There, we'll have to pull ourselves up to the upper floor where we can walk around. Just putting on the gear had me feeling claustrophobic. I forgot how much I hate scuba diving.

It takes about fifteen minutes to get to the opening of the cave, which feels like forever when your heart is pounding and you keep imagining a great white sneaking up behind you. We stop and bob up and down in the waves for a bit to catch our breath.

"You good?" she asks.

Nope. Hating every second of this. "Yup. You?"

"I'm excited."

We flip on our lights and swim through the dark cave side-by-side. It's eerie and dark and, even though I give her a thumbs up every time she looks at me, I am way out of my comfort zone. At least I've moved on from worrying about sharks though. Now, I'm imagining some sea monster with octopus tentacles and sharp teeth appearing out of nowhere. Lola picks up her pace, leaving me behind, which only causes me to keep turning back to make sure I'm not being chased.

Something moves behind me and I scream, only to realize it was my fins. When I straighten out, Lola's staring at me, her eyes wide. She wouldn't have heard it, but she must have looked back at exactly the wrong time.

I give the double thumbs up this time, so she keeps going while I cringe.

Finally, we reach the ledge and we're at the surface. I pull my respirator out of my mouth and breath in the cool air, glad we made it this far. Lola manages to pull herself up onto the floor with ease, then peels off her tank, fins, and mask. I do the same and we start our trek through the dark cave.

"You're scared of scuba diving, aren't you?"

"No," I scoff. "Not even a little."

"Dude, you got startled by your own fins."

"You saw that?" I ask, a wave of embarrassment coming over me.

"Yeah, I did," she says.

"Look, I'll admit scuba diving's not my favourite thing to do, but I want to be here and I'm fine."

She opens her mouth to say something else, but I hold up one hand. "Come on. Let's just get going because in about two minutes, you're going to be four hundred thousand dollars richer."

She grins up at me. "You sure you don't want a cut?"

"A deal's a deal."

We continue on, our bare feet slapping against the cave floor as we shine our flashlights around the cave.

"I just realized we won't even have to sneak the equipment back into the shop. I'll be able to get the keys back as soon as I get the money," Lola says with a huge grin. "Not that I should count my chickens here."

"Go ahead and count them. We both know you're right."

"What else could the clue have meant?" she asks.

"This makes perfect sense. With the high and low tides and Ogden drowning in Lake Shadowmere," I say as if I know what I'm talking about.

"Yeah, the rest of the clue was just to throw people off. That bit about the past participle of vente. Come on," Lola says, rolling her eyes.

"Yeah, could you imagine if you got caught up on that dead end?"

"Right? We'd still be on the dock," she tells me. "Although… I guess there is that one cave with the skylight that they call the Vent to the Heavens."

She stops in her tracks and I do the same. My heart drops to my knees. "But that doesn't have anything to do with the books, right? And they said the clues would only be solved by people who have both the knowledge of the area *and* the series."

She lets out a shaky breath.

"What? Is there some connection to the books?"

"The goddess of life lived in an enormous cave that had a skylight called Heaven's Eye."

Crap. "Wait, seriously?"

She nods at me, looking shocked. "Yeah, seriously. The cave sat on top of an underwater volcano, which is where King Draqen's sword was forged actually."

"Oh, in an underwater volcano in a cave with a vent to the heavens," I say, realizing there's a very good chance we're in the wrong place. "I see."

At the same time, we both shake our heads. "Nah, can't be."

"Definitely not," I say. "It's got to be here."

"For sure. Otherwise, we would have broken the law last night for no good reason at all," she says as we continue to walk. "Although, now that I think about it, why would they send people to a cave that the government considers too dangerous to access?"

They wouldn't.

We both stop walking again and turn to each other. At the same time, we both say, "Fuuuuccckk."

Lola blinks quickly, and I can tell she's fighting back tears.

"Look, we don't know yet," I say, putting my hands on her shoulders. "Let's keep walking. We might still be in the right place."

Nodding, she says, "Right, yeah," but I can tell she doesn't believe it.

We take another few steps to where the cave curves to the left. When we get around the corner, we've reached a dead end.

And there's not a single crown to be seen.

22

Wait a Minute. This Isn't My World. DISAPPOINTED!
(NOTE: IF YOU DON'T GET THE REFERENCE, IT'S TOTALLY WORTH GOOGLING)

Lola

HAVE YOU EVER CRIED UNDERWATER? Like sobbed into your scuba mask? If you haven't, I don't suggest it. It's less fun than you think. Snot fills your mask, making it super frigging hard to see. Plus, it's gross. But I had to get it out and I did, so now I can keep going.

I screwed up. I really, *really* screwed up. I went for the sexier part of the clue instead of the obvious one—the part that most people would overlook. Or at least, I hope most people would overlook it. Because if someone else is finding that crown right now, I'm done.

I lead Aidan out of the cave, swimming hard so he won't see my face. As soon as we get out of the cave, I yank off my mask and clean it out before he can see what a disgusting mess I've become.

Aidan swims up to me. "You all right?"

"Great, yeah. I just … turned both of us into criminals for no reason and there's probably someone right now placing my crown on his greasy head, and I'm actually about to lose everything, but yeah, I'm great," I say, bobbing up and down in the waves. "Tee-riffic."

The look on his face is one of pure empathy. It's not condescending or irritatingly sympathetic. It's just an expression of, 'I get it and I'm sorry.' "It's a setback, but it's not over yet."

I nod, pulling strength from him. "I hope not, anyway." I tear up again, then blink quickly. "It's just…I really needed to be right. I've been wrong a lot—like about The Dirtbag. Penn tried to warn me that he was no good, but would I listen? No. I just jumped in with both feet and handed over not only my heart, but my passwords."

"It's the passwords that'll really screw you."

"It really is." Bobbing up and down in a wave, I say, "I just feel like such an idiot about the whole thing, you know? And I needed to prove to myself that I'm not a complete moron."

"What are you talking about? You are smart. You're a trivia champion."

Sighing, I say, "So I can remember a bunch of useless facts. It's not like that's any help at all when I'm dealing with the bank. To them, I'm just another sucker who got taken for a ride."

"It could happen to anyone, Lola."

"Could it?" I ask, wrinkling up my nose. "Did you give your ex all your banking information?"

He glances out into the horizon to avoid eye contact. "It was different because we weren't in business together."

Nodding, I say, "So at least when you got dumped, you didn't lose everything you had in addition to having a broken heart."

"True."

"Anyway, my point is that I learned my lesson. I'm never going into business with someone I'm romantically involved with again. In fact, I don't even want to have a business partner at all. Whatever happens, it'll be in my hands. End of discussion. At least I can trust myself," I say. "Well, except when it comes to choosing men. Obviously I lack the necessary skills for that."

He offers me a sympathetic smile while he continues to tread water. "I get it."

"I know, and thanks for listening to my rant."

"No problem. Now, I say we get out of here before anyone else shows up. If they see us, they'll know the crown's not here."

Beach, Please

"Good point," I say, even though I'm about a hair's width from losing all hope forever and spending my life curled up in a ball on my couch.

The swim back to the boat is not the celebration I was imagining when we were on the way out to the cave. My lungs burn with disappointment and exertion while my mind races. I have no idea how long it'll take to get to the Vent to the Heavens. It could be two days, for all I know, and by then, I'm sure someone else will have found it. And I have to be at work tomorrow morning at six.

Do not cry again, Lola. Crying never solved anything.

As soon as we're aboard *Zelda*, we strip off our stuff, and I start to feel like I can breathe again with the weight of the tank off my back. Aidan tosses a towel to me, then hurries over to his navigation system. I stand in the sun and dry off while I wait for the news of how far it is from here to there.

"Okay, so the bad news is it's a fifteen-hour ride from here, which would put it at close to midnight when we'll get there. The route we'll have to take, however, means crossing the Windward channel, which is definitely not recommended after dark."

My shoulders slump. "Maybe we should just—"

"Don't say give up," he tells me, walking over and putting his hands on my shoulders. "It's a setback, yes, but it's not over. You can do this. If we leave now, we can anchor off the shore of Solmarino Island for the night. There's a reef there that'll keep us out of the waves. We set off at first light and get there by nine a.m."

I shake my head. "I have to work tomorrow."

"So call in sick. You've come too far to give up now."

I stare into his blue eyes and suddenly everything seems possible. "Okay, you're right. I can't quit."

He lets go of my shoulders and hurries over to hoist up the anchor. "This isn't over, Lola."

My heart swells a little at his faith in me. Even after I got it so wrong the first time, he still trusts that I've figured out the clue. A few minutes later we set off, while my brain furiously goes over the logistics of making this happen. I do have to call into work and let them know I can't make it tomorrow. But there's no way I'm going to have reception out here. Then it hits me. The resort has a radio they use to get ahold of their boats. And Rosy's the one who answers the calls.

"Can I borrow your radio?" I ask.

"Sure, for what?"

"I have to call in to work." I stand next to Aidan and pick up the receiver, then switch the radio to channel 16 and start to talk. "Paradise Bay Resort, please pick up."

I wait a bit, then try a few more times. "This is Lola Gordon, employee of Paradise Bay Resort. I need to speak with Rosy Brown. Rosy Brown at Paradise Bay Resort, please pick up. Over."

Rosy's voice comes on the line and I nearly tear up with relief. "This is Mama Bear at Paradise Bay Resort. Lola? Is that you? Over."

"Rosy! Thank God. I need to talk to you. Over."

"What's wrong? Where are you? Over."

"I'm actually on Aidan Clarke's boat. Do you remember him from the other night? Over."

"Super drunk boy with the cute butt? Over."

I offer Aidan a sheepish grin. "That's the one. Anyhoo, is there a way you can find someone else to cover my shift for me tomorrow? I'm in the middle of something urgent and I can't come in." I pause for a second before remembering to say, "Over."

"Is everything all right, Lola? Is he kidnapping you? Do I need to send the coast guard? Over."

"Everything is totally all right, Rosy. No need for the authorities. I'm just … I found a way to maybe get the money I need to get my shop back. Aidan's helping me. I promise I'll be there on Monday, but I really have to do this. I'm sorry to leave you in the lurch. Over."

There's a crackling on the radio for a second, then Rosy comes on again. "I can find someone, that's no problem, but I do want to know what you're doing that'll get you so much money so fast. You're not making videos for OnlyFans, are you? Because sweetie, you're only going to regret putting naked stuff on the internet. That'll follow you for life. Over."

I close my eyes, embarrassed that everyone on this channel can here this conversation. Good thing I used my first and last name when I was placing the call. "Umm, nothing like that. I'd rather not say on the radio, but if you call Penn, she'll tell you everything. Over."

"Okay, I'll call her, but if something sounds off when I get ahold of her, I'm sending the coast guard out to find you. Over."

"No need. I promise everything is fine. I'm in safe hands. Over."

"You tell that young man that if anything happens to you, he's going to have to deal with Mama Bear and it will not be pretty. Over."

"He's standing right here so he already knows. Over."

Aidan leans closer and I hold the receiver up to him. "Hi, Rosy. Don't worry about Lola. I'm not kidnapping her. I have no ill-intentions. Everything is above board. Over."

"It better be. Over."

I press the button again. "I'll let you go, Rosy. Thank you for giving me the day off. Over."

"Be safe out there. Over."

I place the receiver back in its holder, then let out a sigh of relief.

"She's a little overprotective for a boss, no?"

"She's more than a boss to me," I tell him. "I started working at the resort when I was fifteen. My mom was dating husband number six and was spending most of her time in Florida, so I was alone a lot. Rosy sort of took me in. I used to stay over at her and Darnell's sometimes when I was feeling alone."

"Oh, wow," he says, staring down at me, his face softening. "Your upbringing sounds…"

"It wasn't that bad," I answer with a shrug. "I was lucky, really. The right people always seem to drop into my life right when I need them. Like Penn and Rosy and…" I swallow hard, not sure if I should say it. But I already let the 'and' slip out so I'm pretty sure he already knows what I'm thinking. "You."

He glances at my mouth, then back to my eyes. "Me?" he asks, his voice soft.

"Yeah, I needed a boat captain, and you appeared."

"Must be the universe," he says, taking a step closer to me.

"Must be," I say, unable to tear my eyes from his. I step toward him without meaning to do it and I'm suddenly transported to last night when he was holding me and I had my hands on his chest. I can feel his arms wrapped around me, making me feel so safe.

I look down at his mouth and lick my lips, wanting him to kiss me even though I shouldn't want him to kiss me. When I look back into his eyes, I can see it all—the attraction, the excitement, and then the pain of what a kiss can do. He leans down a little and now our mouths are mere inches apart. I can feel the heat off his body and his warm breath on my skin sends shivers all over me. *Kiss me. Please, kiss me. I need this so much.*

But he doesn't. He clears his throat and looks away. "Um, yeah, so good that you managed to get tomorrow off work."

I nod and take a few steps back, feeling like someone just splashed my lady bits with icy cold water. "Yes, Rosy's the best."

"She seems great," Aidan answers, staring at me with that look again.

I swallow hard, trying to suppress the desire to reach up and wrap my arms around his neck and kiss him hard on the mouth. "She really is."

He runs a hand through his thick, dark hair, looking as frustrated as I feel. I have got to get out of here before I launch myself at him like a missile. I search for an excuse, then say, "Do you mind if I have a quick shower? I'd like to get the salt water out of my hair."

"No, not at all." He gets a strange look and I can't help but wonder if he's imagining me in the shower. I'm sure that's not it. That look is probably more of a 'I can't wait to get away from this woman' thing.

I spin on my heel and hurry into the cabin. When I get into the tiny bathroom and close the door, I lean against it and groan. I should not want this man. There are about a thousand reasons that this won't work. Hell, I don't even want it to work. No matter how good it would feel.

Opening my eyes, I catch sight of myself in the mirror. "He's not in any position to be with someone and neither are you," I tell myself. *So smarten up before you wreck everything.*

23

Pasta, Wine, and Empty Promises

Aidan

"Rein it in, you idiot," I mutter. *Do not, under any circumstances, get an image of her in the shower. Don't do it.*

Dammit. I'm doing it. And she looks amazing.

Don't think about the soap.

Crap. There it is. Now she's all sudsy.

Aaaannd… I'm not going to be able to look her in the eye when she comes back out here.

Okay, quickly think of all the reasons to put the brakes on. Number one: She's clearly very vulnerable. She not only got dumped but also lost her business and her dream job all at once. Number two: Speaking of her business, she's got to focus on that right now, not … whatever we almost did. Number three: I'm never going to fall for anyone again and doing *that* would most definitely mean risking feelings I don't ever want to have again. Number four: She's horribly messy and there's no way I could stand to live with her ever again if this did go somewhere (which it won't for reasons one through three).

But boy, would it ever be incredible. A guy can just tell. The spark is there. Plus, she's a total live-wire, no-holds-barred, kickass girl. I just know it would be explosive. Wild. In fact, I'd have a hard time keeping up with her, but it would be a hell of a lot of fun trying.

The rest of the day is awkward, with both of us being overly polite and slightly formal. "Oh, pardon me, I was in your way." "No need to apologize. If anything, *I* was in *your* way."

The sun goes down and by the time we reach Solmarino Island, the moon is out in full force to light our way. Well, that, and the lights.

I anchor *Zelda* near a deserted beach, then find Lola in the galley, cooking up some pasta. "Are you hungry? I found some penne and a jar of pesto in the cupboard."

My stomach growls in response.

Lola grins at me. "I'll take that as a yes."

I look over at the table and see that she's set out the hummus and veggies that she brought yesterday. "Would you like some wine?" I ask. "I'm pretty sure I have a bottle."

"I'd love some."

I have to squeeze past her in the small kitchen to get to the cupboard. She flattens herself closer to the stove, but our bodies are still so close that we're touching. "Excuse me. Sorry," I tell her, even though I'm not even a little bit sorry.

"No problem."

I open the cupboard and pull down a bottle of red, then get a couple of tin mugs out and take them over to the table, both relieved and disappointed to have made some distance between us. Once I have the wine poured, I hand her a mug. "Sorry about the lack of glasses. We generally try to avoid breakable stuff aboard *Zelda*."

"It'll taste just as good out of a mug."

I hold up my drink to hers. "Here's to adventure."

We clink and she says, "To adventure."

I sit down at the table and watch as she strains the pasta and adds the sauce to it. She scoops out a bowl for each of us, then pops a fork in each one and brings them over.

"This looks delicious," I say when she puts mine down in front of me.

She sits across from me and we stare at each other for a second before coming to our senses and focusing on the food. We finish our meal without speaking, and it's both awkward and somehow comfortable at the same time. Eating with her in total silence is so much better than eating alone in front of the TV.

A gentle rain starts to fall, making a pattering sound on the roof while we eat. When we're done, we get up and start doing the dishes together. I wash while she dries, side-by-side in the small space. Each time I hand her something, I get a surge of attraction and when the hand-off is complete, a surge of emptiness.

I'm just handing her the last fork when she says, "Look, since that moment on the deck earlier, things have felt a little awkward. Maybe if we just talk about it, it'll go away."

"Agreed," I tell her, relieved that she's the one bringing it up.

I pull the plug and let the water run out of the sink while she hangs the dish towel on its hook. "I think we're both on the same page. Neither of us want a relationship right now. Or ever."

"Exactly."

"Because we both know how horribly these things can turn out."

"Godawful."

"Good, so we're agreed. We keep it strictly business."

Nodding, I say, "Definitely."

"Let's just chalk that whole ... moment earlier up to you feeling sorry for me," she says, her eyes glancing away.

I don't like the look on her face. It's like she's somehow embarrassed and I don't want her to feel that way. "It wasn't pity," I tell her.

Her eyes find mine again. "It wasn't?"

"No, not at all." God, she's pretty. "I mean, I don't love what you've told me about your mom. Honestly, she sounds like a total nightmare. But, when we were standing there, I... This whole thing is..."

"Intense?" she asks.

Beach, Please

"Yes, *thank* you. That's the perfect word," I say, turning to face her.

She does the same, straightening her spine. "Agreed. This whole thing has been like a whirlwind. It's been exciting and scary and just … a lot."

"Which can make a person feel certain things they maybe otherwise wouldn't," I say, even though I know what I'm saying is total bullshit. The feelings have everything to do with her and nothing to do with the situation, no matter how badly I want them to.

A flicker of disappointment crosses her face but she hides it immediately. "Exactly what I was thinking."

"Good. Because we've both made it very clear that neither of us are in a position to feel things for anyone."

"Precisely. Been there, done that. Not going back," she tells me.

"Same here. Relationships are a total disaster."

"Amen to that."

I swallow hard, glancing at her mouth again. "It's much better to be alone."

"*So* much better," she says, her voice thick with emotion.

Taking a step toward her, I say, "No one taking up half of the counter space in the bathroom."

"No watching UFC," Lola says.

I wrinkle my nose. "UFC? Really?"

She nods. "Yeah. There were signs."

"There always are," I tell her. "Like, she never used to ask me about my day."

"Really?"

This eye contact is off-the-charts intense. "Not once that I can remember."

"That's awful," she says, stepping toward me. "Talking about your day is one of the few perks of having a person."

"Right? It's nice to share that stuff with your person. Get a little sympathy, some understanding," I say.

"The Dirtbag never asked about my day either. Mind you, we were together most of the time," she says. "Although we traded off who was doing surf lessons and who was at the shop."

"So, he could've asked you about that."

"Yet, he didn't," she says, her eyes doing that thing where they flick down to my lips.

Oh dear. We're dangerously close to kissing again. "Probably lots of signs."

"I'm sure there were. What other red flags did you miss?" she asks, her voice a bit raspy.

"The fact that she was sleeping with my brother," I say, letting my lips curve up a little.

"That's a big one," she answers, nodding as if this is such a novel idea for us both.

Oh my God, just kiss her already.

Nope. End this day before you do something stupid. "We should go to bed."

Her eyes grow wide.

"I mean, get some sleep. We have to be up early if we're going to be first tomorrow."

"Right. Of course."

I rub the back of my neck. "So here's the thing. There's only the one bed. I was planning to sleep out on the trampoline, but with the rain, I'd rather not."

She swallows. "Well, I'm sure we can share a bed without it becoming a problem. We're both adults."

"True. Good point."

Snapping out of it, I take a step back. "Okay, I'll scrounge up a toothbrush for you. I've got some clean clothes in the closet in the bedroom. Help yourself."

She makes a beeline for the bedroom while I head to the bathroom. A minute later, she appears with a T-shirt of mine in her hand. "I hope this one's okay."

"Absolutely." As in, she'll look absolutely irresistible in it.

"You go ahead and get ready for bed. I'm going to take a shower after you're done."

We slip past each other, and I walk back to the kitchen, then pour myself the last glass of wine from the bottle. I take it and walk out onto the deck, under the cover of the overhang, and stare out at the island while I sip my drink and give myself a mental talking-to. The boat bobs a little in the gentle waves, and I drain the mug, looking back inside just as she's exiting the bathroom in nothing but my T-shirt. Well, she's probably wearing underwear as well. I wonder what kind? Nope! Not allowed to wonder that. Then I decide to wait a while before going inside, hoping she'll be asleep by the time I get out of the shower. Because if there's one thing I'm not doing tonight, it's having sex with Lola Gordon.

24

The Point of No Return...

Lola

THERE IS no possible way this is going to work. I will *never* be able to drift off, even though I'm ridiculously short on sleep. Aidan is currently in the shower and will soon climb into this small bed next to me, which is a thought that has every cell in my body on high sexy-time alert. I should be thinking about the crown and strategizing for how to make sure we get there first. That would be the smart girl thing to do. But instead, my brain is absolutely filled with imagining what he looks like in the shower. His lean muscles flexing as he runs the soap over his body. The curve of his ass. His broad chest. And I've already seen the lickable abs on display for the shampoo bottle to ogle. I'm not even *trying* not to think about him like that. I'm just letting my mind wander wherever it wants to go, and in turn, it's sending very clear signals to my lady bits. It's saying, "Time to wake up because it's on."

But it's not on. Even though I really, really, *really* want it to be.

I should stop all this thinking. I know that. It's not going to get me anywhere but more tired tomorrow. The truth is though, I simply don't want to get off the lusty train of thought I'm on. It's delicious, delightful, and isn't harming anyone. Except me, maybe, because in a few minutes, when he gets into bed and goes straight to sleep, I'm going to have an overload of sexual frustration to deal with. But what if I won't? What if he gets into bed and we start to talk a little, then turn to face each other and one thing leads to another and it's 'ride 'em cowgirl' time?

Gah! Why am I so crazy right now? Like seriously. He's just a man. Granted, a super-hot, super-sweet one who has taken such good care of me at every twist and turn during this crazy adventure. I mean, what's not to love about that? Nothing.

Oh, except that he's totally heartbroken and a total neat freak who has taken some weird vow of celibacy. Although he never said he was planning to be celibate. He's just never going to get into another relationship again. So, maybe the door to sexy time is open a crack. Sex without strings attached? Am I capable of that?

God, I wish I could call Penn right now. She'd know if I could be a friends-with-benefits person. I'd just float the idea and she'd immediately give me the yea or nay. Sad that I can't answer the question for myself. But I'm just too close to me to have an objective opinion. Plus, all these pheromones surging through me are making it nearly impossible to think clearly. Damn pheromones. They can definitely get a girl into some trouble.

The door to the bedroom opens and the light of the moon allows me to see him making his way to the bed. He's in a T-shirt and some boxers, and I can't help but wonder if that's for my comfort, not his.

The bed dips, then he gets in between the sheets, careful not to tug the blankets off me. We both lay in silence, and I wonder if he thinks I'm already asleep. I know he's the kind of guy who won't want to wake me up, no matter what, so if anything is going to happen here, it's up to me to make the first move. And what a terrifyingly thrilling thought that is. I don't let myself overthink it. I just whisper, "Hey."

He rolls onto his side, facing me. "You're still awake?"

"Yeah. Can't sleep for some reason."

"Too excited about tomorrow?"

Nope. Too horny. "More like scared."

"There's a lot riding on this."

"So much." I turn onto my side to face him, my heart squeezing. "But it's okay. If I don't get it, I'll figure out some other way to start over. It'll probably take until I'm fifty to scrape up enough money, but hey, better than never, right?"

"True," he says, offering me a small smile. "I love that you're not going to give up."

"Never. Giving up is not in my DNA."

"I'm guessing you get that from your father."

I chuckle a little, knowing he's referring to how many marriages my mom has given up on. "Probably. I don't know who he is, so it's all just a big guessing game."

He stares at me, his expression intense. "I can't imagine not knowing who my dad was."

"It's not that bad. You can't miss what you've never had."

He narrows his eyes a little. "I disagree. I think you can, even if it's just the idea of someone."

"I suppose that's true." I swallow to rid myself of the lump in my throat and change the subject before I let myself go down that road. "Listen, however this whole quest for the crown turns out, I just want to say thank you. You've been amazing these past few days."

"I'm just holding up my end of the bargain."

"No, you've definitely gone above and beyond." I snuggle up to my pillow a little more, wishing it was him. "I've had a few real low points, and you've been so… sweet."

"Sweet," he says, rolling his eyes. "I hate being called sweet."

"Kind then. You've been very kind and you didn't have to be. The deal was you drive the boat, not you drive the boat, help me break into a store in the middle of the night, go scuba diving into a cave, and hold me when I cry."

"All right, fine, I'm a nice guy. Can we move onto a new topic please?"

"Why does that make you feel uncomfortable?"

"Because nice guys finish last," he says.

"Not always," I tell him, glancing down at his mouth. I'd barely have to move at all and our lips would be touching. "Sometimes nice guys win it all."

"When? Because I've been waiting for a long time and it hasn't happened yet."

"Now," I say, closing the distance between us.

I brush my lips against his as gently as possible. So carefully, I wouldn't even be sure I did it at all if it weren't for the fact that every fiber of my body feels like it's on fire. I kiss him again, harder this time, keeping my eyes closed for fear of seeing him looking unpleasantly surprised. I wait a beat to see what he'll do, hoping with everything in me that he'll kiss me back. I don't have to wait long to find out.

He reaches up and places his hand on my cheek, then lifts his head off his pillow and kisses me like he means it. And oh wow, is this ever incredible. It's soft and sweet and hot and urgent all at the same time. It's everything I've been telling myself I don't want. I part my lips, allowing him more access and urging him to take it with a small moan that comes from deep within. Lifting my hand, I cup his jaw, then let my fingertips slide down to his collarbone and over his strong arm while our tongues find each other and do all sorts of delicious things together.

He pulls back for a second, then says, "This is probably a terrible idea."

"Uh-huh," I tell him as I grip his firm ass and pull him on top of me. "Totally."

He plants another huge kiss on me, thrusting his tongue into my open mouth. "We absolutely shouldn't be doing this."

"We should stop," I whisper, even though I'm wrapping my legs around his waist. He grinds himself against me and my brain short-circuits. "Although, what if we agree this is just ... something fun we can do together just this one time?"

"Like something that doesn't mean anything but feels exceptionally good?" he asks, kissing his way down my neck.

"Exactly. It's a release. We're two consenting adults who can absolutely have sex without using words like future or relationship."

I run my hands over his back, feeling every ridge of every muscle while he moves from my neck back up to my lips. I yank his shirt over his head, causing our mouths to have to separate for a second, then I toss it and we get right back to making out.

"Lots of people do this and it turns out just fine," he says, crushing my mouth with his.

"If they can do it, we can do it." We kiss some more, then I say, "If anything, this is a *good* idea. Clearly the sexual tension has been getting in the way."

"So we get it out of the way," he tells me, shifting his weight onto one arm so he can use his other hand to lift my t-shirt up.

"Starting with this." I grab the bottom of the shirt and take it off for him.

"Yes, let's definitely get that out of the way," he says, grinning down at my now bare chest.

"You know what else we should get out of the way?" I ask, panting while he does the most amazing things to my breasts.

"What?"

"Your boxers."

"Totally."

25

Letting Her Down Easy...

Aidan

"Wow."

"Yeah, wow," I say, flopping back onto my pillow. My heart is pounding and I'm completely satisfied, utterly happy, and slightly sweaty. "I think we may have caused a tsunami there."

Lola laughs, turning her face to mine. "Off the coast of Fiji."

"That far?" I ask, dropping a kiss on her forehead.

"Probably. At one point, I was scared the catamaran might tip over."

I wrap an arm around her and pull her close. "Oh, it did, but then you did that thing with your hips and we flipped right back again."

We grin at each other for a second, and I feel a surge of pure joy that starts in my chest and moves out to my fingertips and toes. That was by far the best sex I've ever had. Hands down, no contest. Apparently, surfer chicks rule in the bedroom. Now that I think about it, it makes perfect sense—the balance, strength, agility, and absolute fearlessness it takes to surf. Timing too. And flexibility. And if I keep thinking about it, I'll be ready to go again in about half a minute, even though we were at that for a Very. Long. Time.

She gives me a quick peck on the lips and gets up, giving me a view that drains the blood from my brain before she slides my t-shirt over her head. "I'll be right back."

I watch her exit the bedroom and a second later, hear the bathroom door close behind her, the sound of the click bringing on a gripping fear. This feels too real. Too perfect. Too big. And it's not supposed to feel like anything. It's supposed to feel like something light and fun and easy. It was supposed to scratch an itch. But when I think of the look in her eyes just now, I see more than I bargained for. I see ten thousand nights just like this one—the two of us a glistening heap of naked happiness.

And that's a thought that scares the shit out of me. How can I possibly be making plans when we barely know each other? I can't. Especially since we both have agreed that this isn't the start of anything. It's just a fun bonus while we're out on this adventure together. When the morning comes, we'll find the crown, and this will end because there is absolutely no good reason for us to keep doing this. Other than because it's deliciously satisfying in a way nothing else is. I know we agreed for this to be a one-time thing, but maybe we could continue?

Bad idea. We can't keep doing it because the more we do this, the more danger there is that we'll get attached to each other. Well, more likely that she'll get attached to me. I'm a guy. Guys can handle this sort of thing without it turning into anything.

Crap. I'm going to have to let her down easy when she gets back. It's the only solution. I'll be honest, sensitive, caring. I'll be very Canadian about it. It might sting a little, but it's much better for her to know the truth now, than to let her think this is anything more than what it is. Even though a part of me wants it to be something more. Loneliness, maybe? Nah, it's a simple biological need for wild, uninhibited, vigorous sex. Yeah, that must be it.

She returns to the bedroom, climbing under the covers while I try to think of something that will let her know this isn't the start of something. Oh God, she's going to want to snuggle, isn't she? I'll

Beach, Please

have to say no. Snuggling is off the table. It's too intimate. Although I suppose the things we've just done with each other would also fall into that category.

"You okay?" I ask, deciding that it's a good question for this particular moment.

"Great," she says, smiling over at me. "That was…"

Don't say magical.

"…Fun. Thanks." With that, she flips over so she's facing away from me.

Huh. Well, then. Not magical at all. Not even all that complimentary. Just…fun? Oh, I get it. She's doing that thing where she's pretending to be all coy about the whole thing, but really she's got her back to me so she can snuggle into me and get things going again without making it seem like she's trying to get things going again.

Well, all right, missy. We can do this again. But that's it. Then we move on. I scooch closer to her and am about to wrap my arm around her, but then I hear her snore. It's a light sound. But it's there. She's asleep.

Huh. I guess she doesn't want to go again. Although, it is late and she is tired. I mean, the poor thing's had almost no sleep at all in days.

Okay, then. Not what I was expecting, but it's honestly a relief. Now I don't have to turn her down easy. She seems fine with what just happened. Phew! Thank God. Bullet dodged. No pesky relationship talk needed.

Then why do I feel so… empty all of a sudden?

26

Queen Lola, Ruler of Aidan Clarke's Heart (or at Least His Nether Regions...)

Lola

I'M PLAYING IT COOL. That's the right move in this situation, right? God, I wish I could talk to Penn. She'd know how to play this. She's got a nice boyfriend who loves her to the moon and back. Well, one who hasn't stolen everything and disappeared, anyway, so her gut instincts must be at least marginally better than mine.

Last night was the most incredible sex of my life. Apparently nice Canadian boys can really rock it in the bedroom. If sex were a sport, Aidan would be world champion. He was singularly focused on taking me to orgasm city as often as one can go in one evening. Turns out it's three times when done properly. Who knew a girl could have not just one, not two, but three shiny, fabulous, mind-blowing orgasms? Not this girl, I can tell you that much.

The Dirtbag was competitive in a 'if I finish first, I win,' sort of way. How did I miss all the signs? Seriously? So. Many. Signs.

I jumped in way too fast and ignored all the bad stuff under the guise of 'nobody's perfect.' This time there will be no jumping. Well, mainly because this time it's not going anywhere. We're just having a mature, adult friendship with a side order of deliciously sweet sex. Well, maybe. We did agree it would only be for the one night, but maybe we could do it again.

But if I want to keep having all those orgasms, I better make damn sure he doesn't suspect that I'm feeling *all the feels* for him. And as terrible as it is, I'm having all the feels. It wasn't just the way he played my body like Jimi Hendrix played the guitar either. It was the way he looked at me, his eyes softening in the dim light of the moon and the way he cupped my face so gently with his hand and how he carefully brushed my hair out of the way so he could do the most amazing things to my neck with his lips and his tongue. And it wasn't just what happened in bed last night. If I'm going to be completely honest, it's everything he's done since we got on the boat together yesterday. The way he held me when I cried and how he knows just what to say to cheer me on when I need it. It's the way he listens to me.

It's magic with him.

Which is exactly why I have to pump the brakes, like right freaking now, before it's too late and I cross over from having all these unnamed, intense feelings to being full-blown in love with Aidan Clarke. If he starts to suspect that I'm falling for him, he's going to run for the hills. No more orgasms for me. So in the name of protecting my shot at more of those lovely moments, I'm pretending it meant nothing to me. I'm also going for a fake it 'til you make it thing—pretend I'm not falling for him until I manage to convince myself that I'm not.

So now, I'm standing at the bow of the catamaran sipping my coffee and staring out to the horizon while he drives. This is instead of clinging to him like a baby anteater to her mother, which is what my horrible instincts are telling me to do. Cling to him. Make him love you.

No, thank you. In fact, I don't even *want* to cling to him. I'm perfectly happy with the idea of being sex buddies. That'll suit me just fine actually. No attachment. No chance of getting hurt. Just me being an independent surf-shop-owning businesswoman who gets what she wants from men and tosses them aside.

Well, no. I'm not going to toss people aside. Especially not a guy who can do what Aidan can just with his tongue and one finger because it would be just stupid to say goodbye to that. God, I need to talk to Penn. And I need to find out if anyone has found the third crown, because if they have, I'm officially screwed.

I pull my mobile phone out of the pocket of my shorts and check to see if there's a signal. Nothing. Dammit. I glance over my shoulder at Aidan, who is looking mighty sexy standing behind the wheel with his aviators and a ball cap on. He gives me a smile and a slight head nod, which somehow turns my insides to jelly.

I should go talk to him. It's weird if I don't. I make my way back and offer him a breezy smile. "How much farther?"

"About twenty minutes."

"Would you like another coffee?"

"Sure. That would be nice," he says, handing me his mug. "I didn't get much sleep last night."

I grin in spite of myself. "Sorry I kept you up so late."

He smirks. "I'm pretty sure I'm the one who kept *you* up."

I point to his manly man parts. "Other way around. I kept *you* up."

He bursts out laughing, then says, "You win. That was definitely on you."

I stare at him for a second, wanting so badly to put these coffee mugs down and wrap my arms around his neck. But that would be a girlfriend thing to do. And I'm not his girlfriend. "I'll go get the coffee."

I take my time in the galley, trying to decide if I'm doing a good job of being a breezy, casual sex girl. Yes, I think so. Teasing about what happened is fine. It shows that I'm fun and totally cool with what we did. If anything, *not* talking about it would send the wrong message.

When I return, Aidan points to an island that has appeared while I was inside. "There it is. Your treasure awaits."

I gaze at it, my heart pounding. There it is. My chance to get my life back. Fuegomar is a tiny, uninhabited island with a white sand beach on the south side that gives way to a steep mountain cliff to the east. In the cliff sits the cave. And with any luck, inside that cave sits my crown. "God, I hope I'm right about this one."

"You are."

"How can you be so sure?"

"I just am." The way he says it is so confident, I believe him with my whole heart.

God, he's perfect. I'm gawking at him like a simpleton. But, seriously, that jaw, that mouth, that smile. It almost hurts to look at him.

Okay, Lola, cut it out. You've got more important things to think about right now.

"Are you ready? We'll be pulling up to the beach in about five minutes."

"How close can you get?"

"About fifty yards from shore, give or take. We'll have to swim."

Just as he says it, I hear a sound in the distance. A loud, rumbling sound. I squint my eyes toward the sky only to see a helicopter. My stomach flips. "Urgh. Who do you think that is?"

He grabs his binoculars from the cabinet under the wheel and holds them up to his eyes. "I don't know but whoever it is, they're heading this way."

No! I can't get this close only to lose it. Taking a deep breath, I say, "That's okay. We're still here first. We can make it, right?"

He sucks in some air through his teeth. "It's going to be tight."

I squint up at the sky, only to see two more helicopters flanking the first one. "Oh my God, it's like an invasion. Do you think it's that billionaire guy?"

Nodding, Aidan says, "I'd say that's a good guess."

He slows as we near the beach, while my heart pounds in my chest. The helicopters are almost on top of us now, the sound deafening.

"Lola, grab the rescue board. You can swim out much faster on that," Aidan says, pointing to the red board hanging on the wall. "I'll anchor *Zelda* and meet you there."

Nodding, I unhook it and hurry over to the port side. As soon as

Aidan cuts the engine, I toss it in the water, then slide over the side after it. Hoisting myself on the board, I paddle with everything in me.

"Go, Lola! You've got this!"

Yes, I've got this. I can do it. So what if there's a team of men repelling from the helicopter onto the shore? Big deal. I'm almost there too. I just have to outrun these Navy Seals. No problem.

I move my arms as fast as they can go until I get to water shallow enough to run in, then climb off the board and leave it as I sprint in the direction of the cave. Above me one of the helicopters lowers itself onto the beach, creating a wicked sandstorm.

Well, that's just completely obnoxious. Like seriously, people, have some common courtesy! I stick to running on the wet sand, where the ground is flat and gives you more traction.

Okay, Lola, run, run, run.

I'm doing this. I'm going to win! That money is mine!

I glance to my left and see one of the men running too. He's behind me. It's probably Usain Bolt or some other sprinter that Dick hired to help him cheat.

And now I'm tripping. That did not feel good. Getting back up. No time to wipe sand off body. *Go, feet, go!* Why the hell do helicopters have to be so loud? Honestly. They should be banned.

I sprint up the beach into the cave, then hurry as fast as I can on the slippery floor without falling. My eyes take a few seconds to adjust to the dark, then I see it. The crown. Sitting on a pedestal, just like in the photograph. I hear footsteps pounding behind me and a man says, "Oh no you don't, young lady! That's *my* crown."

"It's MINE!" I screech, lunging for it and wrapping my fingers around it a second before he catches up with me. My momentum propels me forward and I fall into the pedestal, knocking it over. I land with a thud, still gripping the crown with both hands. "It's mine," I say again, rolling onto my back.

He stands over me, panting, and I'm slightly terrified for a second that he's going to try to grab it from me. But he doesn't. He lets out a long sigh and shakes his head.

Two men appear from deeper in the cave. They're wearing long robes like in the TV show. I shove the crown on my head and scramble to my feet.

One of them mutters, "Finally, we can get the hell out of here." He stops in his tracks. "Holy crap, that's Dick Napper."

The other one lets his mouth drop, then seems to remember what they're supposed to be doing. He bends a knee. "As the one to find this crown, you are now our rightful queen."

The other guy kneels reluctantly. "All hail the queen."

Dick Napper doesn't kneel. Instead, he gives me a smirk. "We'll see about that."

"Dude, she won the crown fair and square," one of the men says, standing up.

"Maybe. I doubt it," he says. Turning back to me, he says, "Be careful with that crown. I'll want it in mint condition when I get it back."

He spins on his heel and strides out of the cave, talking into his sleeve. "We're too late. Fuel up the jet and set our course for Morocco."

A second later, a camera crew appears with Aidan right behind them. The moment I see him, I run to him, jumping into his arms. I plant a huge kiss on his lips, forgetting all about playing it cool. He kisses me back, bringing my euphoria to an all-time high. I won. I'm going to get my surf shop back. And wow, is he ever an incredible kisser. I want to kiss him forever. Finally, I pull back long enough to say, "We did it!"

He sets me down and smiles at me, his eyes shining. "*You* did it. You figured out the clue. You raced for it. You won."

He hugs me tightly and lifts me up again, whispering in my ear, "Would it be weird if I told you I'm proud of you?"

I smile at him and shake my head. "Not weird at all."

"No? Not too patriarchal or anything?"

"No, it's just nice to hear," I tell him, glancing at his lips again, then letting my mouth follow my eyes.

We kiss some more until someone clears their throat. "Excuse me. We do need to fill out some forms now so we can make sure you get your prize."

Aidan lowers me back to the floor and I turn to the men, feeling a lot less embarrassed than I probably should. "Right. Of course."

I won. I really freaking won. My nightmare is over. I'm getting my life back, only so much better because I won't be sharing it with The Dirtbag. I glance at Aidan, and my heart whispers to me that he's the one I should share my dream with. But that's not going to happen, is it? There's no way the universe is going to give me the money *and* the man. Or will it?

27

And That's a Wrap, Folks...

Aidan

As soon as we get aboard, Lola turns to me. "I know we said last night was the only night, but I'm wondering if we could maybe… one more time, right now? You know, as a celebration sort of thing?"

I grin broadly. "Will you wear the crown?"

"Obviously."

And so she did. I picked her up and carried her inside. We didn't even make it to the bedroom and instead, went for it right on the counter in the galley. I'm not sure how it's possible, but it was even better than last night. A big win'll do that, I guess. Huh, maybe *this* is why people like playing sports.

We're currently on our way back to Santa Valentina Island, which will be a much shorter trip since we're not taking a giant detour to Caverna Luna Plateada. Lola's having a quick shower while I drive us home. I'm tired but happy in a way I haven't been in a very long time. She won, which in one way feels like justice being done, even though her ex hasn't been caught. After we finished celebrating, she told me this was like the universe righting a wrong. I can totally see why she thinks that's how it happened, even though I know it was just because of her hard work, knowledge, and seizing the opportunity.

I'm not sure what will happen when we step off this boat, but if I have my way, we'll go the route of friends with benefits. That could work, right? I totally think it could with a girl like her—someone cool with a life of her own that she loves.

She comes walking out of the cabin with a perplexed look on her face. Hmm, don't love that expression. "What's up?" I ask, even though I'm not sure I want to know.

"Umm, well, it's obviously none of my business, but my skin was dry after my shower so I opened your bedside cupboard to look for some cream…"

Oh no, no, no. Very bad.

"…and I couldn't help but notice a couple hundred condoms in there?"

My stomach drops. My feet turn to mercury. I search for a good explanation. Then I realize, I don't have to come up with some stupid excuse. I can tell her the truth. "Yes, I believe in being prepared."

"Sure, yeah, it's very responsible," she says, nodding quickly.

Good, so we agree.

"But it's just that… that's a lot of condoms." She wrinkles up her nose. "You didn't buy those just before our trip, did you?"

"God, no," I say with a light chuckle. "I bought those when I first got the boat."

She narrows her eyes and nods some more, as if trying to think. "Uh huh, right. So, how many women were you planning on…" she does a fist pumping motion "…when you moved here?"

Crap. "So this isn't going to sound great, but when I first moved here, my plan was to meet as many women as possible who were up for casual fun. You know, like tourists, women out for bachelorette parties, that sort of thing." Yup, this probably doesn't sound so good to her since we've spent a significant amount of time over the last twelve hours having sex. I scramble to add, "But no one vulnerable, drunk, or in a committed relationship."

Lola stares at me for a second, and I can tell she's thinking hard about this. "So the night we met and you said you don't date locals, that's what you meant?"

"God, you've got a good memory."

"Thanks," she says, although she doesn't seem too happy about the compliment. She turns to walk away, then turns back. "Is that why you bought the boat in the first place? So you could screw as many random women as possible?"

Sort of, yes. "I wasn't screwing them."

She tilts her head and screws up her face in a way that says she completely disagrees. "What would you call it?"

"Consensual sex?" I say, hating the look she's giving me now. "Look, the truth is, I may have started out with that in mind, but it hasn't actually turned out that way."

"No?"

"No, it turns out it's surprisingly hard to find single women who aren't in the middle of a bad break up and who want to have sex with a stranger," I tell her. "In fact, if you made a Venn diagram, the intersecting group would be tiny."

"How tiny? I'm asking because I'm suddenly a little concerned about having slept with you."

"Three in six months."

"Including me?"

"Yes."

She stares down at the deck for a second and runs her tongue over her teeth. "Okay."

"Are you upset?"

Shaking her head, Lola says, "Why would I be? It's not like you and I have a future or something."

Thank God, she gets it. "Exactly."

Giving me a hard look, she says, "So, the fact that this whole thing was premeditated is really of no significance because the end result is the same. We're nothing to each other."

Ouch. That kind of stung. I'm about to protest, but then I realize she's right. I can't exactly fight for us to be something I don't want us to be. "It wasn't premeditated, Lola. Not with you."

"It kind of feels like it was in a way. The boat, the wine, the condoms…"

"You're the one who got things started last night," I remind her.

"Yeah, I did, but the whole set up was already there."

Shit. "It's different with you."

"Different how?"

"Because you live here, and we're friends."

"Are we?"

"I hope so. I really like hanging out with you."

And there it is. The look that says she's hurt but she's determined not to show it. She offers me a small smile and says, "Yeah, great. Me too. Obviously, the sex part has to be over, but we should definitely hang out sometime."

By that, I'm pretty sure she means she never wants to see me again. "Totally. I'd love that."

"Great. I'm going to go tidy up inside a bit so we can head home as soon as we get to San Felipe." She turns and opens the cabin door, disappearing inside and leaving me feeling like a total heel.

It's late evening by the time I pull to a stop in front of her place. Neither of us have said much since 'the talk' but it definitely put a damper on the celebration. We're back to being overly polite and distant.

We both get out of the truck and I help her carry the scuba equipment to her front door. "Thank God we don't have to sneak this back into the shop," she says.

"No kidding. We got away with it once. Twice feels like tempting fate." I stare down at her, wishing like hell that we weren't ending things like this. Or at all, actually. "Okay, I should go."

"Yes, I have to be up super early, but thank you again so much for everything. You really were a total rockstar out there. You kept me going when I was ready to give up and…" She holds up the crown. "I'm just so glad we kept going."

"I'm glad too. You earned it."

She stares up at me. "Seriously, I couldn't have done it without you."

"Glad I could help," I tell her, glancing at her mouth. *Nope. Do not do that.* "So, I'll see you around then."

She nods. "Sure. I'll call you."

No she won't.

I stew about it the entire drive home, right through my shower. Somehow I screwed up, even though technically, I didn't do anything wrong. I think I made her feel cheap, which was the very last thing I wanted to do. I wanted to lift her up, let her know she deserves so much more than what her ex gave her. I wanted us to … I don't know what I wanted.

I wanted nothing because I want to be alone. Being alone is a good thing. Better to be alone than be rejected. Yup. Very good.

I walk over to the wall of windows and stare out into the dark evening, wondering what she's doing right now. Probably having a shower and getting ready for bed. She has to be up early for work, then she's going straight to the bank. Hopefully the money will be in her account by then so she can pay back what she owes. I smile at the thought of Lola being free and clear, and having her shop back. I really do want the best for her. Too bad I couldn't give her that.

28

Huh, Who Knew They Had Dairy Queen in Several Caribbean Countries...

Lola

I'M EXCITED. I am. And honestly, why wouldn't I be? After all, I just snagged four-hundred-thousand dollars (and this very nice crown). So I found a cupboard full of condoms on Aidan's boat. Big deal. It's fine really. Does it take some of the shine off our time together? Sure, a little maybe. But it's not like he wasn't honest about his stance on relationships. I think I just let myself get carried away with the possibility that something more could happen.

But forget about that because Penn is on her way over to celebrate with me. I texted her the moment Aidan left with a picture of myself in the crown. She texted right back saying she was on her way.

I'm just pulling on my pajama pants and t-shirt when I hear some loud knocking. I hurry to answer it, snagging the crown off my kitchen table on the way to the door. I place it on my head and swing the door open, kicking up my right foot behind me while I give her an open-mouth smile.

She wiggles on the spot and squeals, then walks in carrying two

Dairy Queen cups heaped with ice cream, brownies, and lots of gooey chocolate sauce. "Celebratory soft serve."

I take them from her and set them on the table while she comes in and kicks off her sandals.

"Come here, you," Penn says, wrapping me in a big, squeezy hug.

"Can you believe it, Penn?" I ask, tears of joy filling my eyes. "Soul Surfers is back in business!"

We pull back and jump up and down a few times, while Penn shouts, "You freaking did it!"

"I really did!" I take off the crown, then grab my ice cream treat, and flop down on the couch. "Well, Aidan too. I couldn't have done it without him. I'm just so grateful for everything he did."

"So? Did you give notice at the resort?" Penn asks.

"I will as soon as I've been to the bank. I'm not one-hundred-percent sure if they'll let me pay off what I owe and get the shop back or if I'll have to go through the auction, but either way, I'll be done taking room service calls very soon." I smile at her, telling myself it'll all work out. "I'll go straight to the bank after my shift tomorrow."

"Did NBO say when the money will be in your account?"

"A couple of days," I say with a huge grin at the fact that I'm about to be four-hundred-thousand dollars richer. "Can you believe it? I'm still in shock."

"It's unreal," Penn tells me with a huge grin.

"It really is." My mind starts to spin with what's coming. "A few weeks from now, I'm going to be back on the beach every morning doing what I love. It's going to be a lot of work to get things up and running again, but I'm excited about doing all of it. I'll have to find another instructor and build up the staff again. Everyone has already found jobs, but I'm hoping a few of them will come back."

She grins at me. "You've already crossed the biggest hurdle. In fact, you're going to be ahead because the building will be paid off."

"I know. Things will be *so* much better. So much less financial stress. And now that I'll be running it alone, I won't have to compromise. I'll make the decisions. Period."

"I'm just thrilled for you, Lola. Honestly, I didn't know if this was going to happen, but you went out there and got what was yours. It's impressive, *really* impressive."

"Thanks." Letting out a happy sigh, I say, "Can you believe it? Last week I felt like I was trapped in a horrible nightmare and now, it's like the world has opened up with possibilities."

"Speaking of possibilities," Penn says casually. "Anything happening with you and Aidan on the romance front?"

My face instantly heats up. "First, let me start by saying we're never going to be a couple, so don't get your hopes up. Also, huge red flag that I didn't miss this time, so it's definitely better this way."

"So you did *it*," she says.

"Ah, yeah. And even though it's never going to happen again and it turns out he's a bit of a dog, holy multiple orgasms, Batman."

Penelope covers her mouth and lets out a loud laugh. "*That* good?"

"The word incredible doesn't do justice to what this man can do." Flashes of our naked bodies pressed together pop through my mind like a sexy slide show. I'm still slightly raw from his stubble on my skin and just thinking about it makes me tingly all over, even though…dog. "He's surprisingly good at the sex stuff, you know, for a nerdy guy."

"Nerds are where it's at," Penn says, a faraway look in her eyes and I assume she's thinking about Eddie. She snaps out of it and gets back to grilling me. "So? When?"

"Last night. It was raining a little so we had to share the only bed on the catamaran. Otherwise, Aidan would have slept outside on the trampoline. Did you know that net thing is called a trampoline? Which is weird because you can't bounce on it."

"Not at all?"

"No give whatsoever, apparently."

"Who made the first move?"

"Me. Big time," I say, warming at the thought of that first kiss. "There had just been so much build-up of sexual tension for days that neither of us could sleep." I have another big spoonful of chocolate-sauce-covered ice cream. With my mouth still full, I say,

"But it's not going to happen again. As great as it was, today I discovered that he basically started his business so he could hook up with random women."

Her shoulders drop. "Actually?"

"Yeah." I explain how I found the condoms and he told the truth about it. The entire time I'm talking, I feel stupid about having had sex with him. When I'm done, I let out a sigh. "I sure know how to pick 'em."

Penn dips her spoon into her ice cream, then says, "I don't know. Can you blame him? He had just had his heart broken. I can see why he'd think that was a good way to fix it."

"Yeah, but … now I just feel like what happened between us was a bit of a set up."

"But you made the first move."

"That's what he said." I have another bite, then say, "You know what? It doesn't matter anyway. It's not like I thought we were on the path to marriage or something. We both agreed it was only going to happen the one time. Well, technically this morning too."

"Really?" she asks with one eyebrow up.

"Kitchen counter. Right after I won the crown." I grin involuntarily at the memory. "But that was it. I was fine with it at the time, so I can't exactly be upset at him about it now. We really have no reason to see each other again anyway, so it was always going to end today."

"Huh," Penn says. "This is much less fun than I thought it would be."

"Agreed. But the silver lining is that I saw the condoms so I know for sure he's not the guy for me."

"And you're noticing the red flags for once, so that's a positive," she says.

"Right?" I smile a little, then say, "But it is a shame because if it weren't for that, or his absolute hard stance on relationships…"

"He'd be pretty much perfect."

"Pretty much."

"But he's not." She shakes her head.

"Not at all."

"Shame though."
"Definite shame."

I pull up in front of the bank, wishing I had sprung for an air-conditioned Uber instead of taking Bessy. I'm in a skirt suit and am sweating like crazy by the time I step inside the cool building. I find a tissue in my super-professional-looking briefcase and dab at my face a little, hoping it doesn't leave any little white bits on my skin. I don't want them to think I cut myself shaving or something.

I take a deep breath before I walk up to the woman behind the reception desk. *Okay, Lola. You've got this. You're not only the bee's knees at solving* Clash of Crowns*-related clues, you're also a savvy businesswoman who's got what it takes to make it in the cut-throat world of surf shops.*

But mostly, you've got four hundred grand to throw at your problem. That's gotta count for something.

The receptionist offers me a polite smile. "Welcome to Benavente Credit Union. How can I help you today?"

"I'm here to see Mary McNally."

"Is she expecting you?"

"No, but she'll be glad I came in, trust me." Did that sound smug? I think it might have. I'm aiming for confident. I should dial it back a bit.

She taps away at her keyboard for a second, then says, "I'm afraid she's all booked up this afternoon. I can get you in to see her next Friday at ten o'clock."

"Do you know what? That's not going to work for me. We have urgent business."

"I'm sure you do, but she can't see you today."

"It won't take long. Three minutes, tops. You see, I owe the bank a lot of money and I'm about to get a cheque that will cover everything I owe. So I just need to tell Mary that so she can cancel the foreclosure auction."

Her face is pinched as she says, "Hmm, well that's nice for you, but Mary actually is booked."

"I'll wait."

She blinks a few times as though trying to process the concept. "It could be a very long time."

"That's fine. If you wouldn't mind letting her know I'm here, that would be terrific," I tell her. "Trust me. Mary'll want to know."

There. See? I'm a don't-take-no-for-an-answer woman.

Lifting her eyebrows, the woman says, "And your name?"

Right. That might help. "Lola Gordon."

I walk over to the chairs in the waiting area and settle in, deciding to make myself comfortable. Yes, I'm here for the long haul. Even if it's a few hours. Totally worth it.

God, I'm bored. I wonder what Aidan's up to. Probably shagging some horny tourist on his boat right about now.

Oh come on, he is not. Two women other than me in six months? Hardly enough to label the guy a womanizer. But still, the intent was there which means it's at least an orange flag, if not a red one. I could be friends with an orange flag guy. Not friends with benefits. Just friends. Although now that I've tested out his benefits, I'm not sure I could hang out with him anymore because all I'd be thinking about the entire time would be how to get him back into bed. Oh dear, does that make me a manizer? Why isn't that a word?

Let's see, how long has it been? Two whole minutes. I should play Mahjong on my phone to pass the time because sitting here thinking about Aidan is getting me nowhere fast.

I pull my mobile out of my briefcase. Oh! An email from NBO. Maybe they put the money in my account already. That would be perfect. I won't have to come back to see Mary McNally (who doesn't believe in sisterly solidarity) again. Honestly, it would be so convenient to get the keys to the shop back today. I open the email, my heart pounding a little with excitement.

From: NBO Vice President of Marketing and Promotions
To: Lola Gordon@soulsurferssurfshop.bi

Subject: Prize Money

Dear Ms. Gordon,

Congratulations on finding the third crown in NBO's *Blood of Dragons* Quest for the Crown. You are among a very select group of people to solve the difficult clues, so please pat yourself on the back for a job well done.

Unfortunately, you will not be receiving the prize money. As you will recall, you filled in and signed several forms after finding the crown. I am not sure if you read the forms before you signed them, but you are in violation of the rules. Both on the NBO Quest for the Crown website as well as in the forms you signed, it explicitly states that employees of the following corporations are not eligible to enter the contest:

NBO or any of NBO's affiliate networks, or any major advertisers of NBO or NBO's affiliate networks.

TNN (The Nature Network)

Sullivan & Stone Publishing House

Paradise Bay Resort

Nabisco

As you also filled in your current employer as Paradise Bay Resort, and our investigation has determined that you do indeed work for this resort, as recently as today, you are hereby disqualified. This is of course due to author and creator of the *Clash of Crowns* series, Pierce Davenport's close ties to the resort through his wife, Emma Banks.

I am sure this is a great disappointment to you, and therefore, we have decided that you may keep the crown (which has a retail value of $53.87 USD). The cash prize, however, will go to the contestant

Beach, Please

who arrived at the cave just behind you.

We trust that this unfortunate incident won't dampen your enjoyment of the *Blood of Dragons* prequel, launching next week.

Wishing you all the best in your future endeavors,

Brad Johnstone
VP Marketing and Promotions

"No!" I shout, completely forgetting where I am. I glance around, frantically searching for some help.

The receptionist stares at me, looking slightly worried.

Ignoring her, I look back at my phone, hoping that this time the email will say I haven't been disqualified. But it doesn't. And I am.

The air leaves my lungs. My entire body goes weak. This is real. I have really lost my last-ditch effort at getting my dream back. It's over. I'm about to lose everything and this time, there is nothing I can do about it.

Out of the corner of my eye, I see someone standing near me. I look up to see a plump woman in her fifties. "Lola? I'm Mary McNally. I understand you've got the money."

———

Email from Joline.Fita@FitaPrivateInvestigations.BI
To: LolaGordon@BMail.com

Subject: Checking In

Hi Lola,

It's been five months since we started the investigation and I'm afraid I have run out of leads in our search for Mr. Devonrow. He's done a remarkable job of disappearing. No sign of him having made contact with his family or former girlfriends.

Do you want me to continue pursuing him with the thin information we've got to go on or should we call it a day?

As much as I want to find him and bring him to justice, I'm afraid you're going to spend good money after bad here. If it were me, I'd call off the search, but ultimately you need to decide what it is you want to do.

I will await your instructions.

All the best,
Joline

29

Buying Bulk and Other Stupid Mistakes...

Aidan

"Good evening, I'm Giles Bigley at the ANN News Desk. Our top story tonight, bio-medical billionaire Dick Napper has snagged two more crowns in NBO's Quest for the Crown, but one of them has already been found. He not only scooped up the fourth prize, which was hidden in the medieval Predjama castle in Slovenia, he also will take the only one found by another contestant. Correspondent Zachary Jones is live in studio to give us more on this breaking news."

The camera pans out to show a young man with red hair sitting at the desk next to Giles. "Good evening, Giles. Big news today for *Clash of Crowns* fans everywhere. Yesterday, the world rejoiced when a young woman, a Lola Gordon of Santa Valentina Island, bested Napper at what appears to be his favourite game."

"Lola? Like the song?"

Zachary gives Giles a blank look, to which Giles replies, "You may be a little young for that one."

"Or you're just really old, Giles," Zach says with a smirk. "Anyway, as you know, Napper has been racing around the world with a large team of experts to snatch up the crowns in a move many are calling wildly unfair and even evil. Yesterday, he arrived just seconds after Ms. Gordon and was forced to bear witness to her being crowned by the … well, I guess they're actors for the network, aren't they?"

The video feed cuts to footage of Lola being crowned while Giles says, "Yes, I suppose they are actors."

The feed cuts back to the news desk and Zach smiles broadly at the camera. "Anyway, as it turns out, Ms. Gordon was ineligible to enter the contest, as she is an employee of the Paradise Bay Resort, which is partly owned by the wife of Pierce Davenport, Emma Banks."

"Wow, the plot thickens."

"It certainly does, Giles. NBO put out a statement today saying that because there is proof that Dr. Napper arrived at the scene just seconds after Ms. Gordon, he'll be awarded the money, but that they will allow her to keep the crown, which has a value of $53.87 US dollars."

"Fifty-four dollars only?" Giles asks. "But it looks like real gold."

"I guess they were made by the prop department."

"Huh, that's a little disappointing, no?"

Zachary nods. "Indeed. And what a shame for Ms. Gordon. I'm sure a resort employee needs the money a lot more than Dr. Napper."

Shaking his head, Giles says, "Do you ever get sick of reporting how the little guy gets screwed over every time?"

Zach's eyes grow wide. "You okay, Giles?"

Sighing, Giles says, "I don't know." He stares off into space for a second, then looks into the camera. "Up next, spongy moth infestations are on the rise, but is the answer—aerial spraying—doing more harm than good? And just how worried should you be? Find out after a word from our sponsor."

The feed cuts and a commercial for Krispy Kreme Donuts starts up.

. . .

"Shit." Poor Lola. She didn't cheat. She's never even met Pierce Davenport.

Furious on her behalf, I grab my phone and call her, only to have it go directly to voicemail. I grab my keys and hurry out the door.

I guess this answers my question about how it went at the bank today. Here I was the tiniest bit hurt that she hadn't called to share the good news with me. My mind went immediately to her having some sort of party without even thinking of inviting me. But then, I convinced myself that it was probably an ice cream sundae party and she knew I'd hate it. Either that, or she's so disgusted about my condom collection that she cut me out on purpose.

But now I know the truth. No ice cream. No celebration. No money. She must be devastated. I zip through traffic and pull up in front of her place just as the sun is going down. Pocketing my keys, I jog to her door and knock.

Then I wait. And knock louder this time.

After a couple of minutes, I hear a crashing sound, then what sounds like cursing, although I can't quite make out the words. Then the door swings open and I'm faced with a very drunk Lola. She's wearing the crown and holding a bottle of champagne. "Comeonin."

She steps to the side and trips over her foot. I manage to catch her just before she loses her balance completely and smacks into the wall.

"I'd ask if you're okay, but I can see you're not." I stand her up, then let go.

She wobbles back and forth a little. "D'you see the news today? It's a tragic story about not reading the fine print."

"I saw, and I'm really sorry, Lola."

Waving her hand, she says, "Easy go, easy go."

"Easy come, easy go?"

"Yeah, that."

"But it wasn't easy to come by. And as if Dick Napper deserves the prize," I say. "You do."

I suddenly realize something stinks like it's burning. I glance around, only to see the toaster in the sink and a large piece of burnt fabric on the counter next to it. "Did you have a little accident?"

She looks over to the sink. "Um, yup. I did. It's 'cause I have to keep the mirrors away so I put a pillowcase over the toaster, but then I got hungry."

Oh dear. "I'm afraid I'm not following."

"Right." She nods. "I put the crown on because the only place I can't see it is on my head. But then when I walk past a mirror…" She points to the toaster. "Or that awful shiny machine, I keep seeing this stupid crown and it's like knives to my heart, Aidan. Knives."

I look around again and notice that there's a sheet hanging on the wall, presumably covering up a large mirror. "I see. So you're wearing the crown so you won't have to see the crown. And then you tried to make yourself something to eat, but you left the toaster covered."

"Eggos. I was making Eggos." She flops onto the couch.

I walk over to the kitchen window and open it up to get rid of the smell. "Okay, well, why don't I help you out a bit because clearly, you're not functioning at your normal high level."

"That would be lovely," she slurs, taking a swig of the champagne. She holds it out to me. "Oh, sorry. D'you want some?"

"No, but I will take it." I gently slide it from her hand, then pluck the crown off her head.

"No! Now I can see it!" she says, hissing at the crown like a vampire to the sun.

"Just give me a second," I tell her, opening the media cabinet under her television. I pop the crown in it and shut the door. Straightening up, I turn to her. "There. It's all gone."

She stares at me for a second. "So simple. Why didn't I think of that?"

"I'm guessing it's because you've had almost an entire bottle of champagne."

"Yup. I bet that's it."

And with that, she dissolves into tears. "It's over, Aidan. It's all over. Why didn't I read the fine print? Why?!"

"Nobody reads the fine print."

"Well, from now on, I'm going to."

"Smart."

"Not that it'll help me because I really am losing everything for real. And that was my last shot at it. All I have is this stupid crown and I don't even want it. Not at all. It feels like…"

"Knives to your heart?"

She gasps. "How did you know that?"

"Lucky guess."

"You and me are same paged."

Yikes. She's lost the ability to be coherent.

She starts to sob, burying her face in both hands, so I sit down next to her and wrap an arm around her, pulling her close. She heaves into my shirt and I don't even care that there's probably snot getting on my cotton tee right now. I don't care that her face is blotchy and red and her eyes are puffy from crying. She's beautiful to me. And all I can think of is that I need to find some way to fix this for her. Unfortunately, I don't have the cash to get her out of this mess, which is the only thing that will help. So, all I can do is just be here for her right now.

I don't shush her or tell her it'll be all right, both things being totally useless to anyone upset. Instead, I murmur, "Let it out. Just let it all out."

"Okay!" she wails.

Ooh, I should *not* have said that. I really opened the floodgates there. Wow, those are some gut-wrenching, loud sobs.

"And my private dick can't find The Dirtbag!" she cries.

"What?"

"My private dick. Joline. She wrote to tell me she's out of leads, which means that bastard is going to get away with it!"

Anger flows through me as I listen to her. "I'm sorry, Lola. The world isn't fair sometimes."

Sniffling, she says, "Seems like it's only fair to some people."

"Agreed," I say, cupping the back of her head with my hand while she goes back to crying.

After a few minutes, the sobbing slows down a little and she starts making that huffing sound that little kids make after a big cry. I rub her back and say, "I'm here. I've got you."

"Thank you." She reaches for a box of tissues on the coffee table, then blows her nose.

"Can I get you something? Some ice cream maybe?"

Shaking her head, she says, "I just ate a bunch of Eggos." She turns to face me, swaying a little. "Wanna have sex? That'll make me feel better."

"Umm, maybe not right now. Not that you're not totally attractive, but you are definitely way past the ability to give consent."

"Because of the booze?" she whispers.

"Yes."

"I know there's that orange flag, but I still think you might be one of the good ones."

Orange flag? "I'm not sure I know what you mean, but in this case, I'd say I'm just not one of the awful ones."

She flops back, resting her head on the couch and closing her eyes. "Stupid condoms."

Oh right. Those. I cringe, wishing to hell I hadn't ordered the Kirkland Econo-box from Costco.

A second later, she's snoring. And not in a gentle way either. The sound is building all the way from her toes and working its way up to her nose. I get up and shift her so she's laying on her side, then prop her head on a pillow and cover her with a blanket. I consider leaving, wondering if she'd rather be alone when she wakes up, but then I decide to stay. Not because I don't feel like being at my place tonight; it's in case she needs me. Okay, it's a little bit about not wanting to be alone. But mainly it's about looking after her.

I have a feeling that someone as optimistic as Lola probably didn't hit rock bottom when The Dirtbag left, or when the bank started the foreclosure procedures. But today—after having everything she wanted right in her hand, then having it yanked away—is going to be hard to come back from. Even for someone like her. She's going to need people who care to get her through this.

I spend a little while doing the dishes and tidying up, then settle myself on a nearby armchair with a throw blanket and prop my feet up on the ottoman. I sit and watch her sleep for a while, my heart breaking for her. Here she is, trying anything and everything she can to get back what belongs to her. She never gave up and didn't get bitter when she so easily could have. She's an amazing human. Beautiful too. And fun and accomplished. And even though I let her see the real me—the neat freak, sci-fi reading, video-game playing person I am—she wanted me anyway. At least until she found out why I bought *Zelda*. She'll never look at me the same way again after that. If we had been heading down the road to a long-term commitment, that would have been a deal-breaker.

But it's better this way. Honestly, it is. I can go back to my life and she can get on with hers. In a little while, we'll forget we even knew each other.

She frowns in her sleep and I wonder if she's dreaming about the surf shop being auctioned off or The Dirtbag off spending her money. Then it hits me: I can't front her the cash for the shop, but I can at least serve up some justice. Her private dick might not have been able to find her ex, but I sure as hell can…

30

One Girl's Trash is Another Billionaire's Treasure...

Lola

I WAKE to the sound of my alarm on my phone. I'm stiff and sore and for a second, I don't know where I am. I open my eyes to see I'm in my living room. Why am I not in bed?

It all comes back to me in a rush—the email from NBO, me getting ridiculously drunk, Aidan showing up, me bawling my eyes out on his shoulder and, oh yeah, asking him for sex. Gawd, that's *so* embarrassing.

Thank God he's gone. After last night, I never want to see him again.

Grabbing the phone off my coffee table, I shut off the alarm, then force myself off the couch to go shower. Once I'm under the warm spray, my groggy mind starts to wander. I should just call in sick. I am sick. Sick of trying to cling to a dream that is never going to happen. Sick of how unfair life is. Men like The Dirtbag and Dick Napper get ahead while honest, caring people like me get screwed over. Well, I suppose it wasn't completely honest to break into the store and borrow the scuba gear. But that's a grey area really, because it was mine to begin with and I was only trying to right a bigger injustice.

Anyway, the point is other than that one B&E, I'm an upstanding citizen, and more than that, I'm a girl with a dream. Isn't the universe supposed to help girls with dreams? The kind who stay positive and work hard?

Come on, Universe. Do your part, already!

But the universe isn't going to do its part, is it? I'm alone out here. I have been the whole damn time, only I didn't want to believe it. I get it now. I need to stop believing in things that are never going to happen. The money's gone. My shop is gone. I'm never getting it back. Love doesn't last, at least not for me. I need to just accept my fate. I'm doomed to walk this earth alone forever, doing work I couldn't care less about instead of spending my days at the beach, teaching people how to surf. It's fine, really. Who needs a dream? Who needs a man? Not this girl. I've got a crown with a retail value of $53.87, so there's that.

I put my wet hair in a low ponytail, dress quickly in my uniform of a golf shirt and shorts, then hurry into the kitchen where I see a note on the kitchen table.

Lola,

I hope you're feeling all right when you wake up. I wanted to stay but had something urgent I had to take care of. I wish there was more I could do to help you get your shop back.

Aidan

P.S. By the time you read this, the scuba gear will have been returned. If you don't hear from me, it means I didn't get arrested and don't require bail money.

"Oh my God, why is he so bloody sweet?" I mutter. He is totally making me fall in love with him. The bastard.

"This is Giles Bigley at the ANN News Desk. Tonight, our team examines the possible reasons that homicide victims rarely talk to police. But first, Dick Napper, who late last night found the fifth and final crown in Morocco, has announced plans to open a *Clash of Crowns* museum. Zachary Jones is on location in front of NBO studios with more on this breaking story."

The screen splits to show Zachary in a raincoat holding an umbrella. "This is ridiculous. I should be at the anchor desk right now. This isn't even where the museum will be located."

"Zachary, we can hear you," Giles says, looking slightly panicked.

Zach's eyes grow wide. "Giles, hello. Today bio-medical billionaire Dick Napper took to Instagram to announce his plans for a *Clash of Crowns* museum, complete with life-sized wax figures of each of the characters."

"Oh, and what seems to be the response among Crownheads?"

"A bit of a mixed bag. Some are excited while others are still bitter about him ruining the contest for them."

I shut the video off and mutter, "And I'm one of them."

I just got home from my shift, which was awful on account of this hangover. Stupid champagne. I look around my kitchen, realizing how tidy and clean everything is. I was feeling too gross to notice this morning, but now that I'm back home, it's very obvious this isn't how I left it when I passed out on the couch last night.

Aidan must have cleaned it up. And he risked prison time to return the scuba equipment. I tried to call him earlier but he must have been out on *Zelda* with some tourists. Hopefully not beautiful, young, horny ones. Not that it matters, I guess.

Beach, Please

I call him again and wait, my heart pounding as the phone rings. Finally, I hear his voice. "Hey, how are you?"

Damn him and his sexy deep voice. "A little rough today, but I'll be fine. I called to thank you for looking after me last night, and cleaning up, and running that errand."

"Oh yeah, the *errand*," he says, sounding amused. "Don't mention it. I figured you might not be up for it and the sooner it was done, the better for both of us."

"How did it go?"

"Just fine, despite my lack of a nail file and duct tape," he says. "But I may have landed with my foot in the toilet."

I laugh, which feels so good. "You didn't."

"Oh, I did," he says, laughing at himself. "But the good news is, it's done. You don't have to go back there ever again."

My heart swells even though I tell it not to. "Is that why you did it? To save me from having to go back, now that it's over?"

"There was that thought, but there was also the thought of not wanting to go to jail."

"Right. That," I say, wishing I was sitting on his couch instead of mine right now.

"But at least if I had gotten arrested, I'd have had you on the outside with your nail file."

I burst out laughing as he continues, "You would have baked me a cake, wouldn't you?"

"Totally," I say.

"Thought so." His voice grows serious as he says, "How are you feeling today? Really?"

"Surviving."

"Sometimes that's all you can do."

"True." Looking for an excuse to stay on the phone with Aidan, I say, "Did you see that news about Dick Napper finding the last crown?"

"I did. Sometimes life's not fair."

"I guess he wants to open some museum to honour the show," I tell him.

"Too bad he'll be missing one crown for his collection," Aidan says.

"Ha! Exactly. At least I can enjoy the thought of him having one empty spot where the third crown should be," I say. "Not that it makes up for what I'm about to lose."

"No, I guess it wouldn't."

"Did you know the stupid thing isn't even worth fifty-five dollars?"

"Yeah, I saw that on the news," he says. "I wonder what it would be worth to Dr. Evil."

"Good question." I should hang up now because the more I talk to him, the more I'm going to want to talk to him which is going to lead to me wanting to do all sorts of *other* things we can't do anymore. "Anyway, I should let you get on with your..." Life. "Evening. Thank you again so much for everything. You're not only very kind, you're also brave."

"If that's code for stupid, I agree with you," he says.

"Not stupid. Brave." Hang up now before you ask him to come over. "Okay, well, goodnight, Aidan."

"Goodnight, Lola. Let me know if you need anything."

"You, too."

I hang up the phone and close my eyes, wishing that things could have turned out differently. A few days ago, everything was falling into place and now, it's all just falling apart. I get up off the couch and walk over to my laptop to get started on my bookkeeping work (which I'm way behind on due to taking a few days off to go in search of that stupid crown that's sitting in my media cabinet right now).

I glare at the cabinet. "Stupid, worthless crown."

Aidan's words come back to me. *I wonder what it would be worth to Dr. Evil.*

I gasp, realizing that my stupid, worthless crown may not be so worthless after all.

31

Cyber Sleuths, Brotherly Love, and Shit We Tell Ourselves...

Aidan - One Week Later

WHAT I'VE BEEN DOING for the last week is all sorts of illegal, which is why I'm working off of VPNs in the most incognito of incognito modes. The only thing I've figured out so far is that finding a person's location is *so* much harder when you don't have access to a major bank's network. Not that it should be easy for cybersecurity specialists, but it also has to be easy for cybersecurity specialists. Which is why I put in a call to Vivian, my old boss at Scotia Dominion, to lend a hand.

After a bit of begging, some cajoling, and then finally telling her Lola's entire life story, Vivian caved. I'm currently waiting for her to send me the current address of one Reid Devonrow (a.k.a. The Dirtbag).

I get up from my desk and grab a beer from the fridge, then go out onto my deck and lean on the railing, waiting for Vivian to get ahold of me.

Yes, this is nice. Just me, out here listening to the sounds of the waves and enjoying the warm Caribbean air. All alone. Exactly the way I like it.

Or at least the way I liked it before Lola was here. I'm still having a 'the fun is over' hangover, like the kind you get when you've just come home from a trip to Disneyland. It's that restless, empty feeling of going back to your regular life and having nothing special to look forward to. But that's fine. It'll wear off. Eventually. We haven't spoken or texted in the last week, which is for the better really. The sooner we lose touch, the sooner this feeling will go away.

I wander back inside and close the sliding door. "Alexa, play 'Lola' by The Kinks."

The song is about halfway through when my phone rings. I tell Alexa to pause the music and lunge for my phone, thinking it might be Lola. Nope. It's Bennett's face on the screen. Crap.

"Bennett, what's up?"

"Just home from a road trip from hell. Six games with zero wins."

"Ouch."

"Yeah, sucks, but I didn't call to whine about work. I called to find out about this Lola person Mom and Dad can't stop going on about."

I wince, glad he can't see me. "Oh yeah? I'm glad they like her. She really loved getting to know them too."

"Cut the shit, Aid. I know the truth," Ben says. "I spoke to you the day before the 'rents showed up at your place, and you were telling me about having a boat full of single ladies that morning. The next day, you suddenly have a girlfriend living with you?"

I sigh, knowing there's no point in trying to deny it. "Okay, we may have embellished a few details to make it seem like our relationship is farther along than it is."

"Which details?"

"The bit about the relationship."

"Jesus, man."

"I know, I know. I shouldn't have lied to them, but can you blame me? They were talking about moving here. Moving here, Bennett," I tell him. "Can you imagine the pressure Mom would have put on me to find a wife if all she had to do all day was wander around looking for brides for me?"

"It would have been awful," he says.

"Exactly. So, Lola—who's a friend, by the way—agreed to help me out."

"One question, dipshit," Ben says. "What's your long-term plan here?"

"What do you mean?"

"Well, they're going to expect you two to come visit, right? And they're already talking about a big family vacation to Santa Valentina so everyone can meet her. Are you just planning to pretend forever?"

"Only until Mom and Dad are too old to travel," I say, checking my computer to see if Vivian has sent a message via Discord. Nothing yet.

"Dude…"

"I'm hoping that once the baby comes, they'll forget all about me. Well, forget about *worrying* about me, anyway." I have a sip of beer. "You're not going to tell them, are you?"

"I'm no rat."

"And I appreciate that. Thank you."

"But you're going to have to figure out a plan here. Either that or tell them the truth."

"I will. Eventually. As soon as I know they're not going to try to move here."

"Wow, and you're supposed to be the smart one."

"What can I say? I panicked."

He starts to laugh. "Yeah, you did. Dumbass." He pauses, then says, "Man, the way Mom and Dad went on and on about her almost had me fooled." He puts on his best imitation of our mom. "'Lola made the best fish tacos, and Lola taught us to surf. Lola's the best surfer. She'll have to teach you when you go see them. And you should *just see* how Lola looks at Aidan. Her eyes just shine when she looks at him. They just shine with love. Lola's amazing.'"

I picture her smiling up at me and my heart swells in my chest. "Lola *is* amazing."

Crap. I should not have said that.

"Amazing, eh?"

Oh, screw it. I might as well tell him. He knows about everything else. "She's fun and smart and totally adventurous and she's like, the bravest woman I've ever met."

"Is she single?"

"Yeah."

"So, she's amazing and single."

"Yup."

"And would she be into you, do you think?"

"Whether she would or she wouldn't doesn't matter. I'm not a relationship guy," I tell him.

"You were in a relationship for three years."

"Well, things happen. People change."

"Are you seriously going to let Lawson and Cait run the rest of your life like that?"

"They're not running anything. I just realized life is a lot simpler on your own."

He makes a *pfft* sound, then says, "Liar."

"I'm not a liar."

"Umm, hello, guy who pretended he had a girlfriend living with him for a week…"

"Okay, so I lied about that. I'm not lying about this."

"Look, I get that what happened was a massive betrayal and I'm not trying to minimize the pain of that or anything, but it sounds like you might have found someone who, by your own admission, is amazing, and you're going to blow her off because you're 'not a relationship guy?'"

Damn him and his logic. I let out a sigh. "I'm not explaining myself very well. It's complicated."

I hear my computer ping and see a note from Vivian on Discord: *3245 176th Street, San Mariposa, Benavente Island.*

Gotcha, you bastard.

"It's not complicated. You're just scared."

"After what happened, can you blame me?"

"Yes."

"What do you mean yes?" I ask.

"There are roughly four billion women on this planet. *One* of those four billion made a shitty choice, so you've decided they'd all do the same thing."

"That's not——"

"Yeah, it's exactly what you're doing," Bennett says. "And it's stupid, so stop it."

Sighing, I say, "It's not that easy."

"Yeah, it is. Anything else you tell yourself is just bullshit that's going to leave you with an empty, lonely life."

"It's not that easy because she thinks I'm some sort of player who played her."

"You? A player?" He bursts out laughing. "How the hell did she get that idea?"

Not wanting to get into the whole story, I say, "I may have been too honest about why I bought the boat."

"Ooooh, bad move."

Flopping onto my couch, I say, "I already know that. I don't need to hear it from you."

"Well, don't just sit there. Fix it."

"Again, complicated. She's had bad luck with relationships. The last guy did a real number on her so the next one she's with needs to be rock solid, not going anywhere."

"You literally just described yourself," Ben says.

"Tell her that."

"Sure, give me her number."

"Ha! No fucking way am I going to do that," I tell him, having another sip of beer.

"Why? You think I'm going to try to get her into bed?"

"No, but I'm not about to have my little brother call a woman for me to convince her to go out with me," I say. "Not that I want her to go out with me anyway."

"Oh dude, let's not go backwards here. You like her. *A lot.* Mom and Dad are practically in love with her. So make it happen."

"How am I supposed to do that?"

"You're going to have to figure that out for yourself, but you're smart, *apparently*," Ben says, laying on the sarcasm. "You'll come up with something."

We talk for a few more minutes, then hang up, my mind swirling with our conversation. Bennett makes it all sound so easy, but that's just because he's never been in love before. He has no idea how much it can kick your ass.

I make an anonymous tip on the Benavente Police website with The Dirtbag's whereabouts. I can't believe he didn't even leave the country. He's not only a thief, he's also lazy as hell and about to get caught.

I shut down my laptop and sit back in my chair, satisfied that I could at least do this for Lola. I want her to be happy. It's not much, but I can at least give her this.

I think about what I told Bennett about Lola. I meant every word of it. She is amazing. And Mom's not wrong. There was something so real about the way she looked at me. Caitlyn's eyes never lit up when I walked in a room. But Lola's did. I could see it. Feel it. And I just pushed her away, like a total dumbass.

Oh shit. I pushed her away. And she might be the best thing to ever happen to me in my entire life.

Ben's words about 'making it happen' come back to me. How the hell am I going to do that? And do I even *want* to? I'm about to open myself up to a whole lot of hurt. Or a whole lot of wonderful…

32

The Universe Finally Steps Up...

Lola

BILLIONAIRES ARE hard to get ahold of. Like, seriously hard. It's been ten days since I started calling his office, and so far, nada. I keep telling Jane, the woman who answers the phone, who I am and what I'm in possession of, but she's not budging. Apparently, she doesn't know how important this piece of stupid costume jewelry is to her boss.

At least this last-ditch effort at getting my shop back has occupied my mind. I guess that's something. A temporary reprieve from reality—that this is over. Tomorrow afternoon, it'll all go to the highest bidder. I'll be there, on the off chance no one else shows up so I can get it all back for the couple of grand in my bank account. But let's face it, that's not going to happen. I'm going to stand at the back watching as my dream gets sold piece by piece to the highest bidder. Then I'll go home, eat a bucket of ice cream with Penn, and try to get on with my life.

I'm currently at work. It's been slow today, which is only causing each second to feel like an hour as I wait for tomorrow to come. Okay, I've also noticed that time has been moving like a sloth since

Aidan and I parted ways. I know it's for the best, but it's just … not great. I got way more attached to him than I should have. Which means not seeing or talking to him is for the best. But it still sucks sour balls.

I'm on a call with a Canadian who has such a bad sunburn, he wants to eat lunch in his room. His accent tugs at my heart and I find my fingers itching to send Aidan a text.

"It's the worst burn I've ever had, eh," he says. "It hurts just to move."

"That's terrible, sir," I tell him. "I'm sorry that happened to you."

"I should not have had that last beer. Then I wouldn't have fallen asleep by the pool like that," he says.

'Fallen asleep.' Why can't they ever call it what it is? Passing out drunk. "So, just the tropical cheeseburger and fries for you then?"

"Yeah. Oh, and a couple of bottles of Bud."

"Certainly, sir," I say, adding the beer to his order. "That should be up to your room in twenty minutes."

Behind me, I hear the door to the room open and I turn, only to see Pierce Davenport standing there. My mouth drops. My entire body goes numb yet charged up at the same time. *Pierce Freaking Davenport is here.*

He's saying something. I glance around to make sure he's talking to me. Yup. I'm the only one in here so…

Pulling off my headset, I rest it on my neck. "Hi. How can I help you?"

"You're Lola, right?"

I nod and squeak out an "Uh-huh."

He walks over and holds out his hand. I stand, hold out both arms, and go for a hug, only to have my headset cord yank me back. I stumble a little, then catch myself. Dammit. "Oh my God, did that just happen?" I ask him, my face flaming with embarrassment.

"Yup," he says, trying to hide a smile. "You okay there?"

"Great. You're Pierce Davenport."

"I know," he says with a chuckle.

"I'm just making a total jackass of myself," I tell him.

"I've seen worse. Pro tip: breathe."

"Okay," I say, taking a huge inhale. I let it out, then laugh. "You're my very favourite author. I'm sure people tell you this all the time, and I hope you don't mind me saying this, but you're a genius. Like, a *real* one."

He offers me a modest smile, then says, "Thank you. I appreciate your kindness."

"It's nothing," I tell him. "So, did you need to place an order or something?"

"Uh, no, I came to see you."

"Really?" I ask, sitting down in my chair because my legs have turned to jelly.

"Yes, really," he says. "Rosy told me what happened to you with your surf shop and the quest for the crown. Well done on solving the clue, by the way. When I read it, I was certain it was hidden in *Caverna Luna Plateada.*"

"We went there first."

"That's what I would have done. Totally ignore the English grammar lesson."

I am talking to Pierce Davenport. Pierce Davenport knows who I am. He just said well done to me. "I can't believe Rosy told you about me."

"Yes, she actually showed up at our house last night and told me your entire life story," he says, sitting on the corner of my desk. "I might have to write a book about you. You've been through some shit."

"Meh, lots of people have it much worse," I say with a shrug. "I mean, I guess you could say I'm devastated about losing my surf shop, which is going to happen in about twenty-six hours, but in the big scheme of things, I've got … my health?" I ask, as if he might know. "That didn't sound good. I usually can come up with a lot of things to be grateful for but right now, I'm out of stuff. I don't have love. Or money. That's for sure."

"Well, health is important," he says, looking bemused. "Listen, Rosy told me you've been trying to get ahold of Dick Napper, and I wanted to see if I could help you out."

"Seriously?"

"Yes, seriously," he says. "Why don't you dial his number and put us on speaker phone?"

"Okay!" My heart pounds and my fingers go clammy while I place the call.

"Napper Bio-Medical, Jane speaking."

Pierce leans toward the phone. "Pierce Davenport for Dick Napper."

"I'll put you right through."

My mouth drops and I'm filled with a blend of indignant anger and excitement at the same time. The line clicks and a few seconds later, I hear, "Dick Napper here."

"Dr. Napper, it's Pierce Davenport calling."

"Oh my God! I can't believe it. Did you finally get my letters?"

His letters? Pierce and I exchange a grin and I stifle a laugh while he says, "Um, no. They probably ended up at my publisher's in Valcourt. I rarely see them. Anyway, I'm calling about the quest for the crown. I understand that you're opening a *Clash of Crowns* museum."

"I am! I've been amassing the largest collection of memorabilia on the planet."

"That's amazing. I'm guessing you'd love to get your hands on that last crown."

"More than you can imagine, and you've got quite the imagination, so…"

Pierce offers him a pity chuckle, then says, "I may be able to help you with that. I'm here with the woman who has the final crown—Lola Gordon. She's been trying to reach out to you for days now, but she hasn't been able to get you on the line."

"Really? I had no idea," he says.

"Lola wants to sell it to you for a fair price, but she needs the money today for a time-sensitive business venture."

"I'm willing to talk about it. Hello, Lola."

"Hi, Dr. Napper."

"What do you consider a fair price?"

"Four hundred thousand is what I need for my … venture."

"Four hundred thousand? Are you nuts? It's costume jewelry," Dick says.

"Made by the prop department on the greatest series ever made," I answer. "And you need it to complete your collection."

"She's got you there," Pierce says. "And can I just say, before you two make your deal, what a thrill it is to be on the phone with the two biggest Crownheads on the planet?"

"Thank you, Pierce," Dick says. "I'm probably as excited as you, to be honest."

Pierce tucks his lips between his teeth to stop from laughing. "I like to think of my Crownheads as a family. A force for good in this world."

"Agreed. We stand for something—justice, strength, integrity." Dick's quoting the motto on the Dalgaeron family crest.

"Yes, we're a family," Pierce says. "And as such, I expect our members to take care of each other. Lola here has a noble pursuit, and I would hope that someone with the kind of resources you've got would assist her generously. So, the four hundred thousand is the bare minimum she'll need to get herself started. And we wouldn't just want to give the bare minimum, would we?"

"Of course, I'd want to—"

"Generosity is rewarded, Dick. In this case, with an invitation to my home to watch the premiere of *Blood of Dragons*."

There's a pause, then Dr. Napper says, "Are you serious? You would really do that?"

"Yes, depending on the outcome of this call."

"Okay…" Dr. Napper pauses, then says, "Would five hundred thousand be considered generous enough?"

I do a silent scream and start nodding, but Pierce shakes his head. "Come on, Dick, you've got three commas in your net worth. You can do better than that."

"Fine, seven hundred, but that's honestly as high as I can go for something worth $53.87," he says.

"Deal!" I shout.

Pierce chuckles. "You've got yourself a deal. Lola, when do you need the money in your account?"

"Ideally by the time I get off at two o'clock. I'm right down to the wire so I'll have to go straight to the bank," I tell him.

"That's two hours from now," Pierce tells Dick. "Can you make that happen?"

"Of course I can."

"Excellent." Pierce winks at me. "As soon as the money's in her account, I'll call you with the details on the premiere."

He hangs up without saying goodbye, then says to me, "Total baller move if you hang up first."

I burst out laughing, then jump up and give Pierce a huge hug. "Thank you, thank you, thank you!"

Tears fill my eyes and I let him go, wanting to call Penn while I'm running to the lobby to tell Rosy, then drive straight to Aidan's to share the news with him. Only I can't tell Aidan because we're so busy letting each other go.

"You're most welcome, Lola. I better let you go," he says, pointing to my phone, where four lines are flashing. "Rosy'll have my ass if those calls don't get answered."

He opens the door and says, "Congratulations, Lola. You deserve it."

"Thank you again. And if there's anything I can do for you, please let me know."

"Maybe some surfing lessons. My wife's entire family are total pros and it's just so embarrassing to surf with them."

"Anytime."

As soon as the door shuts behind him, I let out a scream, then scramble to get my headset on. "Room service, Lola speaking. How can I help you?"

"Lola? Like the song?"

33

Did I Say Never? I Meant to Say Unlikely...

Aidan

"Can you kids please say thank you to Captain Aidan for a lovely afternoon?" This is coming from a haggard mother of four whose children have spent the last three hours giving their parents (and me) mini-heart attacks. They've all got goat-like climbing abilities which they've displayed on every surface of the catamaran, including the steps to the slide *while* we were en route to our snorkeling spot. I've never cut the engine so fast or sprinted so hard in my life.

I'm sweating and exhausted, but I smile at them while the four children say, "Thank you, Captain Aidan."

"You're very welcome. It's been a fun afternoon," I tell them. Then I look at their father and say, "You must be so, so tired all the time."

"So tired," he says.

The little one, Jordan, a four-year-old boy, scrambles up onto the side of the boat where he teeters precariously while his older brother, Ty, says, "I'll pay you five bucks to jump onto the dock."

All three of the adults lunge at Jordan, shouting, "No!!!"

Luckily, his mom gets to him in time, scolding Ty as they all disembark. The second they're off, I let out a sigh of relief and mutter, "Thank God that's over."

I look around. *Zelda*'s a mess of food, spilled juice, and snorkel gear. My towel pyramids only lasted about ten seconds after they got on. Okay, time to clean up. But first, some lemonade. I go inside and open the fridge, then lean against the counter while I crack it open and have a sip. Memories of Lola on this counter flood my mind and my heart does that thing it's been doing lately—it's like a weird empty stabbing thing that I don't like *at all*.

I push off the counter, grab a garbage bag and set to work cleaning up, the entire time thinking about Lola and my call with Ben. It's been three days since I spoke to him and in that time, I've run the gauntlet of emotions. Irritation, sadness, terror, more irritation, hope, and then back to fear again. I'm doing that cliché thing of not eating or sleeping much. I've accepted the fact that I'm in love with her. There's no denying that anymore because I am. She's the one, even though I promised myself there would never be a 'the one' again. But there is and she's her. And if I've figured out anything over these long, lonely days without her, it's that life is so much better with her in it. So I lay awake every night missing her and thinking of ways to show her I'm a guy who'll stick around. Because Ben's right—I am.

Tomorrow's the big day for her. She'll lose her surf shop forever and I intend to be there to help pick up the pieces. I know she's got her friends, but it'll also be my chance to show her I can be a shoulder to cry on. A dependable guy who *wants* to be there for her and help her figure out her next moves. If only I could think of some grand romantic gesture that would fix everything or some way to make her feel safe starting over with me.

I hurry over to the bedroom, open the cupboard, then dump all the condoms into the garbage bag. There. Done. It's not exactly grand, but it's a start.

An hour later, I'm almost done cleaning up the deck, wishing I had the money she needs to make her dreams come true, when Stogie Stew comes moseying by. "Hey, Aidan, *Zelda*'s looking pretty fine today. You ready to sell her to me?"

I freeze in place, my heart pounding. This is the thing. I can sell *Zelda* and get Lola's shop back for her. If anything says 'I'll be there for you,' it's that. It also says I'm through with the whole 'meaningless sex with random strangers' thing. "Yup."

He stops in his tracks. "Did you say yup?"

"Yes, I did." My heart pounds even harder. "But we have to get the deal done today and I'd need the money by tomorrow morning. I've got a thing in the afternoon."

And that thing is a grand romantic gesture that will either be the greatest thing I've ever done or the biggest disaster…

34

The Moment We've All Been Waiting for...

Lola - The Next Day

"COME IN, come in, and welcome to Soul Surfers!" I call as I hurry toward Penn, Eddie, Rosy and Darnell.

Mary McNally canceled the auction yesterday, and I got the keys a couple of hours ago, when the money transfer was completed. I came straight here to give the place a good cleaning. The overhead doors are open and I've got Bob Marley playing because today feels like a Bob Marley day.

Penn and I exchange a huge hug, complete with shrieks of excitement and happy tears. A quick side hug for Eddie, who's holding a couple of boxes of ice cream sandwiches, then one for Rosy and Darnell, who have brought champagne.

"You did it!" Penn shouts. "I didn't think it was possible, but you really freaking did it!"

"I couldn't have done it without Rosy," I say, tears filling my eyes as I hug her again. "Thank you again so much for going to see Pierce. I still can't believe he came to help me out like that."

"I told him I'd sick Starsky and Hutch on him if he didn't." Those are her dogs, who apparently love to hump Pierce more than they love to eat. "But seriously, there was no way I was going to sit back and let your dream die. Not when you've worked so hard for this."

"You're amazing. This is amazing," I say, lifting my arms and making a big circle. "I have my shop back! I've got money in the bank, so I don't have to worry about how to pay my staff or keep the lights on. I've got everything I ever wanted." *Except Aidan.*

I plaster a smile on my face, even though that thought has been causing this empty feeling in my heart on a day when it should be nothing but full. *Come on, Lola, just be happy. You have so much. You don't need Aidan.*

Darnell pops the champagne bottle and fills the plastic cups they brought. We're just about to toast when my phone pings. I glance at it, only to see a message from Aidan. *Where are you? I need to talk to you before it's too late.*

Too late? "Hang on guys, I have to answer this."

> I'm at the surf shop.

> Be right there.

"Who was that?" Penn asks.

"Aidan," I say, trying to look casual.

"Really? I thought you two were going your separate ways."

Not wanting to get my hopes up, I say, "I probably just left something at his house…"

Rosy holds up her cup. "To Lola, owner of Soul Surfers Surf Shop and Surf School. May today be the start of a new and incredible adventure in your life."

"To Lola," Darnell says.

Penn and Eddie lift their cups and we all have a sip, then Eddie says, "Speech! Speech!"

I blush a little and scramble to think of something poignant to say when I hear the screeching of tires.

Aidan hops out of his truck and runs into the shop. *Hello, Hand-*

some. "Is this where they're holding the auction? At the shop?" He stops when he sees the champagne and his mouth drops. "Did you...?"

I nod, grinning at him. "It's a long story but I got it back. It's all paid for, every brick, fin, and board."

"It is?" he asks, looking completely shocked. "No auction?"

"No auction. Everything has been paid in full. Isn't it incredible?"

Letting out an exhale, he chuckles and shakes his head. "Yeah, it's incredible."

Okay, so that's not a normal reaction. He should be giving me a high five or swooping me off the ground or something other than just standing there looking dumbfounded. "What?"

Rubbing the back of his neck, he says, "Here I thought I was about to save the day."

Something about the look on his face makes my heart pound. "How were you going to do that?"

"I sold *Zelda*."

Gasps are heard around the shop. I let go of my cup and it lands on the floor, splashing my feet. My jaw drops as I stare at his gorgeous face. My brain goes in twenty directions at once. He sold *Zelda*. His livelihood. His means of meeting women. He was planning to buy my shop back for me. "You what?" I whisper.

"I sold *Zelda* yesterday. I've been at the bank all morning waiting for the money to transfer so I could get to the auction in time and..."

I rush over to him, leaping into his arms and kissing him hard on the mouth. He picks me up off the floor and holds me up while we kiss some more. When I pull back, I say, "I can't believe you did that."

"I can't believe you don't need the money."

"But why would you do that?"

"Because somehow, in a very short period of time, the only thing that matters to me is your happiness," he says. "Stupid, I know. There's no logic to any of it, but then again, I don't think logic applies when it comes to love."

"Love?" I ask, my eyes filling with tears.

He nods. "Too soon, right?"

"Yes, but also no," I tell him, planting a kiss on him. "We've already been through so much together, it's like we crammed in six months' worth of dating into a few weeks."

"It really is." He presses his forehead to mine. "I know I said all sorts of shit about being alone and not ever wanting to fall in love again, but it was all just … bullshit. I don't know where this is going. Maybe a month or a decade from now, you'll wake up and decide I'm not the one for you. That could happen. And if it does, it'll hurt like hell and I'll be a fucking mess. But I'm willing to go through that pain because you're worth it. You are, Lola Gordon, exactly the way you are. I want to spend every damn day with you for the rest of my life. I miss you. I miss talking to you and cooking with you and hearing you laugh and seeing you smile. I miss the messes you make in the kitchen, and I miss seeing all your ridiculous little bottles of creams you don't need on my bathroom counter. I miss your stupid cozy throw pillows and your abstract art that actually do make my house feel like a home. I miss you."

"You could've just said that," I tell him, kissing him again. "You didn't have to sell your boat."

"But I did. *Zelda* represented a life I don't want anymore. I'm not that guy. I'm a relationship guy," he says, setting me down on the floor gently. "I want to be with you and only you."

He cups my cheek and kisses me. It's soft and gentle and urgent all at once. It's the start of a future together. It's everything. When it's over, I smile up at him. "I want to be with you too. I've missed you so much, even your stupid little notes you leave for me."

Aidan chuckles. "Really?"

I nod and smile up at him. "Really."

"Good, because I was going to offer to stop writing them, but if you like them…"

I lift myself up onto my tippy toes and kiss him again, my heart surging with pure joy.

A car pulls up in front of the shop, and we all turn to see who it is. Joline Fita, my private detective, gets out and saunters in. "There you are. You're a hard woman to find."

"I am?" I ask her.

"No, just messing with you. It took me about a minute," she says, walking in. "Do you want the good news or the bad news first?"

"Good."

"The Dirtbag is in custody," she tells me, eying the box of ice cream sandwiches.

"Hallelujah!" Rosy says.

"Seriously?" I ask. "How did you find him?"

"I didn't. I got a call from a buddy on the force. I guess they got an anonymous tip. Turns out he was just over on the big island hiding out at a friend's place."

"A tip?" I ask, glancing up at Aidan, who's doing his best to look casual. "Any idea who would have turned him in?"

"No idea. It looked like the tip came in from some small town near the Rockies in Canada."

I look up at Aidan again. "You don't say."

He gives me an innocent look. "That's great news. Someone found him."

"Yes, someone with some mad computer skills," I tell him.

"Probably. I doubt the person was actually in Canada," Joline says, adding, "The bad news is he burned through the money already. All but a few hundred dollars."

I look over at Penn, who says, "Booze and women."

"Booze and women," I answer, not caring in the least that the money is gone. Justice has been served. The universe provided me with everything I needed—the money and the right man. "Any news on my Retro Noserider Longboard?"

She smiles. "It was there."

I grin at her. "That's amazing. Joline, we're celebrating. Would you like some champagne?"

"I'm on the clock, so no thanks," she says. "But maybe an ice cream sandwich for the road."

Beach, Please

"Sure," I tell her while Penn opens the box. "You can have Aidan's."

After Joline leaves, Eddie pours some champagne for Aidan and me. "Lola was about to give a speech before you got here."

"Right," I say, taking my new cup. "To taking chances and good friends."

We all have a sip, then I add, "You're not just friends. You're my family and I love you all with all my heart. Thank you for getting me through this last year."

"You got yourself through this year," Rosy says.

"No, I couldn't have done it without you guys," I say. Looking up at Aidan, I say, "Including you." I stretch so I can kiss him again. "Thank you."

He kisses me again and I taste the champagne on his lips.

Darnell clears his throat. "I think we should go. Give these two some time to … enjoy the moment."

Murmurs of agreement can be heard around the store. Aidan wraps his free hand around my waist and pulls me to him. Penn walks over and takes our cups away from us, then says, "Love you. Call me later."

Without looking at her, I wrap my arms around Aidan's neck. "Love you too. Talk to you tomorrow."

As soon as they leave, I say, "Anonymous tip from Canada?"

"I know nothing about that, other than whoever found him likely did something highly illegal to get that information, so he should never ever tell anyone," he says.

"Not even a woman he sold his boat for?"

"Especially not her. He'd never want to incriminate her."

"That's awfully sweet of him," I say, brushing my lips against his.

"Well, what can I say? I'm a sweet guy. Just ask my mom."

I have never been happier in my life than I am right now. My heart pounds wildly as I pull back and whisper to him, "I'm in love with you."

He grins at me. "Thank God because I'm in love with you too, Lola."

We kiss again and he runs his hands down to my bottom, lifting me up off the floor again. I wrap my legs around him and we make out some more. I pull back long enough to say, "I should probably close the doors."

"Probably."

But I close my eyes instead and melt into him some more, kissing him again. And this is it. This moment right here. With this wonderful, sexy, caring man who has shown me more love in a few weeks than The Dirtbag ever did. He went on a crazy adventure with me, he took care of me when I hit bottom, he sold his freaking boat to make my dream come true. He's seen me at my worst, and he still showed up today. He's the type to stick around. I know it in my bones. This is the beginning of forever with the right man by my side.

Thank you, Universe.

Trivia Geeks, Shiny Rings, and Manly Tears of Joy...

Aidan - Six Months Later

"I REALLY APPRECIATE YOU COMING TONIGHT," Lola says as I pull up in front of The Turtle's Head.

"It's nothing," I tell her, lifting her hand and giving it a quick kiss.

"It's a big deal. You said you'd never go back to The Turtle's Head, so for you to step up when Darnell couldn't make it is very much appreciated."

"Yes, but I also said I'd never fall in love again and look how that turned out."

She leans over and gives me a soft kiss. "It turned out pretty well if you ask me."

I grin at her, thinking about just how much better things are about to get tonight. Getting out of the truck, I hurry around to open her door, then hold out my hand while she steps down, a little thrill going through me like it does every time we touch.

It's been six months since we first said we loved each other. Six shiny, wonderful months. In that time, she's given up her basement suite and moved in with me, complete with candles, plants, and weird art. I started working at the surf shop doing the books and holding down the fort while she takes people out for lessons. I've never been so happy in my life. Having a true partner—someone I not only spend my nights with, but days too—is incredible. We're in this together, side-by-side, through the great days and the not-so-great ones, because those happen too, even when you are living your best life.

Next week, we're flying to Canada to spend Christmas with my family, and to meet my new niece, Rhianne. It'll be the first time I'll have seen Lawson and Caitlyn since I found out about them, but it'll be okay. I'm actually happy for them, and that's in no small part because I'm so happy in my own life. Things turned out exactly the way they were supposed to. If I'd have married Caitlyn, I'd be living someone else's life right now. The wrong one with the wrong woman. But because of what happened and the journey I took, I'm doing exactly what I'm meant to be doing with exactly the right person.

A few months ago, we fessed up to my parents, and told them that we are truly very much in love, even though we weren't at the time when they were here. Although now that I look back, I can see I was pretty much already in love with her but was too scared to admit it, even to myself. They weren't exactly thrilled with either of us for lying to them, but after some time (and conversations with my brothers about interfering), they came around.

We stroll into the pub and Lola weaves through the tables to the one she was at the first time I laid eyes on her. I follow, my heart pounding in my chest as Penn looks up at me and gives me a slight nod.

We sit down and order some nachos and drinks. Wanda, the server, narrows her eyes a little. "Oh no, not you."

"Don't worry. I'm totally sober and completely happy."

"I hope so," she says. Then she looks at Lola. "Is this … the guy?"

She grins and nods. "Yup. And he's amazing."

Beach, Please

"I'll take your word for it," Wanda says before heading back to the kitchen.

I wait impatiently for the game to start while we make small talk. Finally, Buzz gets up to the mic and says, "Good evening, trivia nerds."

He reads the rules out, then gets started on question one. "Name the only person other than bio-medical billionaire Dick Napper to have found one of the crowns in NBO's *Clash of Crowns* Quest for the Crown."

A few people around the bar mutter, "What?" while Lola's face turns red as she writes in her name. "Well, that's a little embarrassing. Apparently, I'm a trivia question now."

Rosy grins at her. "You're famous."

"Question two: Name the most popular place in the world to get engaged."

We all lean in and Lola says, "I'm thinking the Eiffel Tower, but it could also be the Taj Mahal."

"Let's go with The Turtle's Head," Penn says.

"What?" Lola says. "No. Nobody gets engaged at the pub."

"Some people do," Rosy says. "And it's very romantic."

"Very," Penn adds. "Aidan? Do you vote for Eiffel Tower or The Turtle's Head."

"Turtle's Head, hands down."

Lola gives us a strange look. Before she can write the answer down, Buzz moves on. "Moving things right along. Question three. Christ, this is cheesy," he says, shaking his head. "Name the man who wants to spend the rest of his life with the woman in question one."

A guy at the back of the room says, "Seriously, Buzz? Who the hell knows the answer to that?"

Lola freezes and looks up at me. I smile, a lump forming in my throat. This is it. She whispers, "Aidan Clarke."

Nodding, I say, "Yes, put that down."

Tears fill her eyes. "Are you…"

I nod. "I thought it would be nice since this is the place we met."

Murmurs can be heard around the room, as the other trivia teams seem to figure out what's going on. I slide out of my chair and onto one knee, pulling the ring box out of my pocket. "Lola, for the first time in my life, I know what it feels like to be loved back. Really loved back by someone who gets me. I love you so much more than I can even express. I want to spend the rest of my life putting sales stickers on wetsuits and ordering inventory and booking lessons for you to take people on. I want to stay late at the shop with you and count cash and fill in tiny columns of spreadsheets and high five each other when we've had a big day and hug each other when we've had a bad one. I want to go home with you every night and make supper together and walk on the beach and talk and watch stupid TV shows and have sex and fall asleep with you snoring away beside me, heating up my bed like a little furnace, because that's my idea of pure happiness. I want to have a family with you and watch them grow up and take them on adventures with us, and I want us to grow old together, me and you, living a life we both love—"

"Dude, we need to move it along here so we can start the real game," Buzz says, which earns him all sorts of boos from around the room.

"Sorry," I tell him. "I get a little long-winded when it comes to the woman I love." Turning back to Lola, I pull the ring out of the box. "Lola Gordon, will you marry me?"

Lola flings herself into my arms with such force, we both end up on the floor. She kisses me hard on the mouth, then says, "Yes, Aidan. Yes, I will marry you."

Applause erupts from around the bar as we kiss again, then get up. I take the ring out of the box and slide it on her finger. Lola stares at it through shining eyes.

"Do you like it? Because we can take it back and you can pick one out."

"It's perfect," she says, looking up at me again. "You're perfect and I can't wait to be your wife."

She wraps her arms around my neck and we give each other a

mind-blowing, not suitable for public consumption kiss that says everything we're both feeling. This is real. This is going to last. This is the best thing that's ever going to happen to me. The woman I love just said yes, and I know without a doubt that what we've got is a forever kind of love.

ISSUE NO. 356

MUSINGS OF A FANTASY MAN

THE WORLD'S BIGGEST AUTHORITY ON ALL THINGS FANTASY FICTION

LAST CROWN FOUND

NBO has announced that the 5th and final crown in the BLOOD OF DRAGONS QUEST FOR THE CROWN has been found in Morocco. Where in Morocco, you ask? Who cares, because, yet again, I'm saddened to report to you that it's gone to bio-medical billionaire Dick Napper.

This means that four of the crowns, along with the cash prizes for ALL FIVE, are going to a billionaire. So much for justice and integrity of the justice, strength, and integrity values.

Word on the street, though, is that Lola Gordon, the only person to find a crown other than Dr. Crown Napper, has managed to cut a hell of a deal with him. He paid out an unbelievable $700,000 USD for the piece of costume jewelry. So maybe there's some justice after all...

Stay tuned as I start the countdown for *Blood of Dragons* right here on *Musings From a Fantasy Man*...

25% Off

Grand RE-OPENING

Soul Surfers
SURF SHOP & SURF SCHOOL

Sat, May 27
9-5

34 Sea Breeze Blvd.

About the Author

Melanie Summers is a multi-award-winning, Amazon best-selling author of romantic comedies and women's fiction. She's written over thirty books for people who have had it up to here with the real world and need to laugh, feel good, and sigh happily. When she's not writing, she can be found either out for a walk somewhere nature-y with her two dogs and her husband or soaking in a hot bath (i.e., hiding from her three teenage children). Melanie resides on Vancouver Island, Canada where her life goal is to become one of those fabulous people who take daily ice baths in the ocean. So far, she can get in up to her ankles, which is not awful, thank you very much.

If you'd like to find out about her upcoming releases, sign up for her newsletter on www.melaniesummersbooks.com.